ROGUE COMMAND

(A TROY STARK THRILLER—BOOK 2)

JACK MARS

Jack Mars

Jack Mars is the USA Today bestselling author of the LUKE STONE thriller series, which includes seven books. He is also the author of the new FORGING OF LUKE STONE prequel series, comprising six books; of the AGENT ZERO spy thriller series, comprising twelve books; of the TROY STARK thriller series, comprising three books; and of the SPY GAME thriller series, comprising five books.

Jack loves to hear from you, so please feel free to visit www.Jackmarsauthor.com to join the email list, receive a free book, receive free giveaways, connect on Facebook and Twitter, and stay in touch!

CHAPTER ONE

November 10
An Industrial District
Outskirts of Madrid, Spain

Everything glowed a ghostly green, from the blank walls to the carpet beneath his feet.

Troy Stark moved up the narrow corridor, weapon drawn. He was dressed all in black with light body armor under his jumpsuit, protecting his chest, throat, groin, and legs. His helmet's visor was up, and his night vision goggles were on his eyes.

He could feel Agent Mariem Dubois's gloved hand, touching him at the waist. She was right behind him. Touching his body was an old trick. If she lost track of him with her eyes, her hand knew where he was.

People in the office, people they both knew, called her Mari. But not Troy.

"My name is Mariem," she had said to him once. "Only my friends call me Mari."

He hadn't reached that place yet. To be honest, he wasn't in a big hurry to get there. He just called her Dubois.

"Agent Stark," Jan Bakker's calm voice said inside Troy's helmet. "Two unknown vehicles entering the complex. Large SUVs. Pulling to the front doors of the building."

"Copy," Troy said.

He pictured the front doors of the large warehouse building. One was a nondescript steel door that a man would walk through. Three others were large garage-type doors, opening to a vast cement space. That was somewhere up ahead here, maybe a hundred meters along.

Troy wasn't certain. He and Dubois had infiltrated through the rear.

"We need to move it," he said to Dubois, his voice barely above a whisper.

"Okay," came her voice, even softer than his.

He began to pace quickly along the hallway now, catlike, his feet making almost no sound. He could hear his own breathing though, and it sounded loud to his ears. He was taking chances, throwing caution to the wind. There wasn't much time.

1

He came to a corner and turned it, his weapon out ahead. No one.

Twenty meters down, the hallway seemed to turn again. Or maybe it ended right there. The place was like a maze. A bead of sweat rolled down his cheek.

Come on. Where is it?

"Stark," Bakker said. "Six individuals emerging from the SUVs. No. Seven individuals. Very likely unfriendlies. Heavily armed. Three men with automatic rifles. Entire group moving to the doorway."

"Copy," Troy said mechanically.

"Entering the building. Less than sixty meters from your location."

Troy and Dubois had powerful transponder units embedded in their gear. On his monitor, Bakker could see their location with exceptional accuracy. For a split second, Troy pictured the gentle giant Bakker hunched over his various screens, watching all the action: his mind racing out ahead, measuring distances, calculating possibilities, adding, subtracting, and coming up with...

"Abort," Bakker said. "Abort mission."

"Negative," Troy said.

"Stark?" Dubois said behind him.

"Seven men entering," Bakker said. "Three men, by my count, already inside. Ten opponents. You have no chance. Aborting is the best option."

"We've come this far," Troy said.

There was no way they were aborting this mission. The locker had to be in this hallway. *It had to be.* He moved faster now, head on a swivel, pivoting back and forth. It was a small metal door ensconced in the wall, almost like the glass door that holds a fire extinguisher.

"It's here. It's got to be here."

"Abort!" Bakker hissed, his voice like a snake.

"Stark!" Dubois said. Now she spoke above a whisper.

"Ssshhhhh."

"Abort, please," Bakker said. "Agent Stark."

"There's no way out," Troy said.

"Back the way you came."

Troy pictured the winding hallways that led back to the rear of this building. The design was insidious. He'd almost prefer to blast his way out the front than go back through there.

"We'll never find our way back there."

"I'll guide you," Bakker said.

2

Troy gritted his teeth. Frustrating. This was not the United States Navy SEALs. Abort the mission? Go back? In the SEALs, there was GO, and GO HARDER. There was no such gear as reverse.

"Okay," Troy said. "Okay. Just let me check one more door. Then we'll go."

"Stark..." Bakker said.

"One more door. One more hall. And we're done."

He moved to the end of the hallway. It came to a T, with halls moving off in both directions at a ninety-degree angle. To the right, the hall disappeared into the deep, dark distance. From here, he couldn't see the end of it. If they went that way, they could be cut off from retreat.

To the left, there was a door maybe ten feet away.

"Opponents close now," Bakker whispered. "Very close. Wall to your right. Possibly on the other side of that wall."

Terrific. Some of these walls were sheetrock, easy to fire a high-caliber weapon through. Troy was breathing hard. He could hear Dubois's breathing right behind him. If those bad guys heard them breathing, what was to stop them from...

"Very quiet," Bakker whispered in his ear. "Silent."

"SHUT UP!" Troy wanted to scream at him.

This mission was a nightmare.

He went to the door and felt the handle. It had some play. It was not locked. At this point, Troy didn't know if that was a good thing or a bad thing. If it had been locked, he could have just turned around and aborted the mission after all.

It would be an epic journey navigating their way through this confounding maze of hallways again to the rear of the building. And exiting from the rear would be no guarantee of safety. They'd still have to dash across an open lot and duck into some scrub woods on the other side. But going back would mean that he didn't have to open this door.

Very slowly, very quietly, he turned the handle. The door disengaged.

He pushed it open.

There was a large empty space ahead. Dammit. That couldn't be right. Couldn't Bakker see these things?

Troy stepped into the space. He got the sense of a high ceiling two or three stories above his head.

Dubois was right behind him.

3

Suddenly, figures moved in the space. Ahead and to the right, and now to the left, people were moving. It was a set up. Red and green laser pointers appeared. Triangulated fire. There was no way to escape it.

"Duck!" Troy shouted. "Dubois! Move!"

He went counterintuitive on them, diving forward, further into the room.

A shot rang out, and then an entire volley. The sound was loud, echoing off the high walls and the ceiling.

BANG!

Then:

BANG! BANG! BANG! BANG! BANG! BANG!

Behind him, Dubois screamed.

Troy rolled onto his stomach, firing from the ground. He couldn't see what he was firing at. He just aimed for the muzzle flashes.

The sounds were deafening now. A wall of gunshots.

BANG! BANG! BANG! BANG!

He fired until his magazine was empty. He reached for another.

Something hit him then, on his right side. Another one. Another. They'd found him, and now he was sunk. He rolled, but it was too late. Lights flashed on him and found him.

BANG! Another shot him.

BANG! Another.

They could hit him at will. There was nowhere to hide.

The pain was one thing. The rage and the frustration, though, was another. And Dubois. Where was she? She'd been hit right away. In real life, she'd be…

"Dead," a male voice said.

The shriek of a whistle sounded, and the shots stopped.

All around them, overhead lights came on. Suddenly, it was bright in here. In the back of the warehouse space, a door opened. Two assistants came in and pressed buttons that opened two gigantic mechanical shades. Now, weak afternoon light streamed in.

Troy looked around the room. There were six shooters lined up against him. Four were to his right, on an angle, and two were on his left, on a similar angle. It was just as he had suspected. They were dialed in on the door that he came through, triangulating their fire so that it would take he and Dubois down, without any danger of hitting their own team.

4

Standing in the middle of the room was Miquel Castro-Ruiz, the director of this little agency and the producer of this farce of an infiltration exercise. The agency's name was officially the European Rapid Response Investigation Unit, or ERRIU, if you liked. Troy didn't like. He couldn't imagine the word salad that name would become in all the various languages—it was bad enough in English.

Internally, Miquel called it el Grupo Clandestino—the Clandestine Group. He also toyed around with el Grupo Especial—the Special Group. He sometimes even referred to it as "el Grupo." Troy got it. Miquel was trying to build a culture here, from scratch. He was trying to put a stamp on it.

Right now, Miquel wore a pair of khaki pants, black shoes, and a blue dress shirt, all smartly tucked, pressed, and shined up. He was going for the clean shaven look these days, losing the bushy unkempt look from when Troy had first met him.

Troy glanced back at Dubois.

She was sitting on the floor against the wall, about three feet from the door they had come through. Her black jumpsuit was covered in fluorescent green paint splotches. One paintball had hit her square in the helmet. It had exploded and sprayed the side of her face in green. She took the helmet off.

She stared at Troy. She touched her cheek gingerly. The paintballs hurt when they hit. She was almost certainly going to have a welt there tomorrow.

"How does it look?" she said.

Troy nodded. "Nice. I like the color. I'd keep it, if I were you."

"What happened?" Miquel said. He spoke English perfectly, but with the lilted accent of someone who had mastered it later in life. "What did you do wrong?"

Troy shrugged. "Well, I agreed to a canned exercise with impossible odds of success. Those guys had perfect information about us and our whereabouts. That doesn't exist in the real world. If we do our jobs right, the opponent is always guessing. In this case, they knew we were coming through that door."

A couple of the shooters laughed.

Miquel raised a finger. "Incorrect. But a good guess."

He looked around him at the open warehouse space. "Jan?"

"Yes," came Bakker's voice over the loudspeaker system.

"How many times did you request that Agent Stark abort the mission?"

"Uh...no fewer than three times. I also explained why aborting was the best chance of survival and offered to guide them out the way they came in. I would have requested he abort one more time, but he shushed me."

Troy's shoulders dropped. He nearly laughed. Bakker had something like a photographic memory for detail, and he recounted events in a robotically dispassionate tone of voice. If you didn't see giant Jan Bakker in front of you, you might think he was an artificial intelligence come to life.

Troy shook his head. "We were trying to complete a mission," he said.

What he didn't say was *there was no real risk involved.*

Miquel raised a hand. "I'm not picking on you, Agent Stark. I'm only making a point, for all the people here. You're not the only person from a commando background, and this is important for everyone. Yes, your opponents had perfect knowledge of your location. Yes, if you stepped through that door, you were both dead."

"So what's the point of that?" Troy said.

"During your military career, how many men died under your command?"

Troy shook his head. "My military career didn't work that way. I was embedded in teams with highly trained teammates, the best in the world." Troy raised both hands now, as if he were under arrest. "No offense to anyone in this room, but it is what it is."

"Okay," Miquel said. "Continue."

"We went forward. We carried out missions. Everyone knew the deal. Everyone did their jobs. Whether I was in command of a team, or someone else was...that wasn't the important part."

"How many men?" Miquel said.

Troy shrugged. "Under my command. Six. I lost six of my guys. That's true. I live with that. But again, they knew the risks going in. If they had known the outcomes ahead of time, I doubt even one of them would have done it differently."

Miquel nodded. "And how many died that you worked with but didn't command?"

Troy didn't love this line of questioning.

Miquel smiled. "I want to be clear. I'm not putting you on the...how would you call it? The hot seat. I'm not putting you there. I'm not questioning your leadership or missions you carried out. This is a lesson for all of us."

"Okay," Troy said. "In teams I was a part of, including mixed units with personnel from other countries, I must have seen ten times the number of my own men die. Sixty, let's say."

Miquel gestured with his chin at Dubois.

"And now Dubois is dead too. She got shot in the head. You might have survived all that, we don't know for a fact, but she didn't. We do know that much."

Troy looked back at Dubois again. She grimaced and shrugged. Her thick, curly hair had been matted down by her helmet. The green paint dripped down her face.

"I assume you don't want her dead," Miquel said.

"Of course not," Troy said.

Now Miquel pointed at him. "In El Grupo, that's our first job. We protect each other. We keep each other alive, and we live to fight another day. Even if that means backing away when we think the brass ring is almost within our grasp."

There was quiet in the big room.

"I picked the best to be here," Miquel said. "I think so. Jan Bakker is one of the best data intelligence agents in Europe. If he tells you to abort a mission, he has a very good idea what he's talking about."

Now Troy and Miquel locked eyes.

"Trust your team," Miquel said. "And keep them alive."

CHAPTER TWO

"So, you're coming?" Troy's mother said into his ear from five thousand miles away. "Or you're not coming? People do need to know."

Everyone knew. Anyone who needed to, already knew the answer. Troy had been, and was continuing to be, completely transparent about his intentions.

He stood on the steps of the famous Queen Sofía art museum, flanked by the two glass elevator towers, the imposing façade of the building looming behind him (the place was a hospital for more than 160 years, but it looked like a prison to Troy), the early evening swirl of Madrid all around him.

Night had just fallen. The sky was dark, and everything was brightly lit: the streets, the buildings, everything. Hundreds of people were out, strolling across the wide expanse of the stone plaza in front of the museum, bundled against the chill.

His body was sore along the torso. He could feel the throbbing where the paintballs had hit him. Those guys had let him have it today, probably more than was necessary. He had that effect on people sometimes.

Troy glanced up and down the wide boulevard, waiting for *her* to appear. He felt a weird tickle of nervousness. Aliz Willems, the beautiful European heiress from Luxembourg, and Troy Stark, the former United States Navy SEAL from the Bronx, were going on a date.

They had agreed to do this before he came over here. Now, it was happening. His new job had brought him here to Madrid. And when they talked on the phone about that a few days ago, she had said, "I love Madrid. It's one of my favorite cities."

That was it. She didn't have business here or anything along those lines. Troy Stark was in Madrid, and it was one of her favorite cities, so she came here, from wherever she had been, to go on a dinner date. This was how the wealthy did things.

An image of her brother, the international weapons dealer and possible terrorist, flitted through Troy's mind. There were layers and layers to this. Aliz was one thing, and that was…interesting. Getting to her brother was something else entirely.

They were supposed to have dinner at a fancy restaurant in the Plaza Mayor, but for some reason she had asked him to meet her here. He didn't know how they were supposed to get from here to the Plaza Mayor. He was just learning his way around town, and she had been a bit cagey about it. The Plaza was a good half-hour walk. That wouldn't bother him, but it might bother her.

He imagined her showing up here in high heels, then having to limp through the city to dinner. Or maybe she would wear running shoes. Either way, it was a little weird. He smiled at the thought of her in a dinner dress and sneakers.

"Ma," he said into the phone. "I don't know another way to say this that could make it any clearer. I am coming. I have a flight booked for tomorrow morning. I'll be landing at JFK, if everything goes well, in the early afternoon. I'm going to take a taxi up to the house."

"So, you're coming to the wedding, is that what you're saying?"

He shook his head and smiled. "I am coming to the wedding. Yes."

"You know it's up in Worcester, right?"

Troy's young cousin Teddy was suddenly getting married, and in Worcester, Massachusetts of all places. Teddy was a good kid, Troy supposed. He had been about eight years old when Troy left for the military. That would make him about twenty-two now. The truth was that Troy had seen him probably five times in the past fourteen years. Maybe he was a good kid, maybe he wasn't. Troy had no idea.

"Who in their right mind gets married in Massachusetts in the middle of November?" Troy said.

"People who need to get married in a hurry, that's who."

"Ah."

"Yes," his mother said. "Ah."

"Is she showing?" Troy said.

"I haven't seen her. So, I don't know."

That was a lie. It was probably a double lie. It was very likely that his mom knew if the blushing bride was obviously pregnant, and even more, it was likely she had seen photos of her. Troy's mom liked to pretend she wasn't dead center at the heart of the rumor mill.

9

Troy scanned the wide plaza again. On the far side of it, the boulevard was busy with car traffic. The street and the plaza were packed with evening strollers. Aliz could walk right by and Troy might not even spot her. He didn't know what she was wearing. He didn't know what direction she was coming from. He didn't know anything.

This was silly. They probably should have just met at the restaurant.

"So, you're coming?" his mom said again.

"Yes!"

"You know, because I worry."

Here it comes.

He didn't know why he even encouraged this sort of thing. But he took the bait. It was early afternoon in New York. He pictured her, sitting in her living room chair, the TV silently playing a news station across from her. He pictured himself as a large fish, and his mom dangling a hunk of bloody meat above him.

"What are you worried about?"

"You," she said. "I thought you got a job with the police department. You did one assignment for them, down south for some reason, apparently got injured, and then ran off to Europe. Now what? What are you even doing for money?"

"I told you, Mom. I got a better job."

"Working for who?"

"The federal government. A charitable arm of the government. We do medical…"

"What is it called?" she said, cutting him off.

"What is *what* called?"

"The charity." She was implacable. She was the Terminator. She would ask the same questions again and again, phrasing them differently each time, waiting for the mistake to happen.

"Oh. It's called, uh…"

"See what I mean?" she said. "This is why I worry. You work for something, but you don't even know what it's called."

"It's called FOMAP," Troy said, and nearly laughed out loud. "FOMAP, Ma. Okay? The United States Foreign Medical Aid Program. FOMAP for short. US FOMAP, if you like."

"It's a charity?" she said.

"It's the federal government."

"Why do they call it that? FOMAP." She said it as though it tasted bad.

"It's the government. They have funny names for everything."

10

"But what are you doing for money in the meantime? While you're doing all this charity work?"

"They pay me money," Troy said.

Just in front of him, a sleek black Jaguar pulled into a restricted parking spot he had only barely noticed until now. The spot had something written on it in white, on the ground, but Troy didn't know what the words meant, so he hadn't keyed in on them.

"A lot of money," he added, as if that would explain everything. "They pay me a lot of money."

"But why?"

"I don't know. They must like me."

"And what do you do?"

The rear door of the Jaguar opened and a blonde woman in a red dress stepped out. It was her. Immediately, it was if the entire city behind her was rendered in black and white and only she was in color. That was the effect she had.

People turned to stare at her. She reached back into the car and came out with a black leather jacket. It was a chilly night. She shrugged into the jacket. He was going to raise his hand to her, but she already knew where he was. She walked towards him, shimmering in the night, as though walking through a movie.

Behind her, the door to the car closed all by itself. Then the car just sat there. Of course, it was a VIP parking spot. The driver was just going to wait while Aliz and Troy did whatever was on her mind here.

"Troy?" his mother said.

"Yeah, Ma," he said. "I do charitable work. It's a good job. It's safe. I deal with a lot of bigwigs. There are always a lot of important people milling around. I met the ambassador to Poland a couple of days ago. And his wife."

Did the ambassador to Poland even have a wife? Troy had no idea.

"The ambassador to Poland? Our ambassador? I thought you were in Spain."

"Look," Troy said. "I have to run. I'm going to be in town tomorrow. I'll tell you all about it when I see you, okay?"

With any luck, her house would be full of his brothers and their families, and he wouldn't tell her even one word about what he was doing.

"Okay, Troy. Have a good flight. I love you."

"I love you too, Mom."

He hung up. Aliz was here. She walked up the stairs to him. Her heels made her seem tall, but still several inches shorter than he was.

"Hello stranger," he said.

They didn't hug. They didn't kiss. She took him by the arm. "Come inside," she said. "I want very badly to show you something. It'll take just a few minutes. Then we'll eat."

He looked up at the museum. A giant, colorful poster hung over the front entrance, showing several artworks and some writing in Spanish. It didn't seem worth paying full admission price to go inside for just a few minutes.

"How much is it?"

She shook her head and smiled. "It's nothing. Free. I'm a benefactor here. A patron, I think you would say. I come and go as I please."

He stared at her. Of course she was.

She gestured to him, holding out her hand. "Come. Let me show you."

CHAPTER THREE

8:30 pm Central European Time
El Restaurante Paco X (Paco X Restaurant)
Plaza Mayor
Madrid, Spain

Aliz wondered what Troy Stark was thinking.

She had brought him face-to-face with one of the great art works of the 20th century, and he'd said very little about it. Then she'd brought him to one of the best restaurants in the city, and he assaulted his food like a barbarian. Without much information from his brain to go on, she simply watched him work on his food.

He used his entrée fork on his salad. He wielded the fork in the same way a workman would wield a shovel. He shoveled food into his mouth as though he were shoveling coal into a furnace.

At one point, he simply picked up a small, wayward tomato in his long fingers and popped it into his mouth. It seemed that he couldn't successfully spear it, or shovel it, with the fork.

The waiter brought him a beer, and Troy declined the frosted glass, preferring to drink straight from the bottle. The waiter was about to expertly pour the beer into the glass, and Troy held up a hand like a STOP sign.

"No," was all he said. He looked up at the waiter and shook his head.

On the one hand, it was like watching a caveman eat. On the other hand, there was something endearing about it. It didn't hurt that he was tall, handsome, and—given the cut of his jeans and his sweater—very fit.

Aliz was a social scientist above all things, and she was well aware of the so-called "halo effect." People were eager to forgive certain behaviors, or see them in a positive light, when they were carried out by exceptionally good-looking people. She knew that she was as vulnerable to this as anyone. Still, the way he ate was cute.

The surroundings didn't hurt, either. They were seated in the outdoor section of Paco X, a place with three Michelin stars, and

13

perhaps her favorite restaurant in Madrid. Portable jet fireplaces were stationed around the edge of the dining area to chase away the cold night air. All around them, the old grand plaza was lit up and filled with evening strollers. It was a beautiful setting.

Even Troy's response to the restaurant was somehow charming. He didn't seem to notice how special it was. He was a working man, but he also didn't seem to notice there were no prices on the menu. Perhaps he assumed she was going to pay. It was a safe assumption.

The owner, Paco Abrile, was a friend of hers. Paco was famous in the culinary world, certainly in Europe, but maybe even everywhere. When he came out to greet them, he kissed Aliz warmly on both cheeks. Then Troy shook his hand and said, "Howdy."

Paco raised his eyebrows. Aliz nearly laughed out loud.

"What did you think of the painting?" she said to Troy now. "You haven't said."

She did not know why, but his reaction was important to her. They had gone inside the Reina Sofía to look at *Guernica* by Pablo Picasso. Troy was a soldier, she knew that, or had been earlier in his life. He had resorted to violence quickly and with total mastery the night he had "saved" her from her brother in Luxembourg.

Had he actually saved her? She doubted it very much. Her half-brother Luc's men had kidnapped her before. It was Luc's way of bringing her to one of his secret hideouts for a visit. Troy had turned it into a vicious life and death struggle, which he had won. But he couldn't have known what she knew.

In any event, the painting was the most moving, shattering anti-war statement that she was aware of. A protest against the Nazi bombing of the defenseless town of Guernica during the Spanish Civil War, it was probably Picasso's most important work of art. At the time of the bombing, most of the men had left the city to join the war. Of the people who died in the attack, the vast majority of them were women, children, and the elderly. Aliz was curious what Troy thought of the painting. More than that, she wanted to know what it made him *feel*.

He smiled. "Well, it's big."

She smiled too. That was a start. The massive black and white painting was three meters high by eight meters long. It completely dominated the display hall where it hung. People often came in and were struck speechless by its sheer size.

Aliz nodded. "It is. Big."

"Huge," Troy said.

"Enormous."

They both smiled. Aliz sipped her wine. Troy drank his beer.

"The size of it was the first thing I noticed," Troy said.

She looked at him sideways, just a little bit. Were they flirting?

"But you must have…felt something?"

He paused for a long moment and looked out at the bustling plaza. Then he looked back at her again as if he had decided something. She could almost swear that he nodded to himself.

"I was in the military," he said.

She nodded. "Yes, I know."

"I was kicked out because I disobeyed orders."

"I didn't know that."

He nodded again, more forcefully this time. "I'm not really supposed to talk about it, but…this one is on them. I was ordered to take my unit and leave a group of civilians—women, children, and old people—vulnerable to attack. I won't get into the details. A lot of what goes on in combat doesn't make sense. I'll just say that I refused to do it. We accompanied the civilians to safety instead. It seems to have ended my career. Or at least, ended that career. I have a new career now."

There was silence between them. Aliz could feel the heat from the jet fireplace a couple of meters away from them.

"I've spent months wondering about it. What I did, what I should have done. And the painting helped me, if that makes sense."

"What did it help you do?" she said.

"It helped me realize that I made the right decision."

There was a long silence between them. Then the entrées came. Hers was a Bacalao a la Vizcaína, a spicy cod dish typical of the Basque region where Paco grew up. Troy ordered steak. It seemed a bit of a waste—anyone could make a good steak. Paco was a genius of regional Spanish cuisine, and Troy was going to miss that entirely.

They tucked into their meals. Troy ate quickly, very much the Stone Age Man again. An image flashed briefly through her mind—introducing him to her social circle. They would make a strange pair, the caveman and the princess. She had no idea how such a thing might work out.

She gestured with her chin at his plate. "How do you like it?"

He nodded. "It's good." He looked around at the outdoor dining area, the crowds on the plaza, the lights, and the fires.

"This is a nice joint."

CHAPTER FOUR

November 11
5:30 am Eastern Standard Time
A lake cabin
The Berkshire Mountains, Massachusetts

"What are you looking for?" a male voice said.

She ignored him for the moment. She stood on the back porch of the cabin, gazing out at the lake in the predawn blackness. The night was cold, and her breath rose in plumes. The fall tourist season was over now, the leaves were off the trees, the leaf peepers went back to Connecticut or New Jersey or wherever.

The cabins on the far side of the lake, lined up like soldiers in the daytime, were dark now. There didn't seem to be a light on anywhere, except this house.

"Cheri?" the voice said, as if she hadn't heard him the first time.

She called herself Cheri Bomb.

That was as it should be. Everyone in the group went by an alias. Some of them were meant to be humorous, like hers. Some were simple, meaningless, and instantly forgettable, like the name of the man standing behind her now, Mr. Gray. Most people here dispensed with the Mr. and called him Gray.

"You've been standing there for an hour."

It was just safer this way. There had been too many infiltrators in recent years. The FBI, Interpol, and police agencies everywhere just found it too easy to penetrate these groups. Too many cells had been taken down before they ever did anything.

But the groups, and the individuals involved, were getting smarter.

Her long hair was dyed black. She could shave it all off in five minutes. She had done that before. She had several tattoos on her arms that were not real.

A tattoo on her torso said, *Only to the white man was nature a wilderness.* Also fake. All the tattoos were indelible ink, designed to last for a few months. In a pinch, she could scrub them off in an hour. She wore contact lenses that made her eyes brown.

16

She was taking creatine pills, ten grams a day, and doing high intensity body weight workouts—squats, pushups, bear crawls, and pull-ups. The combination made her muscular, like an action movie heroine. If she stopped the supplements and the exercises tomorrow, she would be her normal skinny self again in a few weeks. It took a concentrated effort to force her body to retain muscle.

She was traveling under an assumed identity, one she had shared with nobody here. If things went wrong, she could be five thousand miles away in no time, with short hair dyed white, blue eyes, no tattoos, a body ten pounds lighter and stereotypically female. She could doll herself up and no one would ever expect she could engage in dangerous, "masculine" style behavior.

She had never met anyone in this group before a month ago. They were a good group and very disciplined. They each brought their own skills and personalities, even some quirks, but they had come together as a team and were now something close to a well-oiled machine. After this job, she planned to do one more. Maybe these people would be in on that job, maybe they wouldn't. She had no control over these things. Either way, once that job was done, she planned to never see any of them again.

She turned to look at Gray. She guessed he was about twenty-five, which would make him seven years younger than she was. He had a long, brown beard to go with his long, brown hair. He wore black glasses, which he didn't need. The lenses were clear plastic, with no prescription. He spoke impeccable English, but with just a touch of an accent. Cheri guessed he was from Germany, or maybe Austria.

He was wearing a white t-shirt and jeans. He was barefoot, despite the chill out here on the porch. He was almost ridiculously fit, capable of all kinds of circus-like acrobatics that came from years of calisthenics. He had a very handsome face hiding under the beard, the hair, and the glasses. She could tell by his square jawline. After he disappeared, shaved all that off, and ditched the glasses, he would probably look like a Hollywood movie star.

She had taken him as her lover. Why not? It felt good. It would be over soon. Sometimes she worried that he was catching feelings, but it wasn't her problem. He knew better than that. As long as he didn't jeopardize the mission, he could feel however he wanted. If he did jeopardize the mission…

The way they usually did it was by getting all white knight chivalrous. Old habits, and paradigms, were hard to erase. A lot of the

17

guys in this movement were closet male chauvinists. They were all for risk, militancy, and equality, until it was their girlfriend you were talking about. Then, she shouldn't have to break a fingernail.

Cheri shook her head. That wasn't Gray. The rumor was that he had been on operations where people died, including women and civilians. He didn't seem fazed by it.

"I was out here yesterday morning," she said now. "It was just before dawn. I saw a man swimming across the lake in total darkness, coming this way. That didn't seem right, so I watched him the whole way. You know, you get these ideas sometimes...a frogman FBI agent."

Gray nodded. "I know."

"As he got closer, I noticed his head was too big. I thought maybe it was a helmet. Then he climbed out of the water, just over there by the next house, on that little sandy beach they have. Turned out it was a black bear."

She smiled. "I thought maybe he would come back and do it again."

"I like bears," Gray said.

She nodded. "Yes. I like that they have this whole area to themselves for the next six months."

He held out his arms and she stepped into his embrace. Again, why not? It felt good. Physical touch felt good. Maybe you could even call it love. Not love like in the magazines or the movies, just the love that two sentient beings feel. It could be a cat or a dog. It was better than the camaraderie the members of a movement share.

He was six inches taller than her and very strong. She took a deep breath. It almost felt like safety in his arms.

"You've been at this a long time," he said.

She nodded. "My entire adult life."

"Do you ever worry?"

She shook her head. "Worry about what?"

"Is it wrong?" he said. "Is it right?"

"I don't have to worry about that," she said. "Because I already know the answer."

Indeed, she did. Their enemies were destroying the Earth, plundering it, and someone had to stop them. Someone at least had to try.

In the case of this operation, the powers they were fighting were screwing around with the very underpinnings of reality. They could cause a rupture in time and space, or they could conjure up a black hole,

18

blasting the Earth, the sun, and the entire solar system into it. They thought they were intelligent, and in a very narrow sense, maybe they were. But mostly they were fools.

She sighed. Humans really were like a Disney movie, but a specific Disney movie. They were like the one where Mickey Mouse plays the sorcerer's apprentice. He gets the brooms moving, bringing buckets of water into the house, but then he can't make them stop. Soon he finds himself under water.

Humans liked to tinker. All too often, they liked to tinker with things they didn't understand. Then they claimed to be surprised by the outcome. Nuclear weapons came to mind, but so did leaded gasoline, smog, the decimated ozone layer, gigantic oil spills in the Arctic and the Gulf of Mexico, the clear cutting of ancient forests, and overfishing leading to the die-offs of entire species in the oceans.

Cheri couldn't stop all of it. But sometimes, she could stop one part of it.

"What about when innocent people get hurt?" Gray said.

She thought about it, but only for a second. She was a soldier. She didn't like to think of it this way, but she was also a mercenary, straddling a line between true believer and cutthroat pirate. Either way, she was fighting a war. She had never actually hurt anyone herself, but people did get hurt in war. So be it.

"Darling," she said. "There are no innocent people."

CHAPTER FIVE

November 12
7:30 pm Eastern Standard Time
Our Lady of Warsaw Church
Worcester, Massachusetts

"Well, the bride is definitely showing," big Donnie Stark said.

Troy nodded. "Looks like twins."

"Triplets," Pat said.

"And a half," said Eddie.

"Three and a half children," Donnie said. "That girl's gonna pop like *Alien*."

The four Stark brothers leaned along the bar in the event hall attached to the back of the church, drinking and cracking themselves up. The place was packed with revelers. It was a wedding, after all.

The church was a century-old Roman Catholic parish built by Polish immigrants. The bride's family were descendants of the people who had built the church. Even though most of the original parish had moved away from the old neighborhood and out to the suburbs, they all came back here for church services.

Across the dance floor from them, two catering workers had just carried out a massive, multi-tiered white wedding cake, layer upon layer, bunting upon bunting, with bride and groom figurines at the top. The workers set the beast down on a table. From the way they had carried it, the thing looked heavy.

"You know what they say about babies," Troy said.

Eddie nodded, "Most take nine months."

"But the first one can come anytime," said Pat. He should know. He was in the fire department's Emergency Medical Services and had delivered quite a few babies on the fly in the past 15 years.

The bride wore pink. She looked like she was about eight months pregnant. She was very pretty and beamed with pride. Teddy Stark was a tall drink of water who, at twenty-two years old, hadn't quite filled out yet. His hair was spiked and dyed blue. He had spiderweb tattoos on his hands.

Apparently, he played guitar and sang in a rock band. That was it. That was his plan. No one had informed him that rock had died two decades ago. He was better off trying to rap or sing sweet bubblegum ballads.

"Someone needs to straighten that kid out," Donnie said now.

It was almost as if Donnie could read Troy's mind sometimes. Or as if their minds somehow had a trunk line running from one to the other. Troy was like that when he was in close proximity to any of his brothers, but the effect seemed most pronounced with Donnie.

"Her brothers will do it," Eddie said.

The girl's three brothers were all plumbers.

Troy nodded. "Teddy could be a plumber. It's a good job."

He was starting to feel buzzed. He had met the brothers briefly, just long enough to shake hands. They were all big guys with hands of stone.

Most of the people here were Polish. The wedding band was set up on a small stage off to the left. There were about eight or nine people in the band. They played Polka music. So far, it seemed like Polka was their entire repertoire.

Donnie shrugged and gazed out at the people on the dance floor bouncing to the music. It was a driving, frenzied song about people who like pierogies. "Teddy could be a Polack. He likes pierogies."

"I like pierogies," Troy said.

"You must like Polacks too," Eddie said.

Troy looked at him and nodded. "Yeah. I do. But I think the correct term these days is Polish-American."

They had something going here. They were loyal to the old church and the old neighborhood. They were a tight knit community. Polka wasn't Troy's favorite music, but at least they were keeping the culture alive.

"That's good," Eddie said. "Maybe you should join up. Ma told me you met the Polish ambassador over in Europe. She's been telling everybody who will listen. All the babushkas and mamushkas."

They gazed across at their mother, who was sitting at a round table with a bunch of other ladies from both families. She was regaling them all about something.

"Nah," Troy said. "She's letting them know that Donnie made Inspector."

"What's his name, that Polish ambassador?" Pat said. "In case somebody asks?"

21

Pat was the quiet one, the serious one. You knew it was a drinking party when Pat started to pile on.

Troy smiled and shook his head. He had no idea who the Polish ambassador was. "I told her I met the ambassador to Poland. Not the Polish ambassador. There's a big difference." He had no idea who the ambassador to Poland was, either.

"Did you help him change the lightbulb over at the embassy?"

"Yeah, Troy and about eight other guys," Donnie said.

"One guy to hold the lightbulb..."

"And eight guys to turn the building," said a new voice, finishing the punch line for them.

"Ha, ha, ha. That ain't funny."

Troy looked to his right and saw three big guys standing with drinks in their hands. They were tall and their bodies were thick like Idaho potatoes. They had giant workman hands, the kind accustomed to bending reluctant inanimate objects to their will. Two of the guys were what you'd call heavyset. One was hugely overweight. One of them was a brother of the bride. He was wearing a round button on the lapel of his dark dinner jacket.

Troy figured it must be a button for some union local, a politician, a bowling team, God only knew. He looked more closely at it.

You bet your DUPA I'm Polish.

"Hey friend," Donnie said. "We're just fooling around over here."

"You're talking pretty loud," the heaviest of the three men said. He reminded Troy of some entertainment figure from the distant past. Fatty Arbuckle, maybe, or PT Barnum. He had high rosy color in his cheeks, nearly bordering on purple. Oxygen was probably an issue for this guy. You could almost sense him wheezing and gasping on every word. "A lot of people can hear you. It's disrespectful."

Eddie shook his head. "Nobody can hear us." He gestured at the band. "The oompah music is too loud."

Here we go.

"This is our wedding," the heaviest one said. "This is our church. You punks are just guests here."

Troy shook his head. It was always like this with certain kind of men. No one backed down. No one had reverse as an option. His brothers were this way. These new guys, relatives, friends of the bride, or maybe just denizens of Worcester, were apparently the same way.

Troy was a little buzzed. That didn't matter. It seemed like it was going to be up to him to be the voice of reason here. It made sense.

He'd spent a lot of time in the military. He'd had to deal with all sorts of local people, from all sorts of different places, and in all sorts of complicated situations. The thing to do here was to defuse the tension. He stepped forward, in his mind halfway to a new career as an elder statesman, negotiating settlements to intractable problems all over the world.

He raised his right hand. There was a beer can in his left hand.

"Listen up," he began.

"No, you listen."

"I'm trying to be nice."

BAM!

The man with the DUPA button punched Troy in the nose. It was a hard right hand, with thick tight fingers, and it hit him like a sledgehammer. Troy's head snapped back. Somewhere nearby, a woman gasped. It was quite a hit.

Troy still had his beer. He took a slug of it and shook his head.

"Oh, buddy."

Now the guy nodded. "Yeah?"

Two more local guys were moving in from the left. Behind him, Troy sensed his brothers putting their drinks down on the bar.

"Gentlemen!" the bartender shouted. "Gentlemen, this is a..."

The band was still playing. Wump bump bump bump, wump bump bump.

"Hey!"

If anything, the music was louder and more driving than a moment before. It drowned out whatever the bartender was trying to say.

Troy dropped his beer can on the floor and feinted a jab with his left. The DUPA guy moved to block it, but in the same move, Troy hooked the right around. The guy was completely exposed. It was a hard right, and it hit the guy's chin sideways like a passing freight train. The guy's head snapped to the left.

Then came back to center. His eyes focused on Troy, spaced out for a split second, then found him again. The eyes were bloodshot. The guy had probably been drinking since last night. He smiled.

"You're gonna have to do better than that."

"Okay."

Troy hit him again. The guy's head snapped backwards, then came right back to center again. He either had the strongest chin in the world, or he was so drunk his brain just wasn't registering these hits.

Suddenly, a guy was on Troy from the left. The guy had strong arms and was trying to get Troy in some kind of arm bar or stranglehold. They wrestled, strength against strength, no technique. Troy went for a knee to the groin, but the guy had already twisted to the side, putting his heavy thigh there.

All around them, people pushed and shoved. More people shouted. A mass of big, struggling bodies gathered, like a rugby scrum. It moved out onto the dance floor, crashing into bodies, people falling. Now there were shouts and screams.

Troy could hear punches, fists hitting flesh. Donnie was near him. He had one guy in a headlock. A third guy was trying to get Donnie in a headlock. Everything was intertwined, like a game of Twister, only not sexy. Not sexy at all.

The flashing lights of the dance floor were below Troy's feet now. He didn't know who was who or what was what. The band played on, louder than before.

Troy wrenched his right arm free. He punched the guy holding him, again and again. But he couldn't get leverage, he couldn't get momentum. He was bruising that guy, he bloodied him, but he couldn't get the knockout in.

The DUPA guy was behind him. He grabbed Troy by the hair.

The whole mad scrum surged across the dance floor, moving under its own momentum.

"Not the cake!" someone screamed. "Watch the cake!"

Troy looked up and the tall, white, creamy wedding cake was RIGHT THERE. He noticed how the little bride and the groom at the top were traditional figurines, like you'd see at any wedding. The bride was slim and wearing a white gown and a veil. The groom wore a black tuxedo. His hair was not blue. There were no spiderwebs tattooed on his hands.

It was too late now. There were too many heavy bodies moving, too much force involved. They couldn't stop if they wanted to.

"Watch the cake!" someone screamed again.

CHAPTER SIX

11:40 pm Eastern Standard Time
The New England Heavy Ion Collider
North Adams Laboratory
The Berkshire Mountains, Massachusetts

"One minute," a voice from the front of the van said. "Get ready to engage."

Cheri's heart skipped a beat. It always did at times like this. She got butterflies in her stomach. She shook. She felt like she would throw up. Sometimes, she felt like she would break down and cry.

Over the years, she had learned to start taking Imodium on the morning of any nighttime operation. Having diarrhea on a job was not a good look.

She sat in the back of the van along a wooden bench. She knew that on the outside, the van looked exactly like the utility vans that workers from the laboratory drove. It was a small white van, nondescript, very new, with the cryptic letters NAL in an attractive blue font along the side.

The benign look of the van was meant to disguise the dangerous activities going on inside of this place. She had seen the documents. She knew that they had smashed gold ions here at almost the speed of light, generating temperatures up to 7,500 degrees Fahrenheit, temperatures that existed nowhere else on Earth, except at similar facilities.

She knew that six months ago, they had generated conditions inside their atom smasher resembling a black hole in deep space. For a moment, even the scientists themselves had been terrified at what they'd done.

But the black hole was tiny, and lasted only a fraction of a section, so they had gone right back to what they were doing. But what if it hadn't been so small? What if it had lasted longer? For the scientists, the answer was always, "But it didn't."

She shook her head. Not good enough.

She looked around the van. There were four of them back here, the same four people who had shared the house: herself, Mr. Gray, a guy calling himself Oil Derek, and another guy going by the name Purple Hays. The two men in the front of the van were shadows behind smoked glass. For all Cheri knew, they actually worked for the lab, hated it, and were helping this cell infiltrate.

"Thirty seconds." The man's voice was flat and emotionless.

Cheri glanced out the rear window. They were inside the gates of the complex now. It was going smoothly. It was going exactly according to plan.

Professionalism had taken a huge jump upwards in recent years. It had to. It was either that or do long stretches of time in prison.

She looked at the man called Purple Hays. He was a big guy, an ogre, someone you couldn't miss. His head was shaven. He had hard eyes and a nose broken enough times he seemed to gasp when he breathed. There was a scar running down his right cheek—it was the most obvious thing about him, and almost certainly fake. When he spoke, it was with what Cheri thought of as an Eastern European accent. He seemed to have some sort of military experience. If she was honest with herself, most of the professionalism in this group had to do with the presence of Purple Hays. Everything about him was spare, efficient, no nonsense, and on time.

He was the enforcer. He was the one who would ride in the van with the guards afterwards, and release them, without phones, somewhere in the wilderness of Vermont. His job was also to put enough of a scare into them that they would be reluctant to cooperate with investigators.

He was carrying what looked like a large automatic rifle. Cheri happened to know it was an airsoft gun that role playing geeks used for war simulations. The orange tip that would give it away as a toy had been removed from the barrel. They weren't here to hurt anyone, though Hays could probably kill a man with his bare hands if he had to.

Cheri and the other three all had tasers. They carried them in case of an emergency, and for no other reason. All three of them—her, Gray, and Derek—were chosen for their speed and agility.

In between the benches were three motorcycles. They were fast, of the so-called "crotch rocket" variety. That's how Cheri was leaving here tonight.

Either that or on a slab.

"Ten seconds. Prepare to open door."

"Here we go," Hays said. "Watch my back. Take down any resistance. No games."

He took his helmet and slid it over his massive head. He closed the face shield and picked up the rifle. He was the only one wearing a helmet. It was hard to place charges correctly, and count the timing, when you had no peripheral vision. Cheri pulled the balaclava mask up over the lower half of her face. Gray and Derek did the same.

"Engage," the voice said.

Hays unlatched the rear door and kicked it open. He was out a second later, and the other three piled out behind him.

"Down!" he screamed. It sounded like *Don.* "Down! Down!"

There were two men here, security guards. They had come out to this interior loading dock to meet the truck. They wore white dress shirts and dark blue pants. They had the pleasant blue NAL logos on the breasts of their shirts.

"Down!"

They were armed, with holstered guns at their waists. But they didn't make a move for them. They weren't ready for Purple Hays. They weren't expecting a hulking, six-foot two-inch behemoth in a black smoked helmet with what sure looked like an automatic weapon. They went down, face first. They practically dove to the cement floor.

This place had never been attacked before. They had no reason to suspect it ever would. Despite what went on here, these facilities were soft targets. Most people barely knew they existed.

Hays raised his left hand and made a symbol that Cheri equated with heavy metal music, his forefinger and pinky extended upwards—the so-called devil horns.

Hays had established several hand signals during their training period. The devil horns meant that an action had gone well and according to plan.

He pointed at Cheri and pointed at his own eyes. Then he put his open hand next to his ear. *Watch. Listen.*

She nodded.

"Get the guns," he said out loud. "Check them for other weapons."

Derek and Gray went to their knees, took the guns from the guard's holsters, then patted them down for more.

"GPS?" Hays said.

Neither of the guards spoke.

Hays squatted down and poked one of them in the skull with the rifle. "Answer or I shoot you in the head."

27

"Our identification badges have embedded GPS chips. That's it."

Hays gestured with his chin. "Get the badges."

Derek snapped the leash with the hanging badge of his man. Gray did the same to the other.

"Tie their arms. Tie them tight."

Derek and Gray moved in unison. They pulled the arms of the guards behind their backs, and affixed plastic zip ties to their wrists.

"Now blindfolds."

Derek and Gray had the black cloths out and in seconds were tying them tight over the men's eyes.

"Freeze!" someone shouted. "All of you. Don't move. I swear to God, I will blow your brains out."

Cheri had been wool gathering, watching the action in front of her. She was curious about Purple Hays. She had gotten caught up in how effortlessly he controlled these guards, and how naturally he commanded Derek and Gray. Maybe she was even proud of how efficiently these men all worked as a team.

That was bad. She needed to be more alert. She was supposed to be the sentry.

And now...

Another guard had appeared. He was here in the open warehouse space, moving across the loading dock, his gun drawn, held in a two-handed shooter's grip. He appeared to have come out from the heavy iron door behind him. His breath rose in white plumes.

His eyes said he was afraid. His hands shook the smallest amount. His hair was close-cropped, but it was white at the edges and retreating back from his forehead. He was about twenty pounds overweight. The man was middle-aged.

Cheri was standing behind Hays's giant bulk. She was tiny compared to Hays. She couldn't be sure, but it was possible that this new guard had not seen her here. She looked down at the clunky black M-26 taser in her right hand.

Hays looked at it too. He quickly made his left hand into the shape of a pistol and pulled an imaginary trigger. *Shoot him.* Then he raised his hands in the air. His rifle was high above his head now. He faced Cheri. His broad back was to the guard.

"Yes," he said in a low voice. "Do it."

"Drop that gun!" the guard shouted.

28

The airsoft gun fell from Hays's hand and clattered to the stone floor. It was a toy. A toy for grown men, but a toy nonetheless. Didn't the guard see that?

The guard came up behind Hays. He was close now.

"On the floor, big boy. I swear to God, I'll kill you."

Very slowly, Cheri raised the taser and pointed it directly at Hays's chest. Hays nodded, very subtly, almost imperceptibly.

"You better get down…" the guard said.

Suddenly Hays dropped as if a trap door had opened under him. It was shocking how fast he moved. An instant later, she depressed the trigger on the taser. The taser POPPED, loud, and the two twin probes flew out. They pierced the guard's shirt, right below where his chest met his neck.

"Yes! Give it to him."

The guard screamed as the probes delivered the current of electricity through his body. His gun fell from his hand. For a second, he stood and twitched like he was having a seizure. Then he dropped. He landed on his back, his head bouncing off the concrete floor of the dock.

Hays was on his feet again, as quick as a jungle cat.

He looked at Cheri and nodded. "Very nice. Very good. But pay closer attention next time."

Now he picked up the guard's gun and squatted down next to him. The man was trembling, his face in a seemingly permanent grimace.

"Is he okay?" Cheri said. It was the first thing she had said since they climbed out of the van.

Hays nodded. "Fine. I've seen it before. Maybe a little system overwhelm. I'll put him in the van with the others."

He looked back at them all. "Get to work. Fast. We don't have all night."

"We don't have the codes yet," Gray said.

Hays shrugged. "We only need one."

"We don't have it."

Inside his dark helmet, Hays seemed to give Gray a sidelong glance. He stood to his full height, then walked back to the two guards zip-tied on the floor. Now he squatted again and poked one of them in the face with a large finger.

"You. The code, please."

"What code?"

29

"We're not stupid, you know. The code that goes with your ID card."

The man, blind from the dark cloth tied over his eyes, hands fastened behind his back, shook his head. "I don't..."

Hays moved his big finger to the man's blindfold and slipped it underneath. He pressed it against the man's face near his eye. "I will remove your eye with this finger. Is that what you want?"

"Sir, I..."

"Three seconds, and you are a one-eyed Cyclops. Then I move on to your friend. I think he will cooperate."

"08-28-70," the man said without hesitating.

Hays looked up at all of them now. "Go. I will finish here."

The guard Cheri had tasered was still shaking. Sometimes people had heart conditions and died from being tased. There was nothing she could do about that.

She followed Gray and Derek to a smooth, white door with an electronic lock mechanism and keypad. Gray swiped the ID card, then punched the six-digit code into the keypad. The door clicked and opened a small amount. He grabbed the handle and yanked it all the way.

Now they were in a long, narrow, curving corridor. A set of double doors were to their left. A sign to the right of the doors said simply, CONTROL. Below the sign was an identical electronic lock and keypad.

Gray unlocked those doors and pushed them open.

"Go!"

Derek went into the room.

Gray looked at Cheri. "Ready?"

She nodded. "Ready."

"Run!"

He burst out ahead of her, as they had done many times. He was incredibly fit and fast, much faster than she was. But they both had a role to play. He ran out ahead. His task was to reach a quarter of a mile down the tunnel, then work his way back, planting charges. Hers was to reach half that distance, approximately 200 meters, and do the same.

They passed through an open doorway and now the particle accelerator was on their left. It was a wide cylinder about her height, brown or dark orange in color, segmented every twenty or thirty meters, with wires running along its length, and some sort of grid or catwalk running above it.

The corridor was dark, with only the emergency lights on.

She hit the timer on her wrist and ran as fast as the gear she carried would allow. Repeated practice said that weighed down, she could run the 200 meters in about thirty seconds. When the timer went off, she would stop, and work her way back, setting the charges. Gray would work his way back to her first charge, then sprint for the exit.

"Catch me!" she screamed at his retreating back.

He raised a hand in the OK gesture, meaning he had heard her.

She ran along the cylinder, the only sounds the gasps of her breath and the light slap of her sneakers on the flooring. After what seemed like too long, her timer went off. She was here. She stopped, bent over, and allowed herself five seconds of gasping for breath. Then she took her knapsack off, opened it, and dug out the first charge.

She had ten, one for every twenty meters. They were small round disks, about the size of hockey pucks. Each had a preset timer. There was a plastic backing on each one, which she peeled off. Then she placed the charge against the cylinder. All she needed to do then was press the button.

She moved along the way she had just come, walking backwards and planting the charges. It was easy work. It didn't so much require skill—everything was calibrated ahead of time by people who understood explosives. It required the daring to be here in the first place.

In a few moments, she was all the way back to the double doorway of the Control room. Just as she arrived, Derek emerged. She was sweating and breathing hard. He seemed calm. He gazed at her over the top of his balaclava.

She looked up the corridor. Here came Gray, sprinting.

"Let's go," she said.

They went back out into the dock area. Everything was ready. The three motorcycles were parked in a row, keys dangling from ignitions. Hers was red.

The rear door to the van was open. Purple Hays was lurking there, hanging out the back. He raised his arm and held up his tightened fist, then gave the devil horns again. All was well. He pointed two of his fingers at his own black helmet visor.

"See you," he said. "Good luck."

He banged on the side of the van three times. It began to roll away toward the exit.

"How is the guard?" Cheri said. She hated to show weakness like that. None of the others would do the same.

Hays shrugged. "I think he's fine. Please don't worry for him."

Hays crouched and backed into the van, then slammed the doors shut behind him. A moment later, the van was gone, away from the dock and headed toward the gate. She caught the red rear brake lights of it once before it turned a corner and disappeared.

Gray and Derek were already on their bikes. She climbed on hers. She turned the key in the ignition, pulled the clutch in, and pressed the start button. In front of her, mounted between the handlebars, was a video screen.

It was a map of the back roads she was to take to get her to the Taconic State Parkway in New York, which she would follow all the way south to New York City, and eventually to a scrap yard in Brooklyn. She would surrender the bike to whoever she met there, and that person would crush it into a small cube.

There was a small apartment for her near the Manhattan Bridge, where she would hide out tomorrow. She would shave her head to about a half-inch above the scalp, dye her hair, and scrub off her tattoos.

The next day, with a new identity, she had a flight to Berlin.

She looked at Gray one last time. She fought an urge to lean over and try to kiss him. Who was catching feelings now? She had no idea where his motorcycle was taking him, or where he would go after that. She had no idea if he was chosen for the next operation or not. How this one turned out might be what made that decision.

Derek took off without even looking back.

Gray looked at Cheri, eyes sharp above his black mask.

"See you again," he said.

A moment later, he was gone too. Now she was alone at the dock on her motorcycle. It was an odd moment. It was also a delicious one. This facility was set to blow up in less than ten minutes. And she was sitting here. Everyone else had disappeared.

There was something tempting about the idea of just sitting here on the motorcycle until the place was engulfed in flames, and she along with it.

She shook her head. That was crazy. She let out the clutch, rolled slowly across the complex and exited through the gates. She turned right onto a quiet country road. The mountains loomed in the darkness to her right, the very mountains the supercollider passed under.

She began to move faster and faster, pushing the bike now, freezing wind on her face and on her gloved hands. She had enjoyed her time here in the mountains of Massachusetts. She would miss this place and

32

the quiet empty lake where they had stayed. She longed to see the bear again.

She was miles away when a series of explosions lit up the sky and ruptured the night behind her.

.

CHAPTER SEVEN

November 13
2:35 am Eastern Standard Time
A rural property
Near St. Albans, Vermont

"Well, fellows? I guess it's that time."

Hays felt the van slow down right before it turned onto the property. Now it rolled slowly over the humpbacked road up to the barn. The barn was an old outbuilding that sat on this rustic farmland, all by itself, a thousand meters from the road.

Perhaps it had sat here a hundred years already. There was no house associated with it. It was just a big barn, sitting forlorn below a hillside near some trees, quite far away from its nearest neighbor.

They were very close to the Canadian border here, and in a little while, Hays would cross that border on his way to a flat in Montréal. A car, a change of clothes, and a fresh identity all awaited him in the barn.

In the meantime, the three guards were tied up at his feet. Two of them were alert. They hadn't spoken because, although they were blindfolded, they knew he was with them. They were afraid of him, which was the right call on their parts.

The third guard had never really recovered from the taser blast he had taken. He was breathing, but shallowly. His eyes were closed. His mouth hung open. He was a somewhat overweight man, not old, but also not young. He must have some underlying health problem, and the taser irritated it.

Hays shrugged. It was just as well.

He opened the three small paper packages he had on his knee. Inside each one was an even smaller, premeasured syringe of a powerful sedative. The dose was strong enough to stop a horse's heart.

He took the syringes in hand and kneeled down near the men. One of them must have felt his presence there.

"What are you doing?" the man said, his voice raised in alarm.

"Don't worry," Hays said.

34

He popped the tiny syringe into the man's neck, near the artery there, and depressed the plunger. The drug entered the man's bloodstream.

Not sure if there would be some extreme reaction before death that might upset the others, Hays moved quickly to each man in turn. The entire operation was over in less than thirty seconds. Then he sat back on his bench and watched them.

There wasn't much to see. The three men subsided with a few gasps, but hardly a peep besides that. Then Hays sat with the bodies. Maybe they were dead already. Maybe they weren't. In another minute, they would be.

The van stopped when it reached the barn. The man in the front passenger seat got out of the van and opened the tall sliding door of the barn. Just in the moment that the van door was open, Hays could feel the surge of cold air from outside. Winter had arrived in northern Vermont.

But he already knew that. He had been here a week ago, and there had already been a few inches of crunchy snow on the ground. The van passed into the barn. Hays could hear the man closing the doors behind them.

He pushed the rear door open and climbed out. He carried his helmet and dropped it on the floor of the barn. He would leave nothing behind—no piece of gear, no article of clothing that had touched him. He would dump all of it into the upper reaches of Lake Champlain before he crossed the border. The lake would still be open water now, but not for much longer.

The driver came to the back of the van. Hays barely knew the men who sat in the front of the van. Both were young. One had a beard. The one who drove sported long hair. They looked faintly ridiculous, but young scientists often looked ridiculous these days.

Whoever they were, they had done their job with professionalism. They could be proud of that at least. It was a shame that they were the inside players, the ones who had gotten the rest of the team access to the physics facility. Young men like this, if suspicion fell upon them and they were pressed by the authorities, were very likely to confess. Then they would tell everything they knew.

"How are the guards?" the long-haired driver said.

Their final job was to drop the guards somewhere far from civilization, but not so far that they would freeze to death before they managed to walk to a town.

Hays shrugged his big shoulders. "Come and see."

The man passed him and went to the door. As he did, Hays pulled a 9mm pistol from inside his jumpsuit. The gun had a sound suppressor already attached to the muzzle. Hays had threaded it on during the long drive here. Unlike the Airsoft rifle he had used at the particle collider, this gun was very real.

The young man looked inside the van.

"Are they okay?"

Hays stepped up behind the man and shot him in the head. His head snapped backwards at the top of his neck as the bullet passed through it, back to front. Hays saw a mist of blood spray.

The sound of the gun was like the clack of an office stapler or a single punch of a key on an old typewriter.

Now the man from the passenger seat was coming around to the back.

"What was that?"

He turned the corner, looked at Hays, and then saw his friend slumped on the ground. Hays was already pointing the gun in his face.

Clack!

The man's head snapped back, and he dropped where he had been standing.

Hays looked down at the two dead men on the floor of the barn. He sighed. There were two cars parked in here along with the van. One was the blue Ford sedan that Hays would drive to Montréal. The other car, which Hays barely looked at, was the decoy vehicle these men had thought they would be driving. That car would sit here a while, along with five dead men.

It was cold outside and inside the barn. The barn would act as a freezer until the spring thaw, four or five months from now. The North Adams Laboratory van was a clever forgery. There was no GPS unit inside it and no way anyone could track its location. The authorities would certainly be looking for it soon, if they weren't already.

Soon the real winter snows would fly. The barn would be half a meter deep in snow before too long. No one came out here in winter, and no one had any reason to.

The place would be a silent tomb for months. By the time these bodies were found, other, larger issues would have come to the fore, and greater, more exciting attacks would have taken place. And if a big man had been spotted on video wearing a black helmet and visor, that man would be long gone.

Hays dragged the two men to the van and dumped them in the back with the guards. Then he slammed the rear doors shut. He changed his clothes quickly, trading his black jumpsuit for jeans, work boots, a heavy wool jacket, and a knit green cap.

He started the Ford and drove it out of the barn.

Out in the night air, it was crisp and cold indeed. A light snow was falling. That was good. He felt the cold in his hands as he ran the heavy chain through the metal loops on the barn doors, pulled it very tight, and locked it up with a sturdy Master lock.

He looked out at the dark rolling hills of this farm. No one lived here. No one, except maybe vandals or hopeful thieves, had any reason to break open that lock.

Hays glanced one last time at the doors he had just cinched closed.

"Sleep well," he told the dead men. Then he walked to his waiting car.

CHAPTER EIGHT

6:15 am Eastern Standard Time
Windemere Inn and Suites
Worcester, Massachusetts

"Nice place," a voice said.

Troy opened his eyes. His head felt like a woodpecker had been hammering on his skull all night. It seemed like his veins were pulsating behind his eyes, and that he could see them there, like red neon signs, but the words were a scribble he couldn't read.

His mouth was dry, and his tongue had grown a coat of hair.

Welts on his face, from the punches he had taken, were throbbing a bit. They weren't bad, he had certainly sustained worse, but he could feel them there. If he had to guess, at the very least, he was going to have a shiner under his right eye, and maybe a little something on the left side near his cheekbone.

Across the dreary motel room from him, a man sat near the open sliding door to the terrace. He was smoking a cigarette and blowing the smoke outside. That was against the motel rules, of course. Did this man care? No.

The man was Alex.

The last time Troy had seen Alex, he was crashing a stolen helicopter onto the Brooklyn Bridge, then getting taken away by a swarm of cops.

In the first weak light of dawn, Troy could see past him. They were high on a hillside, and the narrow terrace gave a panoramic view of the city of Worcester, complete with the Holy Cross football stadium. Troy could also feel the cold air seeping in through the open slider. It was late autumn in New England and getting chilly.

"My brother picked it," Troy said. "He said the pictures looked okay."

Alex shrugged, as if he didn't care one way or the other.

"In a few minutes, your phone is going to ring. We should probably talk first."

Troy ignored that statement. He got the sense that Alex liked to feel like he was ahead on everything. He liked to turn up while you were still asleep. He liked it when he knew things that you didn't know. Troy wasn't in the mood for it this morning.

"How did you get in here?"

Alex took a hit from the smoke. "The door wasn't locked."

Naturally. Troy vaguely remembered being inside the room and out on the terrace smoking cigars with his brothers, the bride's brothers, and their cousins and friends. All was forgiven, and the whole group was having a grand old time.

They were all brothers forever now, the marriage a medieval bond between two clans. The coming child was claimed by everyone. There could never be a divorce. The young newlyweds were trapped. This was no longer about their relationship. It was bigger than a marriage. But Troy didn't remember anyone leaving, and he didn't remember going to sleep after that.

He stared down at himself. He was wearing dress slacks, a white dress shirt, and his nice black wingtip shoes—while lying in bed.

He looked at Alex. "Still smoking, I see."

Alex shrugged again. He was dressed in a hunting jacket, wool pants, and green LL Bean boots. Except for the cigarette, he could be in a fall fashion catalog. Troy thought back to when he first met Alex. The man was dressed like a Sikh, and he said he was from Kansas.

"How was the wedding?" Alex said now.

Troy shrugged. "Eh…The bride was eight months pregnant. We got in a fight with her brothers and cousins. There was a big wedding cake and we knocked it over, you know, during the fight. But it ended up on its side, so they managed to save half of it. The half that didn't touch the floor."

There was a long pause.

"Other than that…"

Alex nodded. "Yeah. Typical wedding. How was the cake?"

Troy shook his head. "I didn't have any."

"Sure," Alex said. "Gotta stay in fighting trim."

Troy sat up by the side of the bed and sighed. His head spun for a moment, then stopped. On the bedside table was a can of Rock Star Zero, a couple of blue pills, and a banana.

"Why are you here?" Troy said.

"Missing Persons sent me," Alex said, using the old military nickname for the one-eyed Special Operations colonel, Stuart Persons.

39

Persons was in classified intelligence now. Apparently, so was Alex. Troy wasn't sure what his own relationship to them was.

He had, however, received his first payment from the United States Foreign Medical Aid Program. Eight hundred dollars for consulting services rendered deposited into his checking account. He supposed that meant he was still in.

"You mean Stu?" he said.

Alex nodded. "Yeah."

"Last time I talked to him, he disavowed any knowledge of your existence."

Alex didn't touch that. "He's concerned."

"What did I do?" Troy said.

"You didn't do anything. You did hear about the attack last night?"

Troy shook his head. "I was at a wedding."

"Ah. Well, you could practically have heard it from here. That's what the phone call is going to be about."

"Stu is going to call me?"

Alex shook his head. It was a brief shake, a fragment of a shake, one suggesting it was common sense that of course Missing Persons wasn't going to call.

"Your boss. In Europe. It's early afternoon there. His people want him in on this."

"How would you know that?" Troy said.

He almost asked the question more of himself than Alex. Alex knew a great many things. So did Missing Persons. It wasn't beyond the realm of possibility that the ultimate string puller was Persons, and that he somehow gave assignments to intelligence agencies in Europe. If that was true, it was something he would never divulge to Troy. But Alex would know.

"It was a bombing. It took place about a hundred miles west of here, in the Berkshire mountains. There's an advanced physics laboratory out there. Or there was, until last night. I mean, it's still sort of there, in a sense. The atom smasher they had was blown up and burned, and the central facility, including the control room, was completely obliterated. The place is a dead loss."

Tentatively, Troy reached out, took the Rock Star, and opened it.

"Mostly, the facility was underground. It runs for about six miles along the length of the collider under a ridgeline of the mountains. There are still fires burning down there that no one has been able to reach. There are chemicals on site, various dangerous substances, that make it unfeasible to send firefighters down. Could be a couple of days to a couple of weeks before the fires burn themselves out. That's what I hear."

Troy sipped the Rock Star. It tasted like citrus. There was no sugar in it, just some dangerous chemicals. It was loaded with caffeine and B vitamins. It was fizzy, and he liked the flavor. He swore by these things.

"Or twenty years," Troy said. "Or never. Anybody get killed?"

"Unknown," Alex said. "There are three guards missing, and there were four technical personnel who were deep inside the facility, working overnight on a faulty high-tech gizmo of some kind. It's not official yet, but I'm going to go out on a limb and guess that they're dead. There were multiple explosions, combined with an accelerant which sent a firestorm straight along the length of the tunnel. Whoever devised the charges knew exactly what they were doing. Anyone out in the tunnel, working on the collider in that narrow space, should have been incinerated."

Troy said nothing.

"In any event, as of twenty minutes ago, no one had heard from them."

Troy peeled the banana.

"Who owns the place?"

"You know how these things go," Alex said. "It's a joint project of certain research universities, the Department of Energy, and maybe a couple of entities that prefer to remain silent partners. It was a medium-security facility. That's how the bad guys got in so easily. Its stated purpose was to create the conditions for an elusive sub-atomic particle to appear, one that research suggests should be everywhere in the universe but isn't."

"That's it? Why would someone want to blow it up?"

What he didn't say was, *Why would anyone care about such a particle?* He would say it, but he was too tired. He didn't care enough. Alex probably wouldn't care either.

"In your experience, is anything ever what it appears to be?" Alex said.

Troy shook his head. "No. I guess not."

On the night table next to the bed, Troy's cell phone started to buzz. He must have put it on vibrate. It made that annoying sound where the vibrations made it rub against the surface of the table.

He picked it up. *Miquel Castro-Ruiz.*

Troy pressed the green button. He glanced at Alex, but Alex was looking away, out the door at the fall morning in Worcester.

"Hola," Troy said into the phone. He was beginning to learn Spanish. He figured he should learn some European language, and they were based in Madrid at the moment, so that was a starting place. Everyone there seemed to speak five languages.

"Buenos días, Señor Stark," Castro said. "Did I wake you?"

"No," Troy said truthfully. Alex woke him five minutes ago. "I've been awake for a little while."

"I imagine you have heard about the terrorist attack?"

"Yes. Yes, I have."

"How far are you from there right now?"

"About a hundred miles."

There was a pause over the line while Castro calculated miles into centimeters or milliliters or some damn thing.

"Are you free to go there?" Castro said. "I would like to know the lay of the land, as you would say."

Troy would never say that, but okay.

"Yeah. I can do that."

"No need to get involved or search deeper. It's just that they're holding the intelligence very tightly. Jan cannot get us any information, images, or films at this time. Nothing that isn't already in the news. I would like to know the site from your eyes. Even if they bar you from entry."

"I'll go," Troy said. "I imagine I'll find a way into the site."

"I imagine you will too," Castro said. "That's why I hired you."

"Are we worried about it?"

"Not worried. But of course, we have our own similar facilities here."

"Of course."

They exchanged a few more pleasantries, not much, and then Troy hung up. He liked that about Miquel Castro. The man didn't dilly-dally with a lot of unnecessary chatter.

Troy looked across at Alex again.

Alex stood and pitched his smoke out the open door. "Ready to take a ride? Apparently, you have this motel room until tomorrow. I'll have you back before your family gathers for mid-afternoon brunch."

Troy wasn't ready to take a ride, not really. He was ready to go back to sleep. He was hung over and the last thing he wanted to face was the remains of a terrorist attack.

"Is this part of the charity consulting gig?" he said.

Alex nodded. "I didn't stop by here to reminisce about the old days, as enjoyable as that might be. I was sent here to pick you up."

Troy shrugged and stood up. He was still dressed for the wedding, more or less.

"Remember the time we stole that helicopter?" he said. "And you crashed it onto the bridge, with the rotors shredded off and flying everywhere?"

"Yeah," Alex said. "That was fun. Also the time you left me that dead Albanian gangster in the woods. He had half a pack of Turkish cigarettes on him. It got me smoking again. But I don't blame you for that."

Troy nodded. "Yeah. Thanks. Those were good times. Let me just change my clothes."

* * *

Smoke was rising near a low range of mountains on the horizon.

Troy hadn't spoken much on the two-hour ride out here. Instead, he just stared from the big blue Jeep Alex was driving at the barren trees of the forests lining the road. It made him think of a time after a nuclear war.

Everything lifeless, as far as the eye could see.

"There's also a no-fly zone for ten miles in any direction," Alex said. "They've been chasing news helicopters out of here all morning and jamming drone signals. If we were kids, I'd suggest that we take a walk through the woods and salvage some of the nifty high-tech hardware that's crashed back in there."

Troy glanced up through the t-top roof of the Jeep. A line of helicopters were circling behind them, like insects: off to the east, headed north, and then in the distance, turning to the west. They were so far away, you couldn't even hear them.

Just ahead, there was a checkpoint with three Massachusetts state police SUVs. The first two SUVs were parked facing each other, bumper to bumper across the roadway. The third was parked behind the other two, facing forward. The formation was almost impossible to ram through without a tank.

Alex pulled the car up to the cop and handed him two IDs. "Agent McKinley, Homeland Security. This is Agent Roosevelt."

Troy barely looked at the cop, a big crew-cut duffer, probably graduated from the Marines into the state police twenty years ago. He gave the guy a half-hearted wave. He felt nothing about the alias, or the fact that Alex hadn't mentioned it until now.

It didn't matter. Of course they were going to get in. They were spooks. They could be anyone at any time. If the cops ran the IDs through a computer, they'd almost certainly be real.

The cop gestured along the road. "Drive down in that drainage ditch and come out the other side of our roadblock. Two miles up, there's a command center and a staging area. No one goes past that without hazmat suits." He handed the IDs back. He hadn't bothered to check them at all.

Alex took the cards. "Thanks."

Alex plunged the Jeep into the long ditch, trusting the four-wheel drive. They bucked and slid and scraped along the overgrown bottom until they were past the police, then climbed back up the steep embankment. They drove on, the road well-paved and smooth ahead of them.

"Why does Persons want me on this job? It has nothing to do with Europe."

Alex shrugged. "Well, he figured right now your new outfit doesn't have a mandate. You're just doing trust falls and icebreakers, team building exercises, so you might want something to sink your teeth into."

Troy looked at him. He wasn't in any mood for humor. The pills Alex had given him earlier had pushed back his headache, but now the headache was surging forward again and seizing the initiative.

"Even so."

"No one knows what it has to do with," Alex said. "It's too early to say. But there is this. About ten months ago, a fire burned through a physics research facility in Northeast England, outside Newcastle. It was a small place: old and obsolete. Anyway, that's what everyone thought. It had been developed by the government there back between 1959 and 1961. The stone age of this kind of research. The atom smasher was only 150 meters long. The English government released the place to a nearby college in the early 1990s. The kids could conduct experiments that had been done a thousand times before. That kind of thing."

"Okay, so who did it?" Troy said.

"The original thought was local kids did it. Teenagers. Vandals. They broke in, partied a bit, left some beer cans and broken bottles around, then set fire to the place, maybe accidentally, maybe on purpose. No one was there, no one was hurt, the place was old. Maybe it was no big deal, except to the students who were going to lose the opportunity to do these experiments. And the college couldn't tout the supercollider anymore to attract such students."

He paused as the car rolled quietly along the road. "Turned out whoever did it were pros and deliberately torched the place. They used an industrial flame accelerant, similar to jet fuel, which is wholly consumed. It was a sophisticated attack designed to completely destroy the place and make it look like teenagers had done it."

"To destroy an old, out of date facility?" Troy said. "What did they want, the insurance money?"

"Again, nothing is ever quite what it seems," Alex said. "The place had equipment there, built long ago, to generate and concentrate microwaves. The students, if that's what they were, had concentrated the microwaves to such a degree that they were able to fire them like a weapon."

Now Troy was interested. "What did they fire them at? You know, when I was a kid, we had a dartboard. But we'd get bored and start throwing the darts at each other."

"I knew that about you," Alex said. "I didn't even have to be told. No, they used inanimate objects. It started small, with marbles, pill bottles, things of that nature. Then the cardboard roll at the center of the toilet paper. Books. Shoes."

"They would put the target on a small platform and direct this microwave beam at it. And when the beam hit the target, the target would disappear. It wouldn't melt. It wouldn't explode. It wouldn't burst into flame. It would just be gone. And there would be no residue of it left over. No charred remains, no chunks, nothing. It would be gone like it never existed in the first place."

"Where would it go?" Troy said.

Alex shrugged. "The past? The future? Some other reality? No one ever figured that out. The kids would just have a blast erasing things from the here and now."

Troy nearly laughed. "Come on."

"A Ph.D. candidate wrote a paper on what they were doing. All of this came out after the fact. It was heavily redacted throughout, and the kid's name was removed. We've got the paper, but that's where the

45

trail ends. The British government has nothing to say on the matter. The university claims they don't know anything."

"Could be a forgery," Troy said.

"Could be," Alex said. "Then why torch the lab?"

"Torch the lab first, for kicks, or for practice, or for whatever reason. You're a disgruntled ex-student or former employee with access to flame accelerant. Then someone else releases a fake paper to create a mystique around the event. Not really for any reason other than to foster a legend. People do that kind of thing all the time. The person who wrote the paper probably didn't know the person who torched it and probably never even set foot in the lab."

Troy was tired, so he wasn't in a mood to play along. Frankly, he was a little surprised that both Missing Persons and Alex bought into this idea of microwaves zapping physical objects into the ether. But only a little. Spooks loved their unexplained mysteries. See, because somebody, somewhere, was behind it, pulling strings.

"Anyway, Persons sees a pattern developing," Alex said. "Two attacks on physics research labs. Maybe a little far-fetched, maybe not. He wants our input. They have the security footage here but haven't released it anywhere he can get his fingers on it yet. So he sent us to take a look."

"I thought Castro wanted me to take a look, and you were tagging along."

Alex eyed him but said nothing.

Up ahead was a cluster of heavy, dark green tents in a large dirt parking lot or clearing. There were at least two dozen vehicles—drab green Humvees, a drab green troop transport, several small white vans with the letters NAL across the side in blue, two fire engines, police cars, and several nondescript sedans. A chain link fence with bright yellow aluminum slats inside the links had been hastily erected across the road. You couldn't go past the fence—you also couldn't see past it.

National Guardsmen were congregated around an open-air pavilion with a white, billowy top. A handful of people here were slowly dressing in hazardous material garb, medical personnel hovering around them with checklists on tablet computers.

A young Guardsman in a uniform about a size too large for him stood in front of the Jeep, pointing off to the right. Alex followed the kid's hand gestures.

"Reassuring," Alex said. "His gun weighs about as much as he does."

Troy said nothing. He had no opinion about other branches of the military. He had no opinion about young kids dipping their toes in to get money for college. He was gradually trying to have no opinion about the military at all—who was in it, what they were doing, and why. He didn't care anymore. Or so he told himself.

They got out of the Jeep. Alex seemed to know exactly where he was going. They were side by side now, Troy six inches taller and much broader than this strange partner of his. They walked toward a dark green tent nestled behind some larger ones. Two National Guard, a young man and a young woman, stood at the entrance.

"I'm Agent McKinley," Alex said to them. "Homeland Security. This is Agent..."

He waved his hand at Troy.

"Roosevelt," Troy said.

"They're expecting us," Alex said.

The Guardswoman mumbled something into her radio. Alex was already moving past her. Troy followed, ducking his head as he passed through the entrance.

The tent was a movie theater of sorts. There were nine white wooden folding chairs, arranged in a three-by-three square, facing a projection screen on a tripod near the wall of the tent. A guy in a bright orange fleece jacket greeted them.

"Homeland Security?" he said. "Great." He mentioned his name, but Troy didn't catch it. "I'm security for North Adams Labs. You see I'm wearing blaze orange. Normally we're supposed to wear blue. I recommend orange to everybody this time of year."

They stared at him.

"Hunting season," he said.

Troy nodded. The guy's job had just gotten blown up, apparently on his watch, and he didn't want to get shot accidentally by a hunter.

"I'll run the footage. If you want it to slow down, back up, or freeze, you just let me know, okay? So please," he gestured at the folding chairs. "Have a seat."

They sat, and in a moment, the footage came on. It showed a white NAL van entering a gate, using a swipe card. A hand reached out from the van, waved the card at the sensor, and the gate slowly rolled sideways and open.

"I just want to say," the projection man said from behind them. "That's very clever. That's not one of our vans, but it looks identical. Our vans have tracking chips inside. GPS units to determine their location. Gasoline consumption, productivity, driver road safety, you name it. It's all tracked. The van you see has no chips. Also, the windshield is subtly smoked so you can only see the silhouettes inside. There were two people in the front, but we have no idea who they were. They never exited the truck."

"How did they beat the sensor?" Troy said. "That card he waved must have an ID, some kind of number or other…"

"They exposed a previously unknown vulnerability in the system," the guy said. "Also very clever. Their card was just an infinite series of zeroes and ones, generated randomly. Apparently, the infinity aspect of it opened the loop and never allowed it to close again. The system eventually decides yes or no. But if the loop never closes, it never gets to decide. It turns out if it doesn't decide within a few seconds, the default is yes. We have the sequence to ten thousand digits, but it doesn't matter. No one had any idea that it would work that way."

"Someone did," Alex said.

"Yes," the guy said. "It's possible someone modified it to work that way. Smarter minds than mine are trying to determine that."

"It was an inside job," Troy said. That much seemed clear already.

The guy said nothing in response.

As they watched, the van moved slowly across the compound and came to a large iron door. The door opened and the van pulled inside. Now, the footage changed again. It gave a view from a high corner of what looked like a warehouse or loading dock area.

A couple of men in blue uniforms stood nearby, shifting their feet. Their breath rose in plumes. It was cold last night.

They approached the van. Suddenly, the rear door burst open. A very large man wearing a black helmet came out in a black jumpsuit. He pointed what looked like an automatic rifle at the guards and had them on the floor in a few seconds. By the time the men were on the ground, three more people had emerged from the van. The man in the helmet made an odd hand signal: forefinger and pinky up, thumb pointing straight out.

"Freeze on that rifle," Troy said.

The film stopped.

"Can you zoom in on that and enhance it?"

"I can zoom, but to enhance, that'll take the computer lab. I understand they're working to improve the definition of the entire video."

"All right, well zoom in on it in that case."

48

The video zoomed in on the rifle the man was holding. The definition was bad, but for the life of him, Troy couldn't identify the gun. Troy had handled just about every semi- and automatic rifle available in America, or a variant thereof, and most of the ones available in other parts of the world. The one in the man's hands looked like a toy.

"This is going to sound crazy, but I don't think that's really a gun. I think that big guy was bluffing, and it worked."

"Maybe an Airsoft," Alex said. "Like one of those war simulation guns."

"Maybe," Troy said. "I don't know."

"Well, if you think that's the case, then watch this."

The film rolled on. Suddenly, another guard appeared from a door in the back and to the left. He had a handgun trained on the big guy. The big guy dropped to the ground, and the smallest of the invaders, what appeared to be a woman, shot the guard with a taser. The guard went down like a pile of bricks.

"Nice movement," Troy said.

"And a non-lethal weapon," the projection man said. "We lost four people in the tunnel, but it's possible these terrorists didn't know they were there. Why would they? The video looks like they're trying not to hurt anyone."

The video rolled on. The woman and what appeared to be two young men disappeared into a doorway. While they were gone, the big man rolled three motorcycles down a ramp from inside the van. Then he dragged the three guards inside the van.

In a few moments, not very long at all, the team that dispatched inside the facility were back. The big man made the odd hand signal at them again. There seemed to be a symbol on his jumpsuit.

"Freeze and zoom in on the big guy's jacket. He's got a logo or something there."

The camera zoomed in on him. The logo was a slightly lighter black, against the deep black of his jumpsuit.

"Anything?" Troy said.

"I don't know," Alex said. "Almost like a medieval German rune. I'd almost say it was an SS, but that would be pushing it. Nobody's going to wear a Nazi symbol to a job like this. Especially these guys. They knew from the outset they were being filmed."

In a moment, the last of the three motorcycles had gone out into the night.

"Are they tracing those bikes?" Troy said.

"Trying, sure. One passed a camera on an exit off the Taconic Parkway, then may have turned up again two hours later on street security footage near a strip club in the South Bronx. Another definitely crossed from the Massachusetts Turnpike, onto the New York State Thruway system, heading west near Albany. The third one just evaporated. No sign of it anywhere."

"Now what?" Troy said.

"Now we fast forward to the last moment. A little under ten minutes passed from the moment the last motorcycle left the building until the explosion. From the time the van first entered the bay door, until the last bike was gone, was only four minutes and change. They were moving quickly."

Troy nodded. Although they looked somewhat rag-tag and mismatched, they were fast, no nonsense, and devastatingly effective. They had high-level intelligence about the place before they arrived, and it was all accurate information.

"It was an inside job," he said again. "Maybe not the personnel who actually carried out the attack, but someone got them the intel."

It seemed like a simple matter from here. Figure out who the most likely candidates were—the most disgruntled, the ones with access to security protocols, the ones who might have reasons to sell secrets—then bring them in and grill them mercilessly. In a short while, they would crack and the whole façade would come tumbling down. Any investigator or secret policeman worth his salt knew what to do.

Troy looked at Alex. He had brunch with his newly extended family back in Worcester. If they left now, they could make it.

"We have two employees in mind," the projection man said, as if he could read Troy's thoughts. "We're guessing they were the men in the front of the truck."

Troy nodded. "It's them."

"They've gone missing," the man said.

CHAPTER NINE

November 14
10:50 am Eastern Standard Time
A rural property
Near Monticello, Upstate New York

"What do you want to do about the dogs?" Troy said.

He sat in the Jeep with Alex, at the end of a rutted and pitted dirt driveway. The driveway was itself an offshoot from a rutted and pitted private road, which had seen long winters without being repaved.

The property was rolling farmland, overgrown with tall grasses. At the end of the driveway was a rambling, ramshackle old house. It might have had an architectural style at one time, but it had been expanded and added-on so many times over the years that it was impossible to imagine what the designer had in mind.

A black banner was spread from two windows in the center of the second floor, in an area that might have been part of the original house. It looked like something that would hang from the windows of a raucous frat house at a large state university. There was one simple word stenciled in white across the banner.

LIBERTY.

In the dirt dooryard of the house, at the bottom of the wide front stairs, three large pit bulls had come to life when the Jeep pulled up. They stood at alert now, all three facing the Jeep, none of them chained to anything or controlled in any way.

Alex shrugged. "I don't know."

He lit a cigarette. He didn't seem concerned.

He inhaled, held it, and then exhaled the smoke out into the afternoon. It was overcast here, the sky gunmetal gray, not a hint of blue anywhere. But the air was cool and pleasant.

"I could kill them," Troy said. "But only if I have to. I really don't want to murder dogs. None of this is their fault. They don't decide how they are."

They were dressed as FBI agents. Not in the sense of G-men in suits and fedora hats, but in the sense of heavy boots, blue pants, blue shirts, blue vests, and blue baseball caps with the letters FBI in yellow across the bill. Yesterday, they were Homeland Security. Today they were FBI. Tomorrow they would be emissaries from the planet Nibiru. They could be anybody at any time.

This was Troy's last day in the country. He was leaving tonight on the red eye back to Spain. He would have preferred to spend his last day in town with his brothers. Then again, his brothers were all working. That being the case, he would have preferred to spend it napping on his mother's couch.

But it wasn't in the cards. Missing Persons had an obsession. When Missing Persons had an obsession, he was like one of these pit bulls gnawing on a person's leg. Troy had spoken to him on the phone for five minutes, and the end result was taking another ride with Alex.

They were here to see a man named Hans Erichson. Erichson was a thirty-two-year-old who had lived among underground, militant, anti-government, and white supremacist movements. He had a long history of writing anti-technology screeds on the internet—he saw technology as an instrument of government control.

He was also a very large man, who had done four years in the Marine Corps once upon a time and had active warrants for his arrest. It was a long shot, but everything about him suggested he might be the large man in the video, who acted with military precision, and who seemed to be in charge of the attack on the NAL supercollider. The fact that the man in the video hid his identity so carefully made it seem even more likely that he was Erichson.

This was not Erichson's last known address. This was just a house that was the headquarters of something called the Tree of Liberty, a group of militia members who gathered here to conduct war games on the farmland and in the adjacent woods.

Erichson was apparently an avid participant in these games, and informants said he had stayed in this house from time to time. This fact also pointed a finger at him. High-definition video restoration determined that the gun the man in the video carried was not a real gun at all, just as Troy suspected. It was an Airsoft gun of the type used in military simulations. And the man in the video made frequent hand signals, which was a common practice in the military, but also in military simulations.

There was no one around here today or seemed not to be.

Alex reached behind them into the second row. He pulled a long box from below the seats. It was like a narrow suitcase. He flipped the latches and opened it. There was a dart gun nestled inside.

"By that logic, malaria isn't the fault of mosquitoes," he said. "It's not as though mosquitoes invented malaria and decided to give it to people. Mosquitoes are innocent victims, just like the people they infect. There's no sense in eradicating them."

Troy watched as Alex loaded a syringe into a dart.

"This won't kill the dogs," Alex said. "It will just make them very sleepy. I don't want to kill them any more than you do."

One of the dogs, the biggest and the boldest of the three, had approached the car. It was broad in a way that didn't seem natural, as though someone had been tinkering with pit bulls and making them into Frankenstein monster versions of themselves.

The dog didn't bark. It didn't growl. It didn't run. It simply stepped closer and closer, its eyes somehow blank and aggressive at the same time. It was not being friendly.

Troy imagined that in ordinary circumstances, the approach of this dog was more than enough to make unwanted interlopers turn their car around and leave.

But not today.

Alex sighted down the barrel of the dart gun. "Come here, Rover. I need to talk to you for a second."

The dog moved even closer. He was mere feet from the open window of the Jeep.

"Hey!" someone shouted. "Hey! Don't you shoot that dog."

Troy looked up. Three men had come onto the porch. They were dressed in military-style fatigues. They'd had no intention of coming out before, but now that the dog was about to get shot, things had changed.

Alex pulled the trigger.

Phfffft!

The dart hit the big dog in the neck at his left shoulder. There was no collar or anything there to protect him. The dart embedded into the flesh. Whatever was in the vial hit the dog's bloodstream right away. The dog whined just a bit, high in its throat, then turned as if to go back to the house. It didn't try to run. It just took a few stumble-steps across the yard, swayed, sat down like a good doggie, then rolled over onto its side.

"Too late," Alex said.

He reached to the dashboard, took a small microphone off of it, flipped a switch, then depressed the SEND button on the mike. "The dog is not harmed," he said, his voice booming across the yard. "It's a sedative. This is the FBI. We're coming out to talk. If you have weapons, put them away. Also, sequester the other dogs."

Sequester. That was quite a word. Troy wondered if anyone over there would get it.

"You have no right to be here!" one of the men shouted. He was tall and morbidly obese. He wore an American flag bandana wrapped around his head.

"This is private land."

Troy shook his head. People like this were annoying, with their guns, dogs, banners, and pseudo-military costumes. Didn't these guys have anything better to do? As far as Troy knew, the construction trades were still hiring.

He got out of the Jeep, leaving the door open behind him. Alex didn't get out. Alex, as Troy recalled, didn't do combat. That wasn't what he was for. Troy had to admit that Alex was very good at the things he did do, but it would also be nice if...

Nah. Forget it.

Troy walked across the dusty front yard towards the men. The dogs, momentarily taken aback by watching their leader drop, stood completely still.

"Sequester those dogs!" Alex boomed again.

Troy reached behind him and came out with a standard FBI-issue Glock, solid black, with seventeen rounds of 9mm Luger ammunition in the magazine. They were FBI today. He might as well carry an FBI piece.

"Get off this land!" the man in the front shouted.

The pit bulls began to tremble and growl at Troy's approach.

"If I have any trouble with those dogs," Troy said. "I'm going to shoot them. I like dogs. I don't want to do that, but I will." He held up the gun for their inspection. "And this doesn't fire sedatives."

He never stopped walking. He moved at a medium pace but didn't hesitate at all. He watched the two dogs. He glanced at the three men on the porch. No one made a move. Troy kept coming. The dogs were staring right at him.

"What do you want?" the obese man said.

"I want you to put those dogs away. They're making me nervous. When I get nervous, I kill things."

54

"How do I know you're really FBI?"

Troy shook his head. "You don't. But if your dogs are dead, it's not going to matter who I am, is it?"

The man muttered something under his breath. One of the other men went to a couple of ropes hanging on the wall, took them down, then looped them around the necks of the remaining two dogs. He pulled the dogs by the chokers and took them around to the side of the house. The dogs went willingly enough.

"Now we're getting somewhere," Troy said. He was careful, though. If you pushed guys like these too hard, then they would push back.

"What do you want?" the big man said again.

"I want to speak to Hans Erichson."

The man shook his head. "Nobody here by that name."

Suddenly, the smaller man next to him broke and ran. He darted backwards, turned, and burst through the front door of the house.

Instantly, Troy started running as well. He took the front stairs in two big steps. The obese man stepped in front of him, arms out in front of his body, blocking Troy's way.

"You have no right…"

Troy punched the guy, a hard left to the jaw. At the same instant, he slipped his right foot behind the man's legs. The guy stepped backwards, might have regained his balance, but tripped over Troy's leg. He went down like a large building falling.

Troy burst past him, not even waiting to hear the thud.

Ahead, the other guy was running up a narrow flight of wooden stairs. Troy followed. "Freeze!" he shouted. "You're under arrest."

The guy reached the landing, grabbed the railing, spun, and ran down the hallway. Troy was steps behind him now, watching for a gun to appear.

The guy ran to a door, passed through it, and slammed it behind him. Troy heard a lock slide closed. He didn't hesitate. He lifted his foot and kicked the door. The kick split the wood in a vertical line. Troy took two steps back, then ran at it shoulder first, bursting through the door with his big body.

The door splintered and shattered. Troy fell to the ground, landing next to the guy, who was kneeling by the toilet. This was a bathroom.

The guy had a small, clear plastic bag of white powder. He had torn it open and was trying to dump the powder into the toilet, except his hands were shaking too much. Apparently, he had drugs on him, and he panicked.

Troy jabbed the gun into the guy's back.

"Stop what you're doing. I'm not here for that."

It occurred to Troy that he wasn't really here for anything. He didn't have a warrant. He didn't have a mandate. He didn't work for any American law enforcement agency, and if he did, it certainly wasn't the FBI. The best he could do here was talk, or maybe make a citizen's arrest.

If Hans Erichson turned up, he would do that. If some militia member had cocaine or more likely, crystal meth, and it was for personal use...

That wasn't Troy's business.

The guy on his knees was frozen like a statue. Behind Troy, there was the sound of wheezing, like the hydraulic "kneeling" feature on city buses. It sounded like a deranged bus driver was lowering the bus, then lifting it up, then lowering it again, on and on.

Troy looked, and the obese man stood in the doorway.

"You guys dealing here?"

The big man shook his head. His face was red, nearly deep enough to match the color on his American flag bandana. He gasped, just a bit, when he spoke.

"No. My friend has a problem. He came up here to go cold turkey. I didn't know he got that bag."

The guy on his knees was crying now. "I'm sorry. I'm sorry. I brought the bag in case I couldn't do it."

"You're never gonna do it if you bring a bag," the big man said. He sounded like a den mother who had lost his patience with an unruly kid.

Troy took a deep breath.

"I'm looking for Hans Erichson," he said.

The big guy shook his head. He was regaining his ability to process oxygen—not a bad recovery for a man his size.

"This is the second time in the last three months you guys have been out here. Did they tell you that down at headquarters? Probably not, so I'll tell you what I told the last couple of clowns. Hans is dead. Don't you read the obituaries? You're looking for a dead man. He lost his mind and became an enviro nutjob. He thought we shouldn't eat beef anymore. He wanted to put solar panels on this place. He decided global warming was real, and the world was ending. We told him we couldn't have him here anymore, with the things he was saying. What was the point? He was going down a different path. I guess he got real depressed about that."

The man paused, took a deep breath, and recovered a little more. "A little less than a year ago, he shot himself in the head."

CHAPTER TEN

November 15
7:15 am Central European Time
Berlin Brandenburg Airport "Willy Brandt"
Schönefeld (outside Berlin), Germany

Cheri Bomb had been sick for two days.

Holed up in the tiny Brooklyn flat, she had shorn her hair down to almost nothing, what they called a "pixie cut," then dyed it nearly white. She had taken hours in the old claw foot bathtub, scrubbing off her tattoos. If Gray got picked up by the police, FBI, or the CIA, he would be able to describe the markings on her body. Only the markings were no longer there.

She had painted her nails a pretty light blue. She put big hoop earrings in and did her makeup. She liked it. Even with short hair, she was looking very feminine now. She enjoyed how pretty she was. If this were another life, she could have just been a pretty girl, doing pretty girl things, whatever they were.

In the kitchen, there was canned soup and oyster crackers in cellophane wrappers, and instant coffee and fake sugar, the kind that comes in bright pink packets. She had no need to leave the apartment.

Her new identity was waiting for her in a drawer in the living room end table. So was her flight itinerary.

She could just lay around and relax. She was on the eighth floor of the building, and although the roadway of the Manhattan Bridge was visible right outside her window, there was a wide expanse of park or maybe wasteland between here and there. It was quiet inside the apartment. It was a very nice place to simply stay and do nothing.

It was so perfect, in fact, that she became bored. So, she turned on the television. She flipped around, looking for news about the bombing. She didn't have to flip far, as it was on every news channel.

Four scientific researchers had been killed in the attack. Three security guards were still missing. That couldn't be right.

It couldn't be.

There was supposed to be no one in the facility beside the guards. The guards themselves should have turned up by morning, somewhere in rural...where? Vermont? New Hampshire? That had never been fully explained. Somewhere north. It wasn't her job to know, so she didn't.

Hays. The big man called Purple Hays. He was the one who took the guards. He was someone with a lot of experience. Wherever the guards were, Hays had put them there.

Within ten minutes of realizing that at least four people had died, she was in the bathroom of the flat, kneeling in front of the toilet on the cold tile floor. She vomited until there was only fluid left in her system, and then past that, when there was no fluid.

She ate some canned soup later in the day and vomited that too. She vomited twice on the airplane on the flight here. She hadn't kept any food in her stomach for more than thirty-six hours. It was as if she was suffering from a bad stomach flu. In this case, the flu was being responsible for the deaths of at least four people, and maybe more.

Now, moving along with the early morning crowds under the soaring ceiling of the airport terminal, she was just beginning to feel better. She didn't think she would vomit again. There was no food at all left in her digestive tract. She was empty, her head floating from hunger, her torso tight and sore from all the violent retching.

Moreover, she was finally going to be able to take her ire out on someone. This wasn't right. It wasn't what she signed up for. It could not happen again.

She went outside and stood in a crowd of people waiting for transportation. Traffic was three lanes deep. Some sort of concrete overpass was above their heads, creating a tunnel effect. The car horns and the shouts of drivers echoed off the ceiling.

A gleaming black Mercedes was parked at the curb. The passenger window powered down. A man in sunglasses was sitting there. He gestured at her with his head.

"Get in."

It was the smoothest operation she had ever been part of. Everything was always ready. Everything was top-notch. Everything was new. She glided effortlessly through a world where the mundane issues were taken care of, and the major issues were handled with complete professionalism.

She walked over with her bags. The rear door popped open. She pulled it all the way open, placed her bags inside, and slid into the car.

The driver pulled slowly out into the thick traffic.

59

The man with the sunglasses frowned at her in the rearview mirror. "You look like hell," he said.

"I've been sick."

The man made a gesture with his hand around his own face. "Use some rouge. Put some color in your face. You look like a ghost. Try to blend in a little, if you can."

She said nothing to that.

The man took off his sunglasses. He had dark eyes. "What can I call you?" he said.

She had thought about this on the plane. Her new name reflected her feelings about everything. "Angel," she said.

In the rearview mirror, the man raised his eyebrows.

"Angel..."

"Dusted," she said.

"You can call me Marcus," he said. "The surname is Aurelius. But Marcus is fine for most purposes."

Marcus Aurelius. The Roman Emperor. Who was this guy kidding?

"I need to talk to someone," she said.

The man shrugged. "So talk."

She gestured at the driver. "What about him?"

"He's okay. He doesn't understand English."

The driver was bald and was also wearing sunglasses. He had a thick neck. Tiny silver crosses dangled from each of his ears. That was about all she could see of him. He hadn't shown the slightest interest in her so far. See no evil, hear no evil.

"People died," she said.

Marcus nodded. "You look like you're one of them."

She felt the heat rising up her neck. It was coloring her face now. "Look, who are you? Who are you, really? You're a long way from an emperor. I wouldn't let you clean my flat."

He shrugged. "I'm the one who picked you up at the airport. Does that help? I'm the one who is supposed to commend you for an excellent overall mission, and personally, a job well done on your part. The mission was a complete success, as I'm sure you know. And you received exceptional marks from the team leader."

"Who was the team leader?"

He shook his head. "I'm not at liberty to say. Was it not clear to you?"

Nothing was ever clear. Maybe it was Purple Hays. Maybe it was Gray. Maybe it was one of the anonymous men who drove the van.

Maybe it was someone doing surveillance through security cameras and two-way mirrors.

No. It was Purple Hays. She knew that. The guy was a machine.

"I need to talk to someone real," she said. "I don't need to talk to a flunky, errand boy, whatever you are. You're stupid. Picking someone up at the airport is about all they'll trust you with, am I right? You look like you've never been on an actual mission in your life. You know, unless you call airport runs missions."

Now his face turned red.

"What else do you do? Pick up groceries?"

"There's the temper I heard about," he said. "The fire. I like it."

"I need to talk to someone," she said again. "If I don't get that much, I'm going to walk. No one told me there were going to be scientists in that place when we hit it."

"No one knew."

She shook her head. "I find that hard to believe. The operation went smooth as glass. We clearly knew everything there was to know."

It was true. Someone had gotten them inside the facility. They had maps of the whole place. They knew exactly where to put the charges to do maximum damage. The facility was out of commission now, and likely would never be rebuilt.

"Believe it or don't."

"I'm going to walk away."

"Careful with that kind of talk," he said. "You're most certainly not..."

"Don't even think about threatening me," she said.

"I'm not threatening you. I don't have to. You know the consequences of simply leaving. It would mean you can't be trusted. You're carrying some pretty big secrets right now."

No one had ever put it that way before. She didn't know who any of the people on these jobs were. She didn't know where the information came from. She did her job, then disappeared and turned up elsewhere. The people she had known in Massachusetts, she had no idea if she would ever see any of them again.

There was no reason to kill her. There was no reason to threaten her. She had done everything they wanted to the best of her ability. And she didn't know anything.

Well, that wasn't quite true, was it?

"Please," she said. "This conversation with you..."

She trailed off. That should make it clear to him. The conversation was so pointless, and the man's standing so inconsequential, there was no reason for her to even finish her sentence.

"You want to speak to someone real," he said.

"Yes."

He was holding a slim black mobile phone in his hand. He pressed a few buttons on the touch screen. He passed the phone back to her.

"It's ringing. Make this very brief. And don't reveal anything."

She held the phone to her ear. In a moment, the ringing stopped.

"You're beautiful," a rich, deep voice said.

She looked into the rearview mirror and met Marcus's hard dark eyes again.

Marcus nodded. "Yes," he said. "It's really him."

She knew that. She didn't have to be told. The voice took her breath away. It always had. It was masculine in a way that no other voice was masculine. But it was also caring, loving, and filled with an almost unexplainable wisdom.

"I…I'm concerned," she said.

She was not expecting this. When she demanded to speak to someone real, she wasn't expecting a phone call to the realest person on the planet.

"I know that," the voice said. "I knew you would be. I knew that about you. Of course you would be. Because you are filled with love. My heart almost breaks when I think of how filled with love your heart is."

There was a lump in her throat. To be in the presence of this man…

It was something beyond words.

"We're in a war," he said. "And this war is hardest on the people who love the most. And it hurts me so deeply to know that you are on the front lines of this war, someone so loving, who loves all the creatures of the Earth, who loves the living, breathing Earth herself, with all of your heart, and your soul…I know these things about you. I've always known them."

She couldn't speak. She hadn't seen Silvio in two years. Of necessity, he had gone into hiding. She didn't even know where he was. But he still had this immense effect on her. Just his voice was enough. It was as if she was a part of him, but only a small part, because he was so much more. And she felt safe, being part of him. But she forgot that. Often, she felt alone and afraid.

And she had betrayed him. All the time, with each step closer to the final mission, she was still betraying him. She was doing it right now. She did not trust completely, she found an escape route, and so she became untrustworthy. It was hard to think about, so she shoved it aside, and put it in a tiny compartment. Her betrayal lived in a box, all by itself, but soon it would outgrow the box and be there for everyone to see.

"I put you on the front lines," he said. "And I did it for a reason. Many reasons. You are a woman of such strength, and moral...moral character. And you love so much that you give everything to the struggle."

She finally found her voice. "And to you," she said. She spoke barely louder than a whisper. She was lying. She didn't give everything. She was keeping some for herself.

"And to me, yes. You give me everything. And I put you in this struggle, at the vanguard, because you are the best of the best."

"Thank you."

"Don't thank me. You're so strong. And you're going to have to be stronger than you've ever been before. Because more is coming, very soon, big things, and we're going to win. But it's going to be hard, and it's going to take everything we have, every ounce of strength. Can you do that? Can you be strong for me? Stronger than you've ever been?"

"Yes," she said.

"And can you hold your judgments? And transcend them? Can you understand with all your heart, that our own judgments will defeat us, if we let them?"

She nodded.

"Yes," she said. She forced the word out, and it was almost like the bark of a dog. She wanted to please him. She wanted to show him how strong she could be.

She cast her eyes downward. At the same time, she didn't want to meet the eyes of the idiot in the front row. Who was he? What could he know? Was he the best of the best? She doubted it.

The deep rich voice went on, and its words were soothing music, like a cello in the hands of a master.

"I've always said...to you, and to anyone who will listen, that if I'm the Christ, then you are Mary Magdalene to my Christ. That's our relationship. One of love, a deep enduring love as old as time itself. A relationship across all of history, all eras. But also a relationship of sacrifice. It has to be that way. That's how it is written."

63

"I feel terrible about what happened," she said. "It wasn't...It wasn't what I wanted."

"I know," he said. "And I love that about you. That's the depth of your compassion. You love our enemies, the ones who would harm the Earth. These people are blind, and they would harm us if they could, cloud our minds, separate us, and put us away forever. And yet you feel compassion for them. I love that. It's how I want you to be. It's how I want all of us to be, but some of us don't reach that high standard. You reach it. You've never disappointed me. I've always been proud of you. And never prouder than I am at this moment."

She felt a sudden urge to confess to him. She hadn't seen him in a long time, and yet, she still belonged to him. So, she did confess. She confessed one thing, the easy thing, but not the big one, not the betrayal that involved money.

"I took a lover," she said. "On this..." She wasn't sure how to describe the mission over this telephone call. She didn't know who might be tuning in. She was mindful of the fact that she needed to hang up soon. She would stay on this call forever if she could. There was so much to say. She had taken other lovers before, or course, but this was the most immediate one—a man whose body she could still almost feel next to hers.

As if to punctuate the time pressure of the situation, the man up front stuck his open hand back, indicating he wanted her to give back the phone.

No. It was too soon.

He didn't say a word.

"Trip," she said. "On this trip." It wasn't a mission or an operation. It was just a simple trip. One where a scientific facility had blown up and several people had died.

"I know that," Silvio said. "I know who it is. I want you to know that I sent him for that purpose. Because I didn't want you to be lonely. I wanted you to have a companion."

"You sent..."

"Of course, I did."

"So, you aren't mad?"

"My beautiful lamb. Your love for me spans lifetimes. My love for you spans all eternity, from the spark of the beginning until the ultimate end. It's not a love of the flesh. It is that, yes, but not primarily. It's a love of the spirit."

There was so much to think about. She knew that she would replay this call in her mind, over and over, remembering the tiniest details, trying to understand the gigantic meaning behind all of his words.

She wished she could have a recording of the call. It pained her to think that the FBI, CIA, Interpol, or some other secret police might have such a recording. Low-rent thugs listening to this conversation and drooling over things they couldn't possibly understand.

"My darling, I have to go now," he said. "We will meet again."

She nodded. "I know."

The line went dead. For another minute, she kept the phone pressed to her ear, as though he might return. Of course he wasn't going to. This was life on the run. This was life under the shadow of dark forces.

The man in the front seat snapped his fingers. He still didn't speak.

She placed the phone in his hand.

She just wanted to sit here in the afterglow of that conversation. She wanted to relish it and puzzle over the things that were said. She wanted to remember it all, and she never wanted to forget it.

"Satisfied?" the man calling himself Marcus Aurelius said now, as he put the phone away. "You're okay with death now? You made your peace with murder? We have work to do, and it's more important than a few lives. That's what he told me, and I get it. It really is that simple."

"Don't talk," she said. "Okay? Please don't say a word. It cheapens everything when you talk."

CHAPTER ELEVEN

"Well, well," Agent Dubois said. "Look who is back. That was fast."

"It was a whirlwind tour," Troy said.

She nodded. "Yes. You seem like a whirlwind hit you. In the face."

Troy looked her up and down. He did so ostentatiously, like a sharpie checking her out on a street corner. He had to admit she looked good. She wore a black jumpsuit which fit her tightly, almost like a catsuit. Her black boots were polished to a high sheen. She wore a red bandana or sash around her forehead, and her thick, curly hair was loose and large in an Afro style. She looked like a communist jungle fighter or urban guerrilla from a 1960s movie.

He shook his head and took a sip from his cardboard coffee cup.

They were standing in the conference room of the new headquarters. The room was spare, with an oval table that could squeeze in about eight people. There was a large video screen mounted on the wall at one end of the table—with a low black table below it, piled with various tech equipment. Troy would guess that screen was at least seventy-two inches across. Not that anyone around here would describe it in inches.

She made a hand circle around her own face. "What's with the face?"

"Just call me lumpy," he said and smiled.

He had taken some pretty good shots at the wedding. Over the past couple of days, the welts had swollen and started turning black and blue. There was one on his left cheekbone and one below his right eye. Those new cousins-in-law, whatever they were, could throw a punch.

"Were you in a bar fight?" she said.

"I was at a wedding. You know how that goes."

She shook her head. She seemed to be suppressing a laugh.

"No. I guess I don't."

Troy had flown overnight and landed in Madrid a few hours ago. It was an odd feeling, being here in Spain.

He was staying in the oldest part of the city, La Latina, a charming neighborhood of narrow wandering streets and wide-open plazas. They had gotten him a flat in a 100-year-old building with ornate balconies. It was a long two-bedroom with hardwood floors, three stories above the street.

He could go out on the balcony and look down on the action below. There were several tapas bars and cafes within a block. From inside his flat, he could hear shouts and car horns and the background hum of sound that meant you were in the city. He loved that sound. And he loved that it gradually quieted down to absolute silence in the middle of the night.

All of that was great. The strange part was this headquarters of el Grupo. It was technically in Madrid, but so far out of town that no train ran here. So Troy was a car commuter now. He was doing the reverse commute from downtown to this bleak suburb.

El Grupo had acquired a tiny Smart Car for Troy to drive himself to work. It was neon green with black piping. It had no second row. It was supposed to have a top speed of about ninety-six miles per hour, but that was clearly a lie. Troy could barely get the thing up to seventy. It was just about the most un-Troy Stark car imaginable. More than that, it was un-American. Smart Cars had never caught on in the United States, and there were excellent reasons for that.

But the car was a good pick in a couple of ways. It got excellent gas mileage. And it was easy to park along the crowded streets of Troy's neighborhood.

Troy could see why Miquel chose this place for the Grupo headquarters. What it lacked in charm, it made up for in utility. It was on a large plot of land along a feeder road near a highway. There wasn't much nearby except some high-rise apartment blocks in the distance.

The headquarters building, which seemed about ten years old, was spacious and modern, with bright offices and lots of tall windows. There was a small workout room. There was a kitchen and dining room. In the basement, there was a long room being converted to a shooting range.

There were several outbuildings, which currently were not in use, but which Troy had seen plans for. Miquel wanted to turn them into modular sets for training on various scenarios—much like how he was currently using rented warehouse space. But these would be onsite: hostage scenarios, infiltration, shootouts, rappelling, you name it.

There was a long garage on the grounds, as well. Miquel hoped that one day it would be full of a fleet of specialty Grupo vehicles—a Bearcat-type armored car, fast motorcycles, luxury cars tricked out with James Bond gadgets. There was also a flat, paved area about fifty meters from the garage that might one day serve as a helipad.

The man had a small agency at the moment but big dreams.

All of this was hidden away from prying eyes behind a tall iron fence and an automated security gate. Recently, the word ERRIU had appeared stenciled on the gate in white letters three feet high. That wasn't going to mean anything to anybody.

Jan Bakker came into the conference room, with two black laptops tucked under one arm and a coffee in his free hand. His wide shoulders just about fit through the door, and the skin of his bald head was nearly scraped off by the top of the doorframe.

"Agent Dubois," he said. "Agent Stark. Good morning."

"Good morning," Troy said.

If Bakker noticed Troy's face, he didn't mention it. He was an odd cat. He was big enough, and more than muscular enough, that you would peg him as some kind of enforcer. He was anything but. The blue eyes behind his thin-framed glasses showed a remarkable intelligence and maybe even an unusual sensitivity. Troy thought it possible that Jan Bakker's feelings were easily hurt.

"I'm going to set up for the briefing," he said now. "Miquel told me he will be ready in a few moments."

"Are we it?" Troy said. "Just the four of us?"

Bakker nodded. "For this meeting, yes."

Without coming right out and announcing it, Miquel seemed to be forming a special group within the larger El Grupo. Troy and Dubois, who had fallen into an informal partner relationship as soon as they met, seemed to be partners going forward as well. Troy would almost say they were meant as the tip of the spear.

He liked it. Dubois was not a combat veteran, but she'd held her own on their first go-round. They had weathered some gunfire together, to put it mildly, and dispatched some bad guys.

Bakker was their tech support. At that, he was certainly a whiz kid.

A three-person team with Miquel as their mentor and father figure. Troy doubted that arrangement would last very long—Miquel was ramping up and bringing more people on.

As if summoned by Troy's thoughts, Miquel came walking in. He was quite a bit shorter than Troy, black hair trending toward salt and pepper, the trim body of a long-distance runner. Troy would say that he was handsome, in a middle-aged guy kind of way. He wore a khaki vest over a blue dress shirt, along with khaki pants and light boots that were almost sneakers. A pair of reading glasses were perched on top of his head. His hands were empty.

"Here's my gang," he said.

"Shall we begin?" Bakker said.

Miquel nodded. "Of course." He made a sweeping hand gesture at the table. It was as if he owned this place and Troy and Dubois were his houseguests. "Won't you both sit down? We have quite a bit to go over."

He glanced at Troy. "How was your trip, Agent Stark?"

Troy shrugged. "You know."

"Did you sustain those injuries on agency time?"

Troy shook his head. "Wedding."

Miquel smiled. "Weddings are a time to come together."

Troy slid into a seat at the table. Dubois sat next to him. Miquel sat across from them. Up at the head of the table, Bakker was still fidgeting with his two laptops.

"Agent Bakker is going to brief us on the background of the current situation."

"I'm ready," Bakker said.

"Good. And when he's done, I will ask Agent Stark to report on what he discovered at the site of the supercollider explosion in America."

On the big screen, a multi-colored test pattern appeared. Then a countdown began. 4, 3, 2, 1…and video footage of a protest began to roll. A large group of people with signs and banners were outside the gates of some compound, shouting and pushing on the fence. Troy tried to decipher the signs they were carrying, but they were in another language. There was no sound except the shouts and chants of the protestors.

Suddenly, a piece of the fencing gave away, and fell forward onto some grass. People streamed across the fallen fence but were met by a line of cops behind plastic shields. Now there was pushing and shoving between the protestors and the cops. A smoke bomb went off. Then another.

Jan Bakker began to speak. "This took place in Germany this morning, at a government-funded scientific facility outside of Bonn. To be clear, the facility in question is not a supercollider, and is actually more interested in astronomy, but is thought to carry out some physics experiments."

"Why are the people protesting?" Troy said.

"Since the attack in America, people are protesting scientific facilities all over Europe, especially ones that keep the nature of their research a secret. Here is a similar protest that took place yesterday at another facility outside of Prague, in the Czech Republic. This facility is a supercollider, albeit a small one, and largely obsolete. But it is still operational and still in use. This protest turned violent, and some of the protestors nearly breached the command center of the supercollider itself. More than a hundred people were arrested, and at least forty people were hospitalized, including more than a dozen policemen."

On the screen, there was a pitched battle between protestors and cops, on a stone plaza somewhere. Protestors threw rocks at cops behind plastic shields. As Troy watched, a protestor threw a flaming Molotive cocktail. It hit a cop's plastic shield, and for a second or two until the fuel burned off, the cop was engulfed in flames.

"It's pretty extreme," Dubois said.

"Yes," Bakker said. "It is."

"What are they protesting about?"

It was the second time Troy had asked what was basically the same question. He figured if he kept rephrasing it, eventually Bakker would have to answer. "They're obviously not protesting against the terrorist attack. They wouldn't attack scientific research facilities if they were."

"Correct," Jan said. "The protestors appear to be in sympathy with the terrorists. There is a growing belief out in the public that these research facilities are a bad thing and must be stopped. This is true of the supercolliders certainly, but other types of facilities are also being targeted. The publicity around the terrorist attack seems to have brought a lot of like-minded people out into the open."

"Why do people think they're bad?" Troy said.

"They are playing with things best left undisturbed," Jan said. "Or at least that's the idea. Many people seem to believe that supercolliders are altering the nature of reality. For example, they believe that the Large Hadron Collider outside Geneva has changed the timeline that we live in."

Troy shook his head. "I don't follow. Changed the…what?"

70

Jan shrugged. "In physics, there is an idea that there are many universes nearly identical to this one. They have split off from each other, and in fact do so all the time. The universes are close and move parallel to each other. In each universe, many things take place in an identical manner, but some things are different. The timelines are changed. Certain details are changed. Many people think the Large Hadron Collider is changing this universe, specifically the past. According to people who believe this, details from the past that everyone once agreed upon have changed."

"Do you have any examples?" Dubois said.

Troy had no idea what Bakker was even talking about. He'd ask another question, but he didn't know where to start.

"There are many examples," Bakker said. "The phenomenon is known as the Mandela Effect. Its proponents believe that Nelson Mandela died in prison on Robben Island sometime in 1987 or 1988. That's how they remember those times. But as it stands now, Mandela was somehow alive after that. He was released from prison and stepped into the role of President of South Africa, even though he was already dead. People believe that experiments in quantum physics have changed our past, and therefore have changed the present as well. Mandela is only the beginning."

"Name another," Dubois said.

"There are many examples. There is an American film called *Risky Business*. It appeared in the 1980s, starring Tom Cruise when he was a teenager. In one famous scene, he is dancing in the living room of his house wearing only a dress shirt, tighty-whitey briefs, and socks."

Troy was getting the hang of this now. "I remember the scene."

"Many people remember the dress shirt as being white and recall that Tom Cruise was wearing sunglasses while doing the dance."

Troy nodded. "Sure. That sounds about right."

"In the film as it exists now, he is wearing a pink striped dress shirt, and no sunglasses. Oddly, the scene was widely parodied on TV shows and in comedy movies of the era. Nearly all the parodies show the main character wearing a white dress shirt and sunglasses."

"Why would they do that if he was really wearing a pink shirt?" Troy said.

Bakker showed the ghost of a smile. "Exactly right. Why would they? Believers think that the parodies exist as a residue of what really happened. But the main event changed without them."

"Well," Troy said. "If that's the worst thing these experiments are doing..."

He almost couldn't believe he was even entertaining this as a possibility. At the same time, he seemed to recall the dress shirt as being white. But what did he know? The movie came out before he was born.

"There are larger concerns," Bakker said. "The supercolliders fire particles at each other at tremendous rates of speed, almost the speed of light. The atoms in the particle beams race along the length of the tube from opposite sides. When they collide, enormous amounts of energy are released. Tremendous heat is generated. At the instant of the collision, there is a fireball three hundred million times hotter than the surface of the sun. For a tiny fraction of a second, and on a scale so small it is undetectable without the most sensitive of instruments, the conditions for black holes are created."

Dubois and Stark stared at him. Miquel was looking at something on his phone. It seemed clear that he had heard all of this before.

"Is this real?" Troy said.

Bakker nodded. "Yes. And some believe that a supercollider will one day create a black hole large enough to swallow the Earth, the solar system, and even the entire galaxy. Others believe that black holes are doorways into other dimensions, and perhaps horrifying things will pass through one of these doorways from another dimension, something that we will be unable to deal with."

"Like what?" Dubois said.

"Life forms, diseases, destructive phenomena that we cannot predict and wouldn't understand if they did appear."

Troy watched Bakker. Did Bakker believe in this stuff?

"What's your take on it?" Troy said.

Bakker shrugged. "The physicists I've spoken to are completely confident that the work is one hundred percent safe. They assure me the experiments would not happen if there was even a tiny chance of disaster. If real black holes are being created, they are so small, and they last such a short time, our minds cannot even conceive of it. Approximately ten to the power of minus twenty-three seconds. In other words, ten million billion billionth of a second. Very brief."

He paused, as if considering the situation, then he nodded.

"It doesn't worry me."

That was a lot of trust to put in scientists. These were the same type of people who built the atomic bomb. Build it first, worry about the side effects later.

"If the protestors believe the Large Hadron Collider is causing these changes or might open one of these doorways, why don't they attack there instead?"

Bakker shrugged. "Miquel?"

"The protestors haven't targeted the Large Hadron Collider," Miquel said. "But I believe terrorists will very soon, possibly in the next few days. That's why I called this meeting. Agent Stark, what did you discover at the site in America?"

Troy drummed his fingers on the table. "They weren't letting anyone into the actual site because of a fire below ground, fueled by unknown chemicals."

"Were they unknown or just unspecified?" Jan said.

"They didn't tell me what they were. But I did see the security footage they're not releasing to anyone yet."

"Interesting that the Americans choose to keep vital information to themselves," Bakker said.

Troy shrugged and ignored the statement. He had no doubt that the Europeans did the same thing.

"The attackers were pros. They were dressed in such a way to made them difficult to identify. They moved quickly and without hesitation. They took down the guards easily. They knew their specific jobs and went right to them. They were in and out of there in just a few minutes, each headed in a different direction, three on fast motorcycles they brought with them. They clearly had inside knowledge of the facility, and they entered in a van that appeared identical to the facility's vans in every way, save one: it didn't have a company issued tracking device on board."

"And the van now?" Dubois said.

"Gone," Troy said. "Along with the three security guards. When I left the States, they still hadn't turned up yet."

"Is it possible the American government is holding them in secret?" Miquel said. "Interviewing them, trying to make them crack? They would be the first ones I would suspect as the insiders."

Troy shrugged. "Anything is possible, I suppose."

"Is that it?" Miquel said.

"Yeah," Troy said. "Basically." He decided to skip any mention of the trip to upstate New York and the misadventure there. If the big terrorist had deliberately misdirected by adding elements of military simulation games, it added to the sense that he was a pro. But it also made Troy look like a dope. And even though it was their idea, he couldn't mention Alex or Missing Persons. That would give away the whole game.

"They knew what they were doing," he said. "They weren't protesters who got lucky."

"Professionalism," Miquel said. "That's what concerns me. That's why I want el Grupo to become involved. And that's why we're going to CERN. Tonight, in fact. They are going to humor us tomorrow and give us a tour of their security features ahead of a large gathering being held there starting Friday, and through the weekend."

"What is the gathering?" Dubois said.

"They're holding a symposium," Bakker said. "Or maybe a celebration. It's called the Triumph of Knowledge. It's a gathering of scientists which will last three days. It will involve a tour of the facility for physicists from far and wide. There will be presentations by researchers who work there and by scientists from other facilities. There will of course be photo opportunities with politicians. The food will probably be quite good."

"It sounds like security will be tight," Troy said.

"Very tight security, I imagine," Bakker said. "It will be even tighter, considering the attack in America and the protests across Europe."

Troy turned and looked at Miquel. "What are you hoping to convince them of?"

Miquel nodded. "I'm hoping they will cancel the symposium, temporarily shut down the facility, and recognize the site as a permanent high-risk target for terrorists. Then I want them to reassess its weaknesses and change its protection scheme to the highest possible security, on a par with nuclear weapons installations."

"What do the people in charge think of all this?"

Miquel shrugged. "They think I'm crazy."

CHAPTER TWELVE

10:15 pm Central European Time
Albert Einstein Institute for Plasma Dynamics
Wintergarten University
Wintergarten, Germany

"Why are we here?" Angel Dusted asked.
"It's a target of opportunity," Marcus said.
"What is it?"
"There is a fusion reactor here. It's fake, and therefore lightly defended. But they are studying the concepts that make it work, which will one day lead to building a real one. Children shouldn't play with dangerous toys."

The three of them were in the back of a van, tucked away in the parking lot of a large, modern indoor mall. There was a brightly lit Burger King in a small plaza at the far corner of the parking lot. The mall was closed for the night, but the lot was crowded, and the King was doing a brisk business. Many young people had walked the few kilometers out here to the edge of the city for the protest, but many had also driven.

The group in the van was Angel Dusted, Marcus Aurelius, and a second man calling himself Hy Wire. They each wore black knit wool caps, heavy black coats, black pants, and black boots. They each had black balaclavas they could pull up over their faces once they entered the crowds.

Hy Wire was skinny and had a dark beard. His blue eyes seemed sensitive and intelligent. He didn't speak much.

Angel could hear the crowds from here, just across the main road and down the street, chanting and shouting. She did not understand German, so she had no idea what the chant was.

They had given her a car. It was a nondescript, dark blue, two-door Volkswagen, small and old. It had a few dents and dings, but nothing that would stand out to anyone. She had parked it back in the narrow streets of the medieval town center.

It should have been a two-and-a-half-hour drive from Berlin to this ancient city on the Baltic Sea in northern Germany, but she had gotten lost on the way, and it had taken her closer to four. She was surprised that another operation was underway so quickly. She had been expecting only one more, and a much larger one than this.

She had started to think of it as the Big One. This wasn't it.

"Under no circumstances do we engage with the police."

Marcus had laid out a large map of the facility on the floor of the van. The windows of the van were blacked—they could see out, but people on the outside could not see in. Marcus shone a bright flashlight on the map.

The Albert Einstein Institute seemed to be a long series of buildings, leading to a larger one in its center. All around the complex to the east and south was open land and woods. To the west was the city of Wintergarten, where most of the college campus was located. North was this shopping mall and the ocean.

Marcus pointed to the side of a building on the east side.

"When the police are overrun, that will open access to this alleyway you see that runs along the edge of the building complex. Go there. There will be an iron fence along your right. The alley is a bit overgrown. I understand that sometimes lovers sneak in there during short breaks in between evening classes."

He gave Angel a long look. She met his eyes but felt nothing at all.

"Follow the alley to the end. I will meet you both there. We are promised a window has been left open a small crack at the far end of the alley. I have a crowbar in my pack. We can force it open all the way. From there, we go to the third floor and to the very back of the building. The office we are targeting is there."

"What is the office called?" Angel said.

He shook his head. "You will know when you need to know."

That made sense. If she were somehow identified and arrested, she wouldn't even know what her target was. She would know these two men by ridiculous aliases only. If she were picked up, she could describe the men, but how accurate would the descriptions even be? And anyway, she would never describe them, except under torture.

Marcus tapped his forehead with a gloved finger.

"The items you are carrying are very expensive, and we are reluctant to lose them. But remember that you are more valuable than any material. You are most valuable of all if you remain out of the hands of the police."

He looked at them back and forth.

"Okay?"

Hy Wire nodded. "Okay." His eyes gave away nothing. He did not appear to be afraid or excited. He didn't even seem to be particularly interested. Now he had the baleful look of someone who has weathered tragedy after tragedy.

"Okay," Angel said.

"Angel, you go first," Marcus said. "Just open the passenger door, go out, and close it again. Walk down to the protests and join the crowd. When the surge happens, go to that alleyway and follow it to the end."

She nodded.

"Everything is clear to you?"

"Crystal clear," she said.

He smiled. "That's my girl."

She shook her head, went to the door, opened it, and climbed out of the van.

Outside, the night air was cool. She walked across the vast parking lot, keeping to the darkened far edge of it. It had turned out that Marcus was in charge of the local cell in Berlin. He was a capable operator. He was a jerk, but she could overlook that, for the most part. It just took a moment of deep breathing after interacting with him, and then the emotions he stirred in her were gone.

The main road was just ahead. It was a four-lane road that headed to the east, away from the city. It seemed that this area must have been farms not that long ago. People began to gather around her, slipping between parked cars, all streaming toward the protest. It almost seemed like the crowd headed to a concert or a sporting event. She looked at them, but not too closely, not focusing on any one person for more than a second.

They were young people, college students living in this university town: energetic, excited, and enthusiastic. They were standing up for something, even if they might not be quite sure what it was. She liked them and was glad for their presence. They were not militants. But maybe one day they would be. The movement needed them.

A young man suddenly began to sing. His voice was rich and deep. The group of walkers all joined him in song. It was stirring, whatever it was.

Everyone quickened their step now, not just excited by the protest anymore, but excited to be young and alive. Everything was possible. To change the world was possible. To stop the madness was possible.

She felt it. They gave their energy to her. There was no fear. She could do what was necessary. Not just for herself, and not just for *him,* or for some abstract sense of the world, but for these kids that surrounded her.

Up ahead, across the main road, the wide boulevard was packed with people. To the right were the buildings of the complex, with their undulating rooftops. She imagined they were supposed to resemble a wave function. To the left was a fence and wide-open fields. In the dark, they seemed like they must be a mile across. She crossed the road with a hundred other people and entered the sidewalk on the right side.

Sound came from everywhere now—shouts, chants, and someone with a harsh voice, probably a policeman, issuing instructions or threats over a bullhorn. There were bright lights shining, causing the bodies of the protestors to make strange, elongated shadows. Way up ahead, she could already see the bright red of the main building, where the reactor would be, and the reflecting pool in front of it.

The sidewalk was becoming crowded now. People began to jostle. She was mindful of not becoming hemmed in. She was mindful of the backpack she was carrying, and the things inside of it.

She reached the end of the sidewalk and spilled out into the wide plaza with the crowd. To her left was the densest concentration of people. They seemed to ebb and flow like water. Or perhaps the police were pushing them back after each surge. It was impossible to say from here. But the crowd was like the tide, crashing forward, then falling back again. She was jostled again and nearly tripped over her own feet.

Everything here was like a wall. A wall of people, a wall of sound. She didn't want to be in this spot when 10:30 came. She turned and plunged through the people who had been behind her, moving away from the center now. She needed to get to a spot with some breathing room. If the crowd burst forward now, she would be sucked along with it, unable to stop. She could very well be trampled.

She glanced down at her watch: 10:28.

Two minutes to go.

She was aware of feeling weak and small. There were so many big young men here. People were packed so tightly. She pushed and squeezed through them. People said things, shouted at her as she passed. She didn't understand.

"Malade!" she shouted back at them, the French word for sick suddenly coming to her. *"Vomir!"* she shouted, her rudimentary French

really kicking in now, exactly when she needed it. *"J'ai envie de vomir."*

"I'm gonna puke."

The Germans well understood French. The crowd parted like the Red Sea parted for Moses. Angel looked down, meeting no one's eyes. Instantly, she recognized her mistake—she had called attention to herself. She should be a zero, a cipher, someone no one had seen.

She could imagine the police questioning witnesses: "Did you notice anything before the grenades went off?"

"There was a French girl. She was sick. She said she was going to puke."

"What did she look like?"

That's where it hit a dead end. She wore a black knit cap, black clothes, black boots, black everything. Her hair and eyes were an indeterminate color. Her body was covered by a dark coat. She might have been slight. She might not have been. She looked like everyone and no one.

All of this passed through her mind in a split second as images and not even complete thoughts. She was reaching the far edge of the crowd now, where it began to thin out. She almost breathed a sigh of relief, as if the goal all along had been to get away from the protest. But that was wrong.

Behind her, there was a flash of light, followed by:

BANG!

The sound was loud, ear piercing. Another flash, and then another BANG! followed on the heels of the first one. People screamed. In fact, the voice of the crowd rose as one into a head-splitting shriek. It was the shriek of people at an amusement park, riding the terrifying new roller coaster.

Angel looked, just as another flash went off. It was a hundred meters away, but still blinding. She blinked and white pinwheels spun inside her eyes.

BANG!

Now smoke was rising. People were running in a panic. Many people were running back this way, the opposite of what Marcus intended. A man crashed into her. There was no time to get out of his way. She fell to the ground, the man on top of her. Then he was up and running again, without a word of concern for her.

She climbed to her feet.

Something had changed. Up near the front, smoke was everywhere, obscuring the complex buildings. Another flash went off, but it was like lightning behind the clouds. The crowd, which had been falling back this way, suddenly surged ahead.

They were pushing through.

The floodgates broke. Somewhere up ahead, the men in the vanguard must have broken the police line. The crowd seemed like it was sucked up through a straw. It narrowed into a funnel, young people racing ahead, people being knocked down, but everyone now, everyone, moving forward.

The line was definitely broken. A cheer went up. It was like the roar of a great lion.

Angel ran ahead, angling to her right. It was open space here, seemingly all the way to the buildings. She ran and ran, her breath raw in her throat, her pack bouncing on her back. She could hear herself gasping.

There was a large metal fence erected along the edge of the plaza between buildings, sturdy, and topped with rolls of razor wire. It looked like something from a maximum-security prison. That couldn't be. This fence wasn't on the great Marcus Aurelius's map. She ran to it and nearly crashed into it. She looked to her right.

Ah. There was the mouth of the alley. The fence ran along the plaza until it reached the building. Then there were some bushes and a dark hole between them. The black iron fence began there, maybe three feet from the wall of the building.

She looked around. No one was here. All of the action was to the left now, where the breach had taken place. If police had been stationed this far along the fence, they had abandoned their posts to try to push back the crowd.

She moved quickly to the mouth of the alley, then down its throat. It was dark back here, overgrown with weeds and full of discarded trash: beer cans, wine bottles, discarded pieces of clothing. How very un-German, disorderly, unscientific. She didn't look too closely at any of it.

The end was not far, another fifty meters. She moved through the shadows and came upon them. They were both already there. Marcus was the bigger of the two men. A flat piece of metal glinted in whatever light was there.

He was prying open the window with a crowbar.

He glanced at her. "I thought you had...how do you say it? Chickened out." Then he smiled. Hy Wire laughed, a low chuckle.

"Okay, comedians," Angel said. "Let's do this."

"Well ahead of you," Marcus said.

He put the short crowbar back in his pack. The window was open several inches now. He placed his hands under it and forced it open another inch. He looked at Hy Wire. "Give me some help."

He didn't look at Angel for this purpose. He was too much. He probably thought a woman shouldn't be on this little adventure. He hadn't been in Massachusetts.

In thirty seconds, the two men had forced the window halfway open, enough for them to slide through.

Marcus did look at Angel now. "Ladies first."

She said nothing. She was growing tired of his humor or whatever it was. She went through the window, shrugged out of her backpack, and placed it inside the building. Then she slid through on her stomach, jumped, and put her hands in front of her. She wriggled onto the floor of the building.

She was in. She climbed to her feet and picked up the bag. In another moment, they were all here. They were in a long, modern corridor. It seemed to have no noticeable features at all. They stood in the silence of the school building, the echo of the riots outside sounding far away now.

"Third floor," Marcus said, his voice barely more than a whisper. "The stairs are just along here."

He led and they followed. They opened the door to the stairwell. There was no sound, so they went up, moving quickly, quiet as cats, even their feet nearly silent. The only sound seemed to be their breathing.

On the third floor, they moved along another corridor. At the end was a door with frosted glass. Marcus tried the knob, but it didn't move. Of course it was locked.

He must have a better plan than just trying the doorknob. He must have a key or maybe there was an insider who was going to come and open the room.

He looked back at Angel and Hy.

"Be very careful in here. There are materials stored in this lab that are extremely flammable. Which is why we chose it."

Now he had the small crowbar in his hand again. He turned to the door and simply smashed out the frosted glass with the bar. Angel jerked involuntarily. The sound was loud in the silence of the building. After the smashing of the window came the tinkling of broken glass on the cement floor.

Marcus reached his hand through the window and opened the doorknob from the inside. The door popped open, and they went inside. It was an open laboratory, very clean, with six long metal tables, each one housing several workstations.

"The chemicals are in the cabinets on the far side. I will pry open the locks, then we each set our charges inside the cabinets. Set them for five minutes. Then we run. This part of the building is going to blow sky high."

It took Marcus less than a minute to pry open six ground level cabinets, two per person. The security here was astonishingly lax. Angel's cabinet was closest to the entrance. She kneeled, took the charges out of her backpack and placed the first one inside the cabinet. There were several bottles in the cabinet, but she didn't look at them closely.

One of them said ACHTUNG! on the label in large letters. She thought of it as the German word for danger. It was the most prominent thing about the label.

She looked down at the digital timer on her first charge.

Suddenly there was a flash of light and a shriek to her left. A WHOOOSH of heat washed over her. She dove to the floor and curled into a ball, her back to the flames.

Then Marcus was there, less than a second later, grabbing her by the collar.

"Get up! Get up! Run!"

The man called Hy Wire was on fire. He fell back and away from the cabinet, the top half of his body engulfed in flame. He screamed, a sound like she had never heard before. It sounded like a siren, or the bleat of the damned as they are dropped into hell.

"How did it…"

"I don't know. Come on!"

Then she was up and running, back through the doorway and down the corridor. Another WHOOSH of flame followed them down the hall. The charges! Her entire bag was still in there. And they were going to blow NOW.

They pushed into the stairwell, and Marcus slammed the steel door behind them. The entire hallway behind them was already catching fire. They barreled down the stairs, taking them two at a time.

"Oh my God! Oh my God!"

Everything was a blur. Down the stairs, three leaping steps to the window, then out into the alley.

BOOOM!

Something blew up above and behind them.

She caught a glimpse of it. The entire top of the building had blown out and was now burning.

They raced down the alleyway, plunging through the weeds and the darkness. Angel could feel the heat of the burning building on her back and on her head. She was getting hot. Could she catch fire, just from being this close to the heat?

Please no!

They came to the mouth of the alley. Marcus stopped abruptly, and she crashed into his back. "Run!" she wanted to scream. "Run!"

He held up a hand, watching the plaza outside. He turned to her.

"We split up here. Give me ten seconds. Go to your safe flat. Wait there. Don't speak to anyone unless necessary. Someone will contact you."

Then he was gone. Chivalry was officially dead.

Angel counted to five. She couldn't wait for ten. Another explosion ripped the night behind her. Now tiny chunks of masonry rained down on her. She felt like she was about to cry. The heat was too much. The screams of the protestors on the plaza were too much. The sight of Hy Wire consumed by flame was...

She couldn't think about that.

She burst out of the alley and tore onto the plaza. Ahead of her and all around, people ran in a stampede. Eyes were wide in horror and terror, like giant lamps. People crashed into each other. People fell and were trampled. She sprinted across the plaza as fast as she could, then dived into the frenzied crowd of protestors.

And disappeared among them.

CHAPTER THIRTEEN

10:55 pm Central European Time
Hotel Front de Mer
Versoix, Switzerland

"I just love Geneva," Aliz Willems said. Her voice emanated from the speaker phone feature on his mobile phone. "It's one of my favorite cities."

Troy smiled. He lay sprawled out on the bed, his big body taking up nearly all of it, his head propped up on the pillows. He had a glass of chilled white wine in his left hand. His mobile phone was on his chest.

There was something about living in hotels, moving from town to town, country to country, flying here and there…it appealed to him. In the SEALs, he had moved around a lot on deployment, but then he would return to Coronado, and he might stay there for months before being deployed again.

He didn't stay in hotels that much. They were growing on him. Take this place, for example. It was super modern, a few miles up the coast from Geneva. His room was very small, with fake hardwoods floors and a white tile bathroom. There were sliding glass doors to a terrace that looked out over the lake. There was a tiny refrigerator stocked with snacks, beer, and wine. It was all on the company dime.

"Madrid is one of your favorite cities too, as I recall," he said.

"Yes," she said. "Without hesitation. Sincerely."

"Luxembourg, Madrid, Geneva. Is every city one of your favorite cities?"

"No," she said. "Definitely not."

"What's a non-favorite city of yours?"

"Houston."

He nearly burst out laughing now. "Texas?"

"Is there another?"

"I don't picture you in Houston somehow."

"My family has interests there, of course. It is a hot, humid place. It makes my hair frizz. I find the city drab, flat, and without charm. There is nothing pleasing about it."

"Oil?" Troy said, ignoring her opinions about Houston and what it looked like. It was a modern city. It didn't look like Luxembourg or Madrid. That much was clear.

If her family was in oil, this was the first he'd heard of it. But they seemed to have their tentacles in everywhere, more or less. For a second, he pictured her half-brother again, and the unfinished business without him. It nearly gored Troy's mood. He was trying to forget that Aliz was in any way associated with Luc Willems, or Luc Mebarak, or whatever the man was calling himself on any given day. He'd been doing a pretty good job of it until this second.

"Not oil," she said. "Not directly. But we do have interests in the security apparatus that serves the oil industry, especially in Africa."

"Hmmm," he said. She was a beautiful woman, and he'd had fun on their first date. He didn't want to complicate anything with her. He just wanted things to be easy.

"How long are you there?" she said.

He shook his head. "I don't know, to be honest."

"Why are you there?"

Things were never going to be easy. These could be innocent questions she was asking him, or they could be something more sinister.

Troy had no way of knowing what this woman did with her time, who she saw, or who she spoke to. No, amend that. He had ways of knowing. He just didn't want to employ them. This was a fledgling…whatever it was. A nicely simmering interest. He could put a man on her, follow her, tap her phones, hack her computers, find out everything…and that would surely ruin it.

"No one really knows why I'm here," he said. "Not even me."

"Ah. Mister super spy."

He took another sip of the wine. "Something like that."

"Would you like company, or are you too deep under cover?"

"You would come here?" he said.

"I will come to Geneva anytime. It is not far from here by air, perhaps one hour. It's very convenient for me to come there."

A whole new world was opening in front of his eyes. There were rich people who flew from city to city on a whim. Aliz was one of them. Why wouldn't she be? Troy had spent much of his adult life flying around the world on deployments. Why wouldn't rich people fly an hour or two just to eat out? Maybe he had always known this, and hadn't thought about it.

"Let me, uh…"

"Ask permission?" she said.

"Yeah, if you want to put it that way."

"Is there another way to put it?"

He smiled and shook his head. "No."

Suddenly, a knock came at his door. It was more like a hammer blow.

"Aliz, hold on a second." He raised his voice to the door. "Hello?"

"Troy, are you awake?"

It was Jan Bakker.

"Yes."

"May we come in?"

"Who are we?"

"Agent Bakker and Agent Dubois."

Troy shook his head. "One minute."

He looked at the phone laying on his chest. "Well, my dear. Duty calls."

"I understand," she said. "Please remember to ask if I can visit. Dinner, drinks, overlooking the lake. It sounds lovely to me this time of year. If they say no, I might even come and dine by myself."

For a second or two, Troy entertained a fantasy. There was a beautiful blonde in a red dress, sitting alone at an outdoor table by the lake at night. One of those tall metal fireplaces was going. The lights of the city were shimmering around her. Then a man appeared. The man's name was Troy Stark.

"Do you mind if I join you?" the man said.

She nodded at the empty chair near her. "Please do."

Did he even need to ask Miquel's permission for that?

"I will speak to you soon," he said now and hung up the phone.

He sighed and climbed out of bed, went to the door, and opened it. Bakker and Dubois stood there in the hallway, as mismatched a pair as there had ever been.

Bakker was an ox. He stood every inch of six feet, three inches tall, and his shoulders were wide enough that he would practically have to come in through the door sideways. His big feet were thick and bare. They looked like the feet of a caveman, or a sasquatch, except there was not a single hair on them. He was holding a tablet computer. It looked like a child's toy in his hands. His eyes, as ever, were sensitive and intelligent behind a pair of wire-rimmed glasses. He wore tight blue nylon shorts and a dingy white t-shirt.

86

Dubois stood about five feet nothing. If it weren't for the six inches of curly hair piled on top of her head, and tied with a bright yellow ribbon, she almost wouldn't be there at all.

Even late at night, with no makeup, she was stylish in blue jeans and a yellow shirt that matched the ribbon. Even her slippers matched the shirt and the ribbon. The yellow somehow brought something of the dark cream color of her skin to the fore.

"Have you seen the TV?" she said.

"Have I seen the..."

He turned and looked back into his room. There was a TV mounted on the wall. Certainly he had seen it. He hadn't turned it on, but why would he? The shows were in other languages. Troy had never been much of a TV watcher anyway, even in English.

She had already slipped past him. Bakker followed them both inside.

"There's been another attack," Bakker said.

Dubois went to the tiny desk and picked up the remote control. She clicked the TV set on, waited a few seconds for the picture to appear, then flipped through the stations until she found the one she wanted, a news station. The image was of a raging fire in a building somewhere, black smoke pouring into the sky. The image changed to young people sitting on pavement, faces blackened. A girl was crying. Another was screaming. A person, who looked like a male, lay motionless on the sidewalk. Fire engines and police cars were all over the street, red and blue lights spinning.

The voice of the announcer was in French.

Under the images were the words:

LIVE: Albert Einstein Institute.

"Where's Miquel?" Troy said.

"He's coming," Dubois said. "He was asleep in his room."

"What happened?" Troy said.

Bakker was sitting on the bed now. He was scrolling through pages on his tablet. "The information is very preliminary. There was a protest outside the Einstein Institute at the Wintergarten University tonight. The university is in far northern Germany. It's part of an international science cooperative. What looks like thousands of students turned out for the protests. There is a department of theoretical plasma physics there, and they have a prototype of a nuclear fusion reactor. There's also a department of chemical engineering, housed in the building you see burning."

"If it's a science university, why would the students protest?" Troy said.

"It's a large university," Bakker said. "It takes up the whole town, more or less. They have arts and humanities there, psychology, environmental science, political science. I doubt the physics students were protesting their own work or the work of their professors."

"Hundreds of students were rioting on the plaza between buildings," Dubois said. "They were attempting to break in when the building blew up."

"Did anyone die?" Troy said.

"At least half a dozen were trampled to death," Dubois said. "Maybe more."

"There is no tally on deaths from fire or smoke yet," Bakker said. "No one knows if anyone was in the building. If there were, they're dead now."

"The protest was a decoy of some kind," Troy said, trying the idea on for size, rather than asserting it as a fact. "It engaged the attention of the police…"

"Yes," a voice said from behind him. They all turned, and Miquel was there, in matching blue flannel pajamas, pants and a button-up shirt. It looked like he was wearing a flannel pajama suit. His hair was slicked back.

"And while they were engaged, your professionals slipped into the building and destroyed it."

"But why?" Bakker said. "The facility in question is a center of science learning, but hardly the most advanced. There is no particle accelerator. The reactor they've built doesn't even work. It circulates super-heated plasma but generates no electricity. It's barely more than a mock-up of what a real fusion reactor might one day be like."

"Dig deeper," Miquel said. "I'm sure there's a connection."

"You believe this is related to the attack in America?" Dubois said. "Not just a misguided group of students who…"

Miquel shook his head. "No. I'm certain the attacks are related."

"The attacks have nothing in common. They are in different countries, thousands of miles apart. One took place in the middle of the night when few people were around. One took place with thousands of people present. One was a particle accelerator, one was a prototype fusion reactor."

Miquel said nothing in response. He was the type of guy who became one hundred percent certain of things. And when he did, no amount of reasoning or rational argument was going to discourage him. He'd pull a gun on his bosses and throw away his career before he would back down.

Jan stroked his chin. "If you believe they will attack any scientific facility, no matter how obscure, then it's a target rich environment. That makes it difficult to pinpoint the location of the next attack."

"Yes," Miquel said. "That's why they did it. They want to create uncertainty about their next move."

There was a long silence and no agreement. Troy gestured at the pajama suit Miquel had on.

"You planning to wear that to CERN tomorrow?"

CHAPTER FOURTEEN

November 16
3:45 am Central European Time
Neukölln, near Hermannplatz
Berlin, Germany

"This place will do."

The flat was on the fifth floor of a large apartment block full of what seemed to be, at least this time of night, drug addicts, dealers, and prostitutes.

When she first arrived here, there was a small crowd of people around the entrance way. On the one hand, they all stared at her, and that was bad. On the other hand, probably none of them would remember seeing her by mid-morning.

There was no elevator, so she'd had to walk up the stairwell. A man had been asleep, she thought between the third and fourth floors, lying across the landing. He smelled like piss, beer, and cigarettes, in that order.

She had lost her backpack in the fire. It had probably been destroyed, so she wasn't worried about that. The back of her coat had been singed and nearly burned away. She stuffed it in some bushes near where she had parked the car.

They'd left her some new clothes here. Jeans, a few t-shirts, a sleep shirt, underwear, no-name blue sneakers, a jacket, a green knit hat, and gloves. These were clothes that a normal person might wear. They were in good shape. She might look unusual wearing them when she left here, because there didn't seem to be any normal people around, but that didn't matter now. Either the police knew something about her, or they didn't. A strange, healthy, decently dressed girl leaving a hole like this, and never returning, wouldn't be the most remarkable thing that ever happened.

There were a few cans of beer, some cheese, bread, and mustard in the tiny refrigerator. There was a jar of sauerkraut. There was half a pack of cigarettes and some matches left on the kitchen counter.

She thought she had given up smoking. She was wrong.

She wasn't hungry. She took a beer, the smokes, and a saucer from the cabinet into the living room. She noticed the tin of ground coffee in the cabinet, along with a French press made of glass and a small aluminum pot. The coffee was for later. Beer now, smokes now, coffee later.

In the living room, she sat cross-legged on the ratty carpet. She didn't want to sit on the chair or the couch, not because they were horrible, which they were, but because she wanted to sit in a pose that she associated with a meditative state.

There was a small television, but there was no way she was going to turn it on. She opened the beer and took a sip. Something like a gasp escaped her. The beer was ice cold and delicious.

She opened the flip top on the pack of cigarettes. The smokes were like a line of soldiers ready for action. She took one out. There was a small piece of paper folded and tucked away in back of the cigarettes.

She felt nothing about the note. She thought nothing about it. She was vaguely aware that there were things she could think and feel about it, but none of them were occurring to her at this moment. Every time she blinked, it seemed like she watched Hy Wire go up in flames again.

Hy Wire was now a weak link in the chain. The police were going to find his body, if there was anything left of it. Whoever he was, there must be some record of his existence. If so, Interpol, Europol, Scotland Yard, or some damn thing, was going to know who he was. And that was going to happen soon, maybe later today.

Her breath almost caught in her throat. Hy Wire. It was okay. She had no idea who he really was. She had never met him before yesterday. Outside of the man calling himself Marcus Aurelius, they had no one in common. And Hy Wire was dead.

Marcus. Marcus was the true weak link right now. As the cell leader, he might know the real identities of the people who were sent to him. That would be stupid, and out of character for this organization, but it wasn't outside the realm of possibility.

It came to her that Marcus may have killed Hy Wire. Marcus had given them the backpacks. Marcus had seemed ready to run as soon as the fire started.

If that were so, then why didn't he also kill her?

She took out the note and unfolded it.

There is an incinerator door across the hall. Burn your old clothes. Wear the new clothes.

91

She nodded. This was good. Instructions. She needed instructions at this moment. They were like a lifesaver thrown to a drowning woman.

She lit the cigarette and inhaled deeply. Oh, God. That was good. *Now. Do it now.*

She nodded again, untied her boots, and kicked them off. She had been too tired, too shell shocked, to even take her boots off. Very silly. Boot prints were a way people were sometimes identified and captured.

She peeled off her socks, then stood, took down her pants and her panties, and pulled off her shirt and bra. Now she stood nude in the middle of the living room, with a beer in one hand and a cigarette in the other. She pulled the money, identification, and the keys out of the pants pockets.

She pulled the light blue sleep shirt over her body. Then she rooted around in the kitchen until she found what she was looking for—a large brown paper bag. She stuffed the clothes into the bag and opened the door to the flat.

She looked both ways. There was no one in the hall. The hall itself was long and poorly lit. There was graffiti on the walls, black scribbles of this and that. The walls of the hallway had once been white or maybe a very light yellow. Now they were a deeper, ugly... she didn't have a word for the color.

The color of sickness. The color of the chemotherapy patient.

She took two steps across the hall and opened the incinerator door. She could feel the heat from six floors below. Beautiful.

She stuffed the bag into the incinerator shaft and let it fall. Then she went back to her flat. The door shut behind her. She locked it. Three locks—a regular turn lock, a deadbolt slide, and a chain. No one was coming in here.

She sipped her beer and took another drag from the smoke. It was time for the coffee. She thought she would wait for a while, she thought she might even sleep for a bit and wait until much later, but the suspense was eating at her. She had to know.

She went to the kitchen cabinet, opened it, and took out the coffee can. She placed it on the counter and removed the rubber lid. There was a vacuum seal under the lid. That was very clever. She tore it out.

The smell of the fresh coffee was pungent. She loved that smell.

She pushed her slim hand into the coffee grounds. They spilled out on either side of the canister, displaced as her hand went ever deeper. At the bottom of the can, her hand found what she hoped would be there. Or maybe she knew it would be there. It was a plastic bag.

She pulled it out, coffee spilling everywhere now.

It was the kind of plastic bag that had a zipper across the top. Inside of it was an envelope. Her hands were shaking as she opened first the bag, and then the envelope.

Inside the envelope were a few things. One was a stack of money. She leafed through it. Three thousand euros in denominations of one hundred and fifty. Not much, but enough to get her on the move.

Next was a British passport. There was a photograph of her inside the passport. Her actual photograph. It identified her as Margaret Ainsley, twenty-seven years old, born in London. The passport had three years left on it. She thumbed through it. Margaret had gotten around a bit. She had gone to the United States three times. Canada twice. Barbados. Morocco.

There was another ID in the envelope. It showed Margaret as a graduate student at the University of London.

Okay. She had a new identity. She had a little bit of money in her pocket. She could get out of here. If this was the end of her ride, she could go back to the United States or anywhere.

There was a folded note in the envelope. That was the last thing. She pulled it out and unfolded it. There was an address in Zurich written on it.

Cross the frontier at Konstanz. Proceed to this address. Arrive on the evening of 17 November. It is a restaurant at street level, with outdoor seating. Don't sit outside. Take a table inside. A man there will know you.

Jackpot. They had picked her to go to Switzerland. That could only mean one thing. She had proven herself to them. She was all the way in now. She took a deep hit of the cigarette, held it, threw her head back, and exhaled.

"Compartmentalize," she said.

She had done it. She walked back into the living room and returned to her spot on the carpet. She sipped the beer and smoked. She dropped her ashes into the saucer. She sat that way, just drinking and smoking, not thinking anything, for a long time.

After a while, a thought did come to her.

Was she a true believer in this cause? Was she legitimately part of the movement?

Yes. She was. She had risked her life and freedom for it. She had turned her back on the normal life pursued by so many women her age—career, marriage, family. She was partly responsible for the deaths of other human beings, something she would have to live and struggle with. It was safe to say she had given more than most had.

Was she in love with the leader of the movement, a love that transcended time and maybe even lifetimes?

Without a doubt. Silvio had opened her eyes to so much. She would not be the person she was without his presence in her life, a presence that she felt even now, after not seeing him for two years, and after the disaster earlier tonight into which he had sent her. She loved him more than she could speak in words. The sacrifices she made were more than just for the movement. They were for him.

Was she also about to make the biggest payday of her life?

Yes. If she had really made it onto the final assault team, and it seemed like she had, then…yes. All of these things were true. She was part of the movement, she loved its leader totally, and she was also working for other people. Those people were the ones who paid her. Her work for them was to get all the way inside.

"Compartmentalize," she said again.

CHAPTER FIFTEEN

"Watch everything carefully," Miquel said. "From the large to the small. Take nothing for granted."

They were sitting in a smallish black SUV, waiting in a line of three cars stopped at the gate of Entrance A. The gate was a simple metal arm with red and yellow reflectors that came down after each vehicle passed through. There was a scanner next to the gate that read ID cards. A couple of people had passed through by opening their windows and waving their cards at the scanner. There was one guard on duty, a man in a smart-looking police-type uniform, and he was stationed in a small building that reminded Troy of a tollbooth.

Miquel was in the driver's seat of the SUV, with Dubois in the front passenger seat. Troy and Jan Bakker, by far the largest humans in this group, sat in the back with their knees pressed against the seats in front of them. This was like some bizarre family outing, with Dubois and Miquel as the mother and father, and Troy and Bakker as the two big teenage sons.

"Okay Dad," Troy nearly said.

As he watched, a man on a racing bicycle zipped around the gate and onto a pedestrian sidewalk. He waved a card at the security guard as he passed. The guard raised a hand as if to say, "Hi."

"You mean like that guy who just entered the campus with no security check of any kind?" Troy said. "That's the kind of thing you don't want us to take for granted?"

"Yes," Miquel said. "But don't stop there. Keep your eyes open."

"I imagine," Dubois said, "he's an employee who the guard recognizes."

"I'm sure he is an employee," Troy said. "He's a man who everybody likes, and everybody trusts, and he was planted here three years ago by Iranian intelligence to quietly collect data."

Jan smirked and shook his head. "I doubt he's an Iranian intelligence asset, but I do agree with you. The security is lax."

They reached the guard. He came out of his little tollbooth and up to the window. Miquel handed him his identification.

"We are the contingent from the European Rapid Response Investigation Unit."

"You said a mouthful," Troy said.

The guard looked down at the ID card, then back at Miquel.

"Again?" he said. "Please?"

"Interpol," Miquel said. "We're from Interpol. We have a meeting with Dr. Tremaine from the public information office. She is expecting us."

A light went on in the guard's eyes. "Ah. Yes. You are expected." He disappeared into the tollbooth, then came out again with four plain black badges. Each one had a silver metal clip on it. He handed them to Miquel.

"Day passes, for both campuses. Attach to your clothing, please, in a visible place. Dr. Tremaine will meet you in front of Building 432. Building 432 is straight ahead, and then bear to your left. It's where her office is located. Enjoy your visit."

The gate opened and Miquel drove through. Now they were inside. They cruised slowly through what resembled a fairly typical university campus. In this case, the cluster of buildings and thoroughfares was set against the backdrop of low green and brown mountains in the near distance.

"He checked your ID, but no one else's," Dubois said.

Miquel shrugged. "Well, mine was probably good enough in this case. I am the director, after all."

They passed what appeared to be a large brown orb, eight or ten stories high, possibly made of wood. There was a parking lot and open plaza across the road from it. The parking lot had several school buses and dozens of cars in it. Flags of different nations fluttered in a light breeze.

"The Museum of Science and Innovation," Jan said. "It has a lot of informational programs for kids."

"Are you the tour guide?" Troy said.

A little way farther, and they pulled into the parking lot for Building 432. The building was a concrete and glass modern construction three stories high. It was probably designed to bring in natural ambient light from the outside.

An older woman with white hair close cropped to her scalp stood waiting for them in front of the building, in a long skirt and light jacket. Miquel pulled up next to her. She came up to the SUV and Miquel powered down the window.

"Hello!" the woman said. She had deep crow's feet around her eyes and smile lines around her mouth. Her eyes were bright, intelligent, and pale blue. She was very pretty and seemed to give off an almost animal energy. She was cruising into late middle age without hitting any speed bumps.

Troy reflected that she was perfect for greeting the public.

"Are you the…"

"Yes, we are," Miquel said. "Are you Dr. Tremaine?"

"Please call me Sylvia," she said. "Are you ready to have a look around?"

Have a look around.

Troy noticed a glance pass between Dubois and Bakker in the rear-view mirror. These people simply refused to believe they could be the target of an attack.

"It should be fun," Troy said.

Sylvia looked back at him. "Oh, most definitely. It will be fun. And I hope very informative. And I suspect it will put your minds at ease."

"I will be happy to have my concerns eased," Miquel said. His voice was flat and deadpan.

Troy nearly laughed. He was just coming to know Miquel a little bit. This was a man who had pulled a loaded gun on his superiors so they couldn't stop a mission in progress. This was a man who deliberately set up an exercise where Troy got his partner killed, just to teach him a lesson. If ever there was a person whose concerns would not be eased, it was Miquel.

Sylvia's smile redoubled, brighter than ever.

"I'm excited to show you."

* * *

"Our name is actually a misname," Sylvia said.

They were sitting in a conference room in Building 432. Troy imagined that this was how the dog and pony show tended to begin— with food and drinks and some general information. It was still early, and since this little meeting was scheduled to take the entire morning, might as well start the day out right.

97

He sat next to Dubois, with Miquel and Jan across from them. Sylvia stood at the head of the table, in front of a large video monitor mounted to the wall. The room was sleek, long, and very clean. The table could have sat twenty or more. Behind Troy was a line of windows, looking out on the campus with the ever-present mountains in the distance. With the touch of a button from Sylvia, a set of near transparent blinds had slid down silently, limiting the outdoor light, but still giving the view.

There was delicious coffee, which Troy took black. There was fresh bread and soft cheese, along with sugary confections. There was orange juice in tiny four-ounce glasses, the way God intended orange juice to be served. Miquel was the only one who didn't eat. It seemed that the very pleasantness of the presentation was putting him in a sour mood. He did drink the coffee, though.

"We are called the European Organization for Nuclear Research. We don't really do that. And our acronym CERN is even more inaccurate. In French, it stands for the European Council for Nuclear Research, which stems from a treaty agreement signed by the original twelve member states in 1954, before there even was an organization."

She looked at each of them in turn. They stared back at her. Troy sipped his coffee. Man, it was good.

"What we really are is the European Organization for Particle Physics Research. And even that is a slight misname, because Israel was granted membership in 2014. Now we have twenty-two European member states and Israel. We have ten more associates that are in the process of applying for membership, and these include Turkey, India, and Pakistan. So, we are gradually moving beyond a strictly European focus."

"Any questions so far?"

"Who makes the coffee?" Troy said.

Sylvia smiled. It would take a nuclear bomb to make that smile falter. Apparently, nuclear bombs weren't what they did here.

"A local service provider in a nearby town brings it. It's very good."

Troy nodded. "Yeah. It is. If everything here is this good…"

He let that hang there.

Sylvia marched on. Coffee was on the menu, but not on the agenda. "Any other questions?"

"Russia?" Jan Bakker said. "China?"

Troy realized that Jan must already know the answer to that.

Sylvia shook her head. "Not at this time. They have their own programs. And perhaps they are less interested in the spirit of cooperation that we try to foster here."

She clicked a button on the device in her hand and two photographs abruptly appeared on the screen behind her. The first image was of what looked like a large pipe, disappearing into the distance down a long, curving corridor. Two men wearing safety glasses were in the foreground, one on his knees, and they appeared to be elbow-deep in the guts of the thing. Troy was well familiar with photos like this by now. She was showing them a particle accelerator.

He glanced at his watch. It was 8:45.

In the second photo, there was a map with two circles superimposed on it. One was big and took up nearly the entire space of the map. The other was smaller, a concentric circle within the larger one. The two circles touched at a point on the left side of the photograph.

Sylvia pointed at the photo.

"Our work here is primarily with the Large Hadron Collider, or LHC, which you probably know is recreating the conditions of the universe that existed right after the Big Bang. In 2012, we were very excited because we believe that the LHC discovered evidence of the Higgs Boson, the so-called God Particle, a subatomic particle which had been proposed nearly fifty years earlier. And as you can see from this image, both the Meyrin site in Switzerland, where we are now, and the nearby Prévessin site in France, are quite small, when compared to the size of the LHC."

"Therefore, the name," Jan said.

Sylvia nodded. "Yes. The collider is very large, twenty-seven kilometers long, which is about sixteen miles." She looked directly at Troy, who was the only one in the room who couldn't instantly understand the size of twenty-seven kilometers.

"Thank you," he said.

"The LHC lives in a tunnel that runs underneath the surrounding Swiss and French villages, and out into open country. The smaller ring that you see is the old Super Proton Synchrotron collider, or the SPS, which was built in the early 1970s. The SPS is not to be confused with the original Proton Synchrotron, which was built in the 1950s, and is still in operation. The SPS is seven kilometers long, which seemed enormous when it was first opened. Nowadays, it mainly exists to speed up particles and feed them into the LHC. But also bear in mind that there are a dozen accelerators and decelerators currently active here, including the LHC, and that there are no fewer than eight large-scale individual experiments being conducted along the length…"

Miquel raised a hand, like a kid at school. "Sylvia?"

"Yes? Miquel."

"This is all very interesting, and we are grateful for the education. But we are mostly interested in a looming terrorist attack, which we think may occur here, possibly as soon as two days from now, when your big celebration begins. It's probably best if we learn about the security provisions you have in place."

The smile faltered…for a second. Then it was back, not quite as bright as before.

"There's just a bit more of the science to cover," she said. "I find it fascinating, and I hope you will too."

"We aren't science students," Miquel said. "I'm sure you understand."

She nodded, the smile wilting and dying now, like a piece of lettuce on a bright, hot day. Miquel could kill anyone's smile. He was worse than a nuclear bomb.

"I do," Sylvia said. "Of course."

Half an hour later, they were in a control room in France. They had traveled through a car tunnel across the border, open only to the denizens of CERN. The setup was similar to the entry gate they had first passed through—a narrow security arm, a card reader, and a single guard in a glorified tollbooth.

Now, they stood back from a large bank of stacked video displays and computer monitors, taking up three entire walls. A counter ran along the length of it, a desk of sorts, where eight people, most dressed in business casual, a few dressed in white lab coats, sat in rolling desk chairs, typing into keyboards and watching the information on the screens. On several of the screens, people were inside the collider tunnel, apparently examining the machine itself.

The group from Interpol had added one more. His name was Eduard. He was a tall man with a mustache. He wore work pants and a red linen button-down shirt. He was not the Director of Security. He had been very clear about that. He was an Associate Director.

Eduard had just given a rundown on cyber security, which was similar to just about any government agency or large corporation with giant network systems. They had a modern firewall to guard against external attacks, which had been upgraded in the past two years. They had a single sign-on portal for all system users, with enhanced security key features for remote logins. They had mandatory operating system upgrades, which happened automatically on start-up when the system detected a machine that was behind the times. They had permissible and impermissible software packages. They had training for all staff not to click on malicious email messages or download malicious attachments.

Troy shook his head. You didn't have to be Jan Bakker to know that it was just about impossible to make thousands of people conform perfectly to computer security measures. People weren't paying attention. People made mistakes. People had their little guilty pleasures they liked to indulge, which brought them to the shadier parts of the internet. These were scientists, not saints.

Troy caught himself musing about this, even though it was Jan's department. In the meantime, Eduard had moved on.

"As you can see," Eduard said, gesturing at the busy control room around them, "there is a great deal of work happening today, in preparation for the upcoming celebration."

"How do people go inside the collider?" Miquel said.

"There are several access points, two of which are in this facility. Others are offsite, along the length of the device."

"What are the security arrangements?" Dubois said.

"It is the highest-level clearance we have. No one can enter the tunnel without authorization. Generally, the only people with authorization are scientists and mechanics who maintain and repair the device. I would take you inside, but we couldn't grant you authorization in this short of a time frame. I don't have authorization myself, and I've worked here twelve years."

"How do you keep unauthorized people out?"

"We use iris scan technology, which examines the colored part of the human eye. It is a much more accurate scan than either fingerprints or facial recognition. The iris has 240 specific data points for comparison, making each one unique to the individual. Even identical twins have starkly different iris readings. The scans are done by devices at each access point, and take just a couple of seconds. The door will only unlock if the scan is an exact match to the existing digital file."

"Are the access points manned by security personnel?" Troy said.

"No. The scans make it unnecessary. Redundant, if you will. Also, people with authorization may enter the tunnel twenty-four hours a day, at their discretion. To have a security guard posted at an access point in the countryside all night on the chance that a scientist might appear there..."

Eduard trailed off, as if the sentence finished itself.

"Let me give you a hypothetical scenario," Troy said. "Suppose a scientist did decide to enter the tunnel in the middle of the night. And suppose I was waiting there with a gun, which I put to the scientist's head. He does the iris scan, and I go in with him. What then?"

"It seems a bit extreme, does it not?" Eduard said.

"No. Not to me. Where I come from, things like that happen all the time."

Eduard shrugged. "Well, the system would detect one iris scan and two people entering the tunnel. It would alert security staff, who are on-call in the command center twenty-four hours a day, and they would bring up the scene on a monitor. Within a short time, they would intervene, both by mobilizing CERN personnel and by contacting the local police in the area where the offense took place."

"What if I were dressed like the scientist and went in by myself?"

Eduard shook his head. "What would you hope to accomplish?"

"I'd hope to lay down a series of connected explosive charges and blow the whole thing sky high."

"Sir, this is all very far-fetched. This facility was in operation during the depths of the Cold War, the collapse of the Eastern Bloc, civil war in the Balkans, through decades of war in the Middle East and in Africa, and Islamic and left-wing terrorism on the continent. We came through it all."

A man in a lab coat turned around to face them. He was an old man with bright white hair. His face was deeply lined. He was holding a clipboard.

"In the Cold War, security was much tighter than it is now," he said. He spoke with an accent. Troy guessed Russian. "I promise you that."

"Thank you, Oleg," Eduard said. Troy wouldn't be surprised if the next words out of his mouth were, "Now please sit down."

Oleg smiled. "Things are much more, what would the capitalists call it? Things are more *laissez faire* now. We must let nature take its course."

"Thank you," Eduard said again.

The old man shrugged and turned back to whatever he had been doing.

Eduard looked at Troy again. "Anyway, nothing like you describe has ever happened here."

There was a long, somewhat awkward pause. Troy stood silent. He hoped he didn't need to mention all the things that happened, that until they happened, had never happened before.

The Oklahoma City bombing came to mind. The Chernobyl meltdown came to mind. People hijacking and then deliberately crashing passenger planes into tall buildings came to mind.

He could stand here all day, thinking of these things, and he was pretty sure a new one would pop up every ten seconds or so. Things that never happened before tended to happen with startling regularity.

"In any event, CERN security will be fully staffed, and there will be an additional one hundred Swiss and French police on the sites during the ceremonies. That doesn't count personal bodyguards that a handful of our guests will also bring with them, and whom we have extended the right to carry..."

"You will do a demonstration of the collider in operation during the symposium?" Jan Bakker said.

Eduard nodded. "Yes. It will be a centerpiece of the entire event. People are coming from all over the world, including media. The leaders of CERN imagine that our visitors would like to see the device work. It's a great opportunity to showcase the frontiers being reached here."

"The device generates a great deal of radiation while in operation, does it not?"

Eduard was still nodding. "Enormous amounts, as I understand it. But they are captured within the collider. If the integrity of the collider were to fail, which is nearly impossible, and all these people you see here now are making sure of that..."

He gestured at the mostly young people working the monitors.

"But if its integrity were to fail, it is still deep underground, in a tunnel made of thick concrete. In a worst-case scenario, the radiation would be captured within the tunnel. Which again, is why access is so limited. In the event of such an accident, the countryside would be evacuated, and highly trained teams would go into action, either sealing the radiation underground permanently, or more likely, releasing it in a controlled fashion over a long period of time."

"How much?" Jan said.

Eduard looked at him. "How much what?"

"How much radiation, exactly, is generated?"

"I'm not a scientist," Eduard said.

"Maybe you should ask one."

103

Abruptly, Eduard called to one of the workers sitting along the counter. He said something to the man in a language Troy neither understood nor even recognized.

The young man said something back.

"He is the lead scientist here today," Eduard said. "His name is Yuri. He and I both come from the Czech Republic. We are proud that our country became a CERN member state in 1993. I asked him how much radiation is generated. He said we wouldn't understand the amount, but it's a lot. A terrible amount."

"And you feel there is no chance the radiation could be released to the surface?"

Eduard nodded calmly. His faith wasn't shaken by this line of questioning. "The official policy of the organization, and the member countries, is that such an event is of such vanishingly small probability, as to be the closest thing to impossible. The facility wouldn't be located here if it was possible."

"How many people live in this region?" Miquel said.

"Well, obviously Geneva is nearby. That's 200,000 in the city."

"And in the village near the CERN sites?"

Eduard shrugged. "Oh, I imagine about 40,000 in the villages and towns right here."

"Some of whom live directly above the accelerator?"

Eduard nodded. "Some do, yes."

"In a couple of days, they could be sitting on top of a bomb," Miquel said.

"If it puts your mind at ease," Eduard said. "I assure you we will take your concerns into account during our preparations."

CHAPTER SIXTEEN

10:05 pm Central European Time
Nightclub The Wall
Mitte
Berlin, Germany

"Identification?" the big man at the door said.

She still looked younger than her years. The man towered over her. She gave him the passport from England. She did it nonchalantly. Of course it would pass. It was a real passport. And of course she was really Margaret Ainsley.

The club was just a few blocks from the glimmering and touristy Potsdamer Platz, on the old East Berlin side. The club's façade showed a brick wall with a screaming face similar to, but not exactly the same as, the cover of the old Pink Floyd movie, "The Wall." The movie was before her time, but she remembered the picture well. Her mother had owned the movie on DVD. What, if anything, it had to do with the Berlin Wall, she wasn't sure.

The bouncer held the passport under a red scanner, then handed it back to her. He smiled. He was quite young, and his huge size belied the fact that he barely needed to shave yet.

"You changed your hair."

"Yes."

She was wearing a brunette wig. It was the closest thing she could find to Margaret's hairstyle, and in the same color. She blushed, completely involuntarily. Even though she didn't control it, and would have preferred if it didn't happen, it was still good. The man reached down and touched her face.

"Very pretty," he said. Then he waved her into the club.

Inside, dance music was pounding. Over the insistent beat, a man sang the same line over and over again.

"Relax! Don't do it!"

After a few minutes of this, she realized it must be some kind of remix. No song would simply have the same phrase repeated a hundred times in a row, would it? She moved through the club, the sound thumping in her ears, as she slid between knots of people in leather jackets, tight bodysuits, and garish makeup. A few people wore leashes or brightly colored neon tubes around their necks.

The place was very dark, punctuated by strobes of multicolored light that seemed timed to the music. Reds, blues, greens, and yellows. The place was like a rabbit warren, with hallways and open spaces, dance floors, seating areas, then narrow hallways again.

It was crowded in here, but not nearly as crowded as it would become. The night was young. She went to a bar at the back of a dance floor, ordered a beer, and looked around. Out on the dance floor, a few people made crazy gyrations. One young guy saluted an invisible sun god, raising his arms to heaven.

Later the real party would start. Later the dances would become more frenzied. The people were just getting warmed up.

A man approached her from out of the crowd. He was tall and wore a long leather coat. His hair was bleached blonde and stood up in spikes. Maybe he was handsome. Maybe he wasn't. It was hard to tell in this darkness. He walked up to her as though they were old friends.

"The tower will fall," he said.

"And we are the ones who will bring it down," she answered.

He smiled.

"We are lovers. Do you understand?"

For the first time, she caught a hint of his accent. He was from the east, Russia probably, though he had spent some time learning to hide it.

She nodded. "Yes."

"Come with me, then. We need to talk."

He held out a hand to her. She took it, and he led her away from the bar. This was how it went. Being led by others, ever deeper, into a world she could barely understand. She liked that world, though, what she knew of it.

The man led her through the people, up a short flight of stairs, then down another narrow hallway. It dead-ended at a door. There was very little light back here, just shadows from the laser lights downstairs.

He placed her against the wall, then pressed his body against hers. The sound of the music thumped through the floorboards and the walls. The whole building seemed to shake with the bass line. The man put his face very close to hers. She could feel his breath on her ear.

"We understand you have been chosen," he said.

She put her hand on the back of his neck. "Yes. I think so."

"You don't know?"

"I'm being sent to Zurich. They don't tell you until they tell you."
The man seemed to shrug that off. "Zurich is close. It must be."
"Right. That's what I think too."
"When are you going?"
"I'm supposed to arrive tomorrow night."
He nodded slowly, the hairs on his face touching her cheek. "Okay. Money was deposited in your account today. Did you see it?"
"I can't look. I can't access anything. I don't know when they're watching. I assume they're tracking my computer usage."
The man nodded again. His hand reached for her waist, but then slipped something into the inside pocket of her coat. It was heavy. She felt it pulling on her coat.
"That is an envelope. There are twenty thousand euros inside. They thought you might not be at liberty to look into your account. So, they felt like you might not trust. That is a small taste of the money, so perhaps you can relax just a little bit."
"I'm relaxed," she said. "The money has always come before."
Every step of the way, every increment as she inched closer and closer to this final mission, they had paid her a little bit more. It was understood that the big payoff came if she made it all the way to the end.
"I am going to put another envelope in your pocket. Inside of it is a device, similar to a mobile phone. It has your instructions. It has maps of the facility, and the location of the materials they want retrieved is marked. Some photos are included, the best that could be taken without raising suspicions. There is a passcode to open the device. Six digits. The date your president John Kennedy died, presented the way Americans think of it—month, day, then year. Two digits for each. Do you know it?"
"Not off the top of my head."
"But you can discover this date on your own, I imagine?"
She shrugged. "Sure."
"How will you do it without accessing a computer?"
"I'll snatch someone's phone on my way out of here tonight."
"What if it's locked?"
"I'll take another one."
He nodded. "Very nice. The device is also a satellite tracker. It is currently in disabled mode. If you make it out, you must turn on the tracker immediately. They will pick you up wherever you are and accept the materials from you."

"What if I don't have the materials?"

He pulled back, just a touch, and looked at her. There was humor in his eyes.

"Have them."

"I'll do my best. But I can't control everything."

Now he smiled. "This is a long way to travel, and a lot to be paid, to emerge without the materials."

"Did you see that fire last night?" she said. "On the television. You saw it on the news?"

He nodded, eyeing her closely.

"Unlike you or our employers, I was there. Inside the building. It happened very fast. Instantly. There was almost no time to get out. The flames took skin off the back of my neck. The fire burned away the coat I was wearing."

"I understand," he said. "If you don't have the materials, I will understand that too. But our employers won't. And it's not my decision. So if you don't have the materials, my advice to you is to not turn on the satellite tracker."

There was a silence between them. They were still pressed together, body to body.

"If you tell someone I said that, of course I will deny it."

She nodded. "Okay."

His hand moved inside her coat. It deposited another item in her inner pocket. The new item was lighter than the money.

"This is the last time anyone will be in contact," he said. "Until afterward. You understand, right?"

She looked up into his eyes, as though they really were lovers. "Yes."

He touched her face. It was a gentle touch, more familiar, and more loving than what the bouncer had done. "Goodbye," he said. "And good luck."

He hugged her tight. It lasted for a long moment. She pressed herself against him. She was vulnerable to this. Human touch.

There was so much secrecy in her life, and so much hiding. It was impossible to become close to anyone. It was impossible to tell anyone the whole truth. One day, maybe one day soon, she would like to disappear somewhere for good. The Greek isles, or the southern Caribbean. Anywhere no one could find her. And when she arrived at that place, maybe she could just...

What?

"If you don't have the materials, I suggest you run like hell," the man said now, adding one last parting thought. "And never stop running."

Then he released her, turned, and walked to the end of the hall. He went down the stairs without so much as a backward glance.

CHAPTER SEVENTEEN

11:20 pm Central European Time
Hotel Front de Mer
Versoix, Switzerland

"We know the man who set the fire."

It was late. Troy and Dubois were sitting at a table on the ground floor patio of the hotel, overlooking the lake. As Troy watched, a motorboat moved quietly through the darkness on the water, its running lights the only sign it was out there.

In the late afternoon, Miquel had gone to Lyon to try to convince his superiors of what he believed, but the people in charge at CERN thought it was a joke. He had left Troy, Dubois, and Bakker here because he hadn't given up yet. They might as well stay another night.

That was fine with Troy.

The night was cool and crisp. Dubois was dressed in pant and boots, what Troy thought of as a hunting jacket, and a knit cap squashing down her curly hair. Troy was wearing jeans, a black t-shirt, and sneakers. He liked the cold.

They had a bottle of red wine open between them. They had demolished a box of crackers and a chunk of Swiss cheese. It wasn't quite the same as being at a restaurant on the lake with Aliz Willems, but it was still pretty good.

Troy and Dubois turned, and Jan Bakker loomed behind them. He was dressed similarly to Troy: in jeans, a blue t-shirt, and sandals. There was no way the cold bothered this guy. He was carrying his ever-present attachment, a laptop.

"Do you mind if I join you?" he said.

"No," Dubois said. "Of course. Please sit down."

Troy wouldn't say he minded. He also wouldn't say he didn't mind. So instead, he said nothing. A dozen people had died in the fire, including the man investigators thought had set the fire. So, Troy understood the motivation of Jan's to continue working on the problem night and day. It was just that Jan never seemed to stop working, even when there wasn't a problem.

There was always a problem, Troy supposed.

"Who was it?" Dubois said.

Bakker raised a large finger. "It's very interesting. Interpol was finally able to match the man's teeth to dental records of a Dane named Lars Casperson. He was thirty-one years old. He has a long history of arrests dating back to his teenage years."

Suddenly, Troy was hooked. A minute ago, he would have been happy to sit here half the night, chatting amicably with Dubois about this and that, until the wine was gone, and it was time to turn in. Now that idea was gone. It always seemed to work that way.

It was fascinating work, Troy realized. What brought a relatively young guy from Denmark to his death in a massive firestorm that he caused at a scientific institute in Germany? He could have been doing anything else. There were a million other things he could have been doing. He could have lived to doddering old age, bouncing grandchildren on his knees, but he chose what he chose.

"What kind of arrests?"

"He was an environmentalist. He was arrested at the age of sixteen for attempting to sabotage a whaling vessel at harbor in Norway."

"Sabotage?" Dubois said.

"He and another boy had homemade gasoline bombs. They were going to blow up the ship. They had traveled from Copenhagen on their own for this purpose. No one put them up to it. Or so they said."

"What else?" Dubois said.

"Lots of things. He was involved in attacking and blocking Japanese whaling vessels in the southern Atlantic Ocean. He was arrested for infiltrating the grounds and pouring what turned out to be human blood on a facility housing NATO nuclear missiles in Belgium."

"Whose blood was it?"

"It was his own blood," Bakker said. "That, and the blood of several volunteers. They had been collecting it from themselves for months for this specific purpose."

"Sounds like a fun guy," Troy said.

"His behavior turned darker in recent years."

"Darker than collecting his own blood?"

Bakker nodded. "Yes."

Troy loved that about Jan. His sense of humor had gone missing in action. Sarcasm, irony—these things didn't reach him at all. On the rare occasion he told a joke himself, it wasn't funny.

111

"Okay, let's hear it."

"It seems that he joined a cult."

"A cult."

Bakker put a large hand up as if to say STOP. "Well, it calls itself a movement, but it's similar to a cult. For the past two or three years, Casperson was involved in this group. It's hard to say exactly how long because the members often mask their identities and obscure their movements. At least, the members of the paramilitary unit do."

"It's a cult," Troy said. "With a paramilitary unit."

Bakker nodded. "Indeed. The group is called Espíritu, or Spirit, if you prefer the English. The paramilitary unit is the Army of the Spirit. They claim to worship the spirit of nature, of the Earth. Fortunately, the spirit is embodied in the person of a man."

Dubois smiled. "Of course it is. It always is."

"Who is he?"

"His name is Silvio Strukul. He is fifty-four years old. Born in Milan, Italy. He's from a wealthy family. As a young man he went to the London Business School and earned an MBA. He began publishing magazines in Italy, mostly related to the environment, environmental causes, natural wonders requiring protection, corporations degrading the environment, and that sort of thing.

"Later, he diversified into magazines and one-off publications covering spurious and unfounded stories about things like alien abductions, unidentified flying objects, an ancient nuclear war that destroyed civilization on Mars and stripped the planet of its atmosphere, and far-fetched theories about the origin of the human race.

"After that, he diversified further into publications touting unproven medical treatments and fad diets. Everything he published seemed to be met with success. Many of his publications were translated into French, German, English, Spanish, Dutch, and other languages, and were distributed throughout the continent. To his original wealth, he added his own pile of money."

"So, he started a cult?" Dubois said.

"He gathered a group of people to himself. There were once thought to be as many as fifty people, mostly young women, living in the house and in guest cabins on the grounds of his mansion at Lake Como. He may have had a Svengali-type relationship with some of the women. Or maybe they were just young women attaching themselves to money. For his part, Strukul has denied ever forming or leading a cult."

"Of course he has," Troy said.

"As the internet matured and competition increased, some of Strukul's publications began to falter. He was using a subscription model, where the physical magazines were mailed to readers. His one-off publications were available at newsstands. That era of physical publications was dying out.

"His publishing empire was crumbling, and he was running up massive debts. It's thought now that he was simply acquiring debt in the names of his businesses, accessing the money, and then moving it offshore. He may have sent as much as a hundred million euros to offshore accounts. He was embezzling from himself, more or less. Then his offices in Milan were raided. It turned out he hadn't paid taxes in more than a decade, not in any country where he did business, but especially not in Italy. It is possible he was being protected from government scrutiny by the Mafia, but then he stopped paying the protection money."

"What did he do?" Troy said.

"He fled the country. He tried to sell the Lake Como property, but it was seized by the authorities."

"Where is he now?"

Bakker smiled. "He moved his community to another property, not even that far away, on the Adriatic coast of Albania. If the Italians want him, they don't want him too badly. And Albania..."

Bakker shrugged, as if to say, "You know, it's Albania."

"He seems free to move about Europe, especially Eastern Europe, as well as North Africa, with a degree of impunity. There is a long Interpol sheet on him. Despite the collapse of his publishing efforts, his fortunes have only grown."

"He has all that stolen money," Dubois said.

"Yes, and he has also been trading in stolen antiquities, which he buys at black-market auctions, then turns and sells to retail buyers, who are willing to pay a fortune for them. It seems that the very wealthy don't like to mix with the organized thieves and murderers who traffic in stolen goods, but Silvio Strukul has no such compunctions. Which makes Albania a good place for him."

"And the cult?" Troy said.

"Hard to know," Jan said. "There appear to be a couple dozen people living at his property in Albania. Others may be salted across the continent, and for all anyone knows, the entire world. The estimate is he may have between 200 and 500 followers.

"They believe, and Strukul himself seems to believe, that humans cannot be trusted with technology. We need to go back to a time before science, when we lived in harmony with the planet. Most recently, intercepted communications among them suggest they've come to believe that scientists are going to accidentally destroy the world by uncovering knowledge that they shouldn't. For example, by playing with quantum physics."

"And creating the conditions for black holes," Dubois said.

Bakker nodded. "Yes."

"So Strukul looks like our man," Troy said.

"Yes," Bakker said. "He may be. I feel strongly that he is involved. The evidence is circumstantial at the moment, but it points at him."

"Why weren't we looking at him before?"

Bakker shrugged. "Earlier today, there could have been a thousand different culprits. The terrorists, as you say, seem to be pros. Few would suspect that a small European cult who follow a rich man, and are expecting the end of the world, could carry out a sophisticated attack across the ocean in America, and then disappear without a trace. Or that they would choose to attack centers of advanced technology.

"We still don't know for a fact that it's them. But if it is, it makes perfect sense. They believe that technology is going to destroy this world. And it appears that Strukul has been actively recruiting fanatics with operational experience to his cause. The exposure of Lars Casperson makes that clear. Casperson carried out small-scale environmental attacks most of his life. We don't know if he was in Massachusetts, but we know he was in Germany."

"Has the identity of the Casperson man been made public yet?" Dubois said.

Bakker shook his head. "No. It's a misdirection. Tomorrow morning, it will be announced that the body was too badly damaged by the fire to retrieve DNA or dental samples."

"So Strukul lets down his guard?"

"Strukul or whoever else might be involved."

"Why don't we just go get him?" Troy said. "Go to his house in Albania, pull him out of there, and round up his followers."

"It's not as easy as it sounds," Dubois said. "It would require the cooperation of the government and Albanian State Police. That cooperation is hard won and goes to the highest bidder. Most likely, what would happen is a series of frustrating delays, during which Strukul would be tipped off and the entire group would leave the property. Then they would spread out as far as they could go. We'd be left trying to hunt them down one by one, never knowing which one might have the information we need."

Troy shrugged. "It's harassment. It breaks up his little Albanian beach party and forces him to reboot somewhere else."

"But it doesn't address the questions we want answered. For instance, is he even involved?"

"I guess we'd have to catch him out and about somewhere and ask him those questions ourselves."

Now Bakker was smiling.

Try smiled with him. "Are you anticipating that he's going to be out and about somewhere?"

"I have been able to track his whereabouts. I've also intercepted a few messages involving him."

"Anything about the attacks?"

Bakker shook his head. "No. I suspect he's much too clever to discuss something of that nature in a way that can be traced. In fact, the messages I was able to track were from third parties outside his circle. And I only have their halves of the conversations."

"So..." Troy said.

"So, in a roundabout way, it appears there is going to be a black-market auction in Algiers tomorrow night. It's common to hold such auctions outside Europe. It's comparatively easy for the thieves to move stolen property across North Africa. It's harder to bring it into Europe or transfer it to America. That's why it's an auction, and that's why the middleman gets a discount."

"He has to figure out how to get it to its final destination."

"Correct," Bakker said.

"And you think Strukul is going to be there? In the flesh?"

"Strukul is a very hands-on trader," Bakker said. "He goes to these events."

"He's up for grabs in Algiers," Troy said.

"More so than in Albania, certainly. I'm sure he will have some personal protection with him, like any bidder there will have, but he won't be walled inside a compound, and guarded by an entire country."

"What's being sold?" Dubois said.

Bakker shrugged. "I can't say. It seems that figurines, plates, and other antiquities looted from Iraq and Syria may be for sale. There's some hint that something more valuable or rare may be available at this auction, but I could not determine what that might be."

"A weapon?" Troy said.

Bakker shook his head. "Doubt it. The weapon traders are a different group."

"So maybe we go down there and obtain evidence that the man is trafficking in stolen merchandise," Troy said. "This might put pressure on him."

"A man like Strukul doesn't feel that kind of pressure," Dubois said. "He has been avoiding criminal charges for years."

Troy shrugged. "A different kind of pressure, in that case. Everyone feels pressure, as long as it's the right kind and correctly applied."

He looked at Dubois and smiled.

"You feel like going down there and having a word with our new friend Silvio?"

She returned the smile. "As long as you don't get me killed."

"Nothing like that would happen. It's just a friendly conversation." Now Troy looked at Bakker. "What do you suppose Miquel would think of this idea?"

"I think he would like it," Bakker said.

"Yeah? And why do you say that?"

Bakker shrugged. "Because I spoke to him forty-five minutes ago. He said whatever we need to arrange to put you inside that auction tomorrow night—false identities, costumes, travel arrangements—go ahead and do it."

"How do we get into an event like that?"

Bakker looked at Troy. "Have you ever fallen out of an airplane before?"

"I was a Navy SEAL," Troy said.

"And this means…"

If he really didn't know, there was no sense telling him. Troy turned to Dubois.

"How about you? You ever jumped out of a plane?"

She suppressed a smile, like a cat trying to swallow a canary.

"Really?" Troy said.

"There are things about me you don't know, Agent Stark."

* * *

Troy was just back in his room when a man came out of the bathroom.

116

The man was a blur, emerging from behind Troy, in a dark jacket. Troy spun, all reflexes, swept the man's legs out and took him to the floor. In an instant, he had one foot on the man's right wrist, a knee on the man's left forearm, and was about to drive a sharp punch into the man's exposed throat.

"Wait," the man said.

It was Alex.

Troy stopped, his entire body going slack at once. "Do you ever knock?"

Alex's face was impassive. He didn't seem rattled in the least that a professional killer was kneeling on him, half a second from delivering a death blow.

"I knocked. You weren't home. So I let myself in. It wouldn't do to have me standing around in the hall, would it?"

Troy took a deep breath.

"Listen, I've had a long day. Do you mind getting off me?"

Slowly, Troy climbed off Alex and sat on the floor next to him. Troy was tense, wound up, and he wasn't sure why. He needed to relax.

Alex sat up and pushed himself against the wall. He was dressed in a dark jacket, pants, and a white shirt with dark suspenders. He looked like one of the room service delivery guys. Apparently, he was one of them, at least tonight.

"What are you doing here?" Troy said.

"What am I always doing? Checking in."

"Keeping tabs."

Alex shrugged. "Whatever you prefer. Missing Persons wanted a check in. So here I am. We knew you went to CERN today. What did they say?"

"They said don't worry about it. It's under control."

Alex eyed him. "How does it look?"

"It looks like they have a nice university-type campus. Two campuses, in fact, one in Switzerland and one in France. It looks like they do a reasonably good job of processing thousands of entries and exits a day, all while keeping it a friendly, collegial atmosphere where no one gets their feelings hurt. They have ten entry points, along with a tunnel that connects the two different sites. Each entry point has exactly one security guard on duty at all times."

"Yeah," Alex said. "I guess I kind of knew that."

Troy shrugged. "I watched the guard at our gate wave a cyclist in before he issued visitor IDs to us without really checking to see who we were. They assured us that there will be a souped-up police presence for the gala gathering, with cops from both France and Switzerland, and the personal bodyguards and security services of some of the attendees, but..."

"Who vets the cops?" Alex said.

Troy nodded. "Right. And never mind the cops, who vets the contractors? Dozens of contractors come in and out of that place on a daily basis, from construction workers and other trades to food service and laundry trucks. Who vets the visitors? There's a hotel on site with 450 rooms. It's entirely booked. Who are those people? Who vets the public? There's a museum with programs for kids, and schools come in there all the time. For all intents and purposes, the place is wide-open."

"Help," Alex said.

"Yeah. They do have an anonymous mechanism for tattling verbal abuse and other unwanted behavior among co-workers, and they encourage everyone to report suspicious behavior. They're proud of these things, which is nice. And they have iris scans for people who need to access the most sensitive areas, like the colliders themselves, but otherwise...eh. With all these people coming and going, a terrorist group that thinks ahead in the most marginal way could have planted people there months ago."

Alex nodded. "And been bringing in and hiding weapons, explosives, whatever they might need. Casing the people with high-level clearances and learning their habits."

"Right," Troy said. "The security they have there is enough to keep good guys honest. Bad guys? Not really. And determined bad guys with training and resources, who have been out in front the whole time? Forget it. I was told the terrorists went in an open window in the Wintergarten attack. They planted someone in there. Could have been a week ago, a month ago, a year ago. Who knows? And that person just left a ground floor window open along an alleyway. It was that easy."

"What else were you told?" Alex said.

"The guy who burned. He was from Denmark. In the environmental movement most of his life. He wanted to save the whales and that kind of thing."

Alex nodded. "We have that much. I think everybody has that by now. What else?"

"Jan Bakker thinks the guy belonged to a cult called Espíritu. Jan followed a digital trail, not one that's there, but one he made up from bits and pieces of other trails. Shadows of trails. Deleted files. Whatever it is. You know how he does."

"He's the best," Alex said. "What is the cult?"

"It's a doomsday thing. Environmental catastrophe. They think humans shouldn't play with technology. It's run by a guy named Silvio Strukul, a bit player, a rich Italian who's been hiding out in Albania because of embezzlement and tax evasion charges. Supposedly he's got a bunch of young people living at a mansion on the water over there."

Alex made a face and a sort of half shrug. It was the look of a man who wasn't convinced. "I don't see how a group like that would have the training to do what these people have been doing."

"Bakker thinks Strukul has been recruiting these green terrorists, people with experience, to join the cause."

"But why?" Alex said. "Why would a rich cult leader get embroiled in this? If he has money, followers, a place on the water, and he's in a fast and loose country like Albania, probably under protection, why would he risk all that? Those guys usually want to keep that sort of thing going as long as possible. The perks are too good to voluntarily give up. Is he some kind of true believer?"

Troy shrugged. "I don't know. That's what I plan to ask him when I see him."

Alex smiled. "When will you be seeing him?"

"Tomorrow night. In Algiers. Seems the guy has a soft spot for looted treasures from the ancient world. There's a black-market auction. Hush-hush. We're dropping in on it. We'll land on the roof, come down through a skylight or fire exit, so I'm told."

"Your girl knows how to jump?" Alex said.

"I guess we'll find out."

"Why don't you just use the tunnels?"

Troy didn't answer. He didn't know about tunnels.

"Algiers is full of tunnels. They're all over the place, especially in the older parts of the city. The resistance used them when they were fighting the French. I'm part Algerian. Those tunnels are in my blood."

"I thought you were a Sikh," Troy said.

Alex nodded. "Yeah. That too."

He gave Troy a long look.

"You know where the auction is?"

Troy shrugged. "I can get the location for you if you want."

"I don't really want it, but I guess I'm gonna need it," Alex said. He shook his head. "Man, I hate Algiers."

CHAPTER EIGHTEEN

November 17
1:15 pm Central European Time
Interpol Headquarters
Lyon, France

"You're not going to shoot us, are you?" Gregory Fawkes said.

Miquel Castro-Ruiz stared across the conference table at the three Interpol officers lined up in opposition to him. And it really did seem that way. Miquel and they all worked for the same organization, and yet, when his three colleagues filed into his windowless room, none of them chose to sit next to him. Indeed, all of them chose to sit across from him as though they were his adversaries.

The most important of the three was Maxim Davidoff, Director of Special Projects. Max had become Miquel's boss when Miquel was given the green light to begin El Grupo. Miquel didn't get the sense that Max was happy about this arrangement, but it may be that he didn't need or want the additional responsibility.

Miquel was not coming in with the best of reputations. They had given him El Grupo, not as some celebration of his many years of exceptional work, but because they had no other choice. He had been insubordinate, he had pulled a firearm on superiors in the line of duty, but he had also guessed right. He had protected the work of his people, and those people had saved New York City from a potentially devastating terrorist attack.

The powers at Interpol had no choice. It was either give him his own sub-agency or fire him. If they fired him, they would have to cope with the accompanying publicity, which they did not want. In sum, they seemed to want Miquel as far away from them as they could make him. It was no surprise that when he asked to headquarter his sub-agency in his Madrid, no one even blinked. They didn't want him here in Lyon, and Europol certainly didn't want him in the Netherlands.

In addition to Max, Gregory Fawkes of the Internal Affairs Department, was here. It was perhaps an indication of Miquel's place in the organization that whenever he requested a meeting, Internal Affairs felt the need to send a representative.

And finally, Grace Pastilha was here. She was a young woman who Miquel didn't know well. She was a liaison from International Cooperation. Her presence at this meeting seemed reasonable. She was from Portugal, and Miquel hoped that might mean she would be well-disposed toward him. But then, you never knew.

"No, Agent Fawkes," Miquel said. "I'm not going to shoot anyone. I'm not even armed at this moment."

"Captain Fawkes," Fawkes said, his voice flat.

It was their little game. Fawkes was a young guy from Canada, Miquel thought Toronto. He was shooting up the ranks, largely by making life difficult for people who were trying to do their jobs. Miquel refused to call Fawkes by his title. Fawkes never failed to remind Miquel what the title was.

"What can we do for you today, Miquel?" Max said.

Miquel nodded. "Good. Thank you. I will get right to it. I met with staff at CERN yesterday. Myself and three members of my staff."

"Was the American with you?" Fawkes said.

"Agent Stark?" Miquel said. It was more game playing. Thus far, he had no other Americans. That was about to change, later this afternoon in fact, but these people knew nothing about it.

Fawkes nodded. "Yes."

"Of course he was," Miquel said. "He is one of my best agents."

"It's interesting how not that long ago, you were disavowing any responsibility for his actions and claiming you had no idea of his whereabouts."

Miquel shrugged and smiled. "He didn't work for me then."

"Do you know where he is now?" Fawkes said.

Miquel looked at Max. "What is this questioning?"

Max made a face designed to show boredom. "Just please answer. It's the easiest way forward."

"He's still in Geneva. He's with my other agents."

That was true earlier today, but by now it might be a lie. There was a chance that his people were already en route to Algeria. Miquel had left that scheduling to Jan. But there was no sense in sharing information about it in this meeting. Anyway, Max was sure to find out soon enough. They were flying across the Mediterranean in the older, unmarked Interpol jet he had granted Miquel use of. The flight manifest was certain to be part of the monthly reporting.

"And they're all still in Geneva…why?"

"That's why I'm here," Miquel said. "I'm asking permission to continue my operations there, just for the next few days."

It was galling to be on this tight of a leash. There was little he could do about it, though, except play along.

"What did the representatives of CERN tell you?" Max said.

"They told me they will take my concerns very seriously."

He smiled.

"They will give them," Fawkes said, "the level of attention they deserve."

See? Even Fawkes could have a sense of humor. If he could show more of his humanity from time to time, perhaps he and Miquel could spar less than they did.

"Yes," Miquel said. "Exactly right."

"But you want to stay there and continue to monitor the situation?" Max said.

Miquel nodded. "For the time being."

Grace spoke for the first time. "Without any buy-in from them?"

Miquel shrugged. "Ah…I'm concerned that the terrorists who have attacked scientific facilities in America and Germany have CERN as their next target."

"There's no evidence that the incidents in the United States and Germany are even related," Fawkes said. "Certainly they appear to be unrelated. As a result, you've conjured up some relationship in your imagination, complete with a shadowy organization that is now moving on to attack CERN."

Miquel didn't answer.

He knew that in this line of work, personal biases could cloud a person's reasoning. Did he have a bias here? He thought not. Other than that morning in the Atocha train station in Madrid nearly twenty years ago, in the aftermath of the bombings, amid the smoking carnage and the chaos, the woman lying on the platform who was missing below the waist. She was his bias.

He had been a young police commando then, just thirty-two years old. If he lived to one hundred, he doubted he would ever clear the image of that woman from his mind. It was good. He wanted to remember. He never wanted to forget her. He kept her forever in front of him.

She was dressed in a white blouse and brown leather jacket. Her hair was pulled tight in a bun. She wore makeup. Her eyes were open and staring, blank and dead, like a doll's eyes. She had probably been an office lady, on her way to work.

Sometimes, he woke in the middle of the night, eyes wide, his heart pounding in his chest, and she was there, in the room with him.

"Save me," she said.

He couldn't save her. But it was possible he could save others. That was his bias. The desire to keep innocent people alive.

Did Gregory Fawkes have a bias? Yes. He wanted to make Miquel look bad.

"What makes you think CERN is a target?" Max said.

Miquel didn't have a good enough answer. He knew that.

"Gut," he said simply.

"That's all?"

"One of the previous attacks was against a particle accelerator," Miquel said. And then suddenly, he was on a roll. "CERN has the most important, and most advanced, particle accelerator in the world. They are hosting an event this weekend. The Triumph of Knowledge is what they're calling it. Hundreds of visitors will be there, including esteemed scientists from all over the world. If the two previous attacks are related, clearly they were carried out by enemies of science. If I were them, I would find CERN a tempting target."

There was silence as they chewed on this.

Miquel shrugged. "What harm will it do if we're there? We're observing from a distance. If nothing happens, fine. We go home. If something happens, perhaps we can be of some assistance."

He had to choose his words carefully these days. If he were to say, "Perhaps we can kill the terrorists before they hurt anyone," he wouldn't find a sympathetic audience in this room.

"I want to remind you of something," Max said. "Interpol is an entity that assists in investigations, data and evidence sharing, and collaboration between police forces. We are not commandos. The name of your sub-agency is the European Rapid Response Investigations Unit. I take that to mean that after a crime occurs, you can be on site quickly, gathering evidence and conducting an investigation. Your people are also not commandos."

Miquel nodded. "I understand that completely."

He didn't understand that at all. He didn't agree with it. When he thought about El Grupo, its present composition, and his future intentions for it, none of what Max was saying played any role.

Now Max nodded. "Maintain a skeleton crew in Geneva through the end of the event. No more staff than you already have deployed. Four of your people met with CERN? Fine. Maintain that number. Monitor the situation. But keep in mind, you can't stay there forever, like some guardian angel. The event will end. CERN may not be the target. Life goes on."

Miquel nodded. "Understood."

"What organizational resources will you need?"

"We have two surveillance drones that we can deploy," Miquel said. "Along with the equipment and the expertise to operate them. We could use surveillance satellite access as well. That way we're not in anyone's way."

Max nodded. "Granted."

They were giving him what they wanted, and it seemed he didn't have to give anything in return. But Miquel knew the nature of the exchange here. They were giving him the rope with which to hang himself. The further he stepped out on a limb, the more likely he stepped off. Fawkes, for one, would be happy to see Miquel fall.

"Anything else?" Max said.

"We could also use a rapid deployment helicopter."

Miquel raised his hands as if to say, "Don't shoot."

"Only for use in an emergency," he said instead.

CHAPTER NINETEEN

10:45 pm Algeria Standard Time (Central European Time)
The skies over the Casbah
Algiers, Algeria
North Africa

"Five minutes," a stern voice said over the intercom. "Prepare to jump."

Dubois was ready. She checked the altimeter function on the smart watch she wore on her wrist. They were flying at a little over 1,300 meters. This was a good altitude for her. She'd made jumps from this altitude several times. They had geared the jump to her abilities. Apparently, Stark had jumped from just about every height imaginable.

In her helmet and heavy goggles, she felt more like a downhill skier or motorcycle racer than a secret agent, or whatever she was. She wore a dark jumpsuit that concealed the form of her body. Her deployment bag was attached by a harness to her back.

The sound of the engines was loud. It was dark outside the jump door window, but she could see the lights of the city below them, sprawling out toward the south. Cool air rushed in from somewhere. It was a good, familiar feeling. She shivered just a bit. Her body always felt cold—colder than the air around it—right before a jump.

They had come into the country on a private jet less than an hour ago. They had landed at an airfield west of the city sprawl and changed to this beater of a jump plane. Dubois hadn't gotten a good look at the outside of it in the dark.

On the inside, it was very small and cramped. They sat on a wooden bench that ran along on side of the fuselage. The plane was not well sealed, which caused the wall of sound inside here.

Stark was staring at her. From inside his crazy goggles, he almost looked like he was underwater. But his eyes seemed concerned, and concern was something she rarely saw in them. He was usually some sort of cross between a cowboy and a kamikaze.

"How you doing?" he shouted.

She nodded. "Good."

"You've done this before, right?"

Now she smiled and shook her head. "No. Never."

How many times did she need to tell him? When her father was young, he was a paratrooper with the French military. He never really got it out of his blood, not for himself, and not for the people around him. She had been jumping out of airplanes since she was eight years old. But Stark didn't seem to believe it.

It was starting to make her nervous, how nervous Stark was for her.

"Once we're out, keep your eyes open. It's going to be dark out there. It's easy to get disoriented. We're going right for the infrared strobe. Just home in on that, and steer right to it. Understand?"

Dubois nodded. A tiny drone flown by Jan had dropped a strobe on the roof of the building where they believed the auction was to take place. Both she and Stark had an attachment on their helmets that could see infrared, which they would pull down over their left eyes right before they jumped.

"Got it, Dad."

Stark shook his head and smiled. The smile didn't reach his eyes.

Now Jan was coming up the line. His giant bulk didn't fit well in this tiny airplane. She would never tell Stark this, but Dubois happened to know that Jan didn't like heights, and he didn't like airplanes, making it all the more surprising that he was here. It was one thing to fly in a modern jet. This was not a plane for someone who didn't like flying. But she knew Jan well. Duty meant everything to him.

"Let's see what this guy has to say," Stark said, gesturing at Jan with his head.

Jan was holding a tablet computer. She imagined that for him, it was an anchor to the ground.

"You both know about the strobe, yes?"

They nodded.

"Let's go over the operation one last time, if you don't mind. Once out of the plane, you will use your parachuting skills to target the infrared strobe, and land on the same roof. It will help your cause if you land as lightly as possible. Satellite data suggests that there is a heavy door to a stairwell on that roof. It will likely be locked, but Agent Stark has a device that can defeat most typical door locks."

He looked at Stark. Stark nodded. "Got it."

"Few people will expect an infiltration from the roof. This auction is something of a fly by night operation, and we are supposing that security will be lax coming from that direction. I have been monitoring the roof since late last night. There have only been a few moments when people appeared there."

He looked back and forth at them. Dubois hoped he was right about this.

"Once you've landed, remove your jump clothes, and proceed down the stairwell. Intelligence suggests that the auction will take place in the basement. So anticipate heavy security once you reach the ground floor, and perhaps one or two stories above."

The plane hit a patch of turbulence. For a moment, Jan didn't say anything. Dubois watched his face. He almost winced but controlled himself.

"You have your stickers." It wasn't a question. Jan had given them both sheets of stickers, light colored ones and dark ones. The idea was to get close enough to Strukul to touch him, and smoothly attach a sticker, or more than one, to his clothes. If he was wearing dark clothes, use a dark sticker. If he was wearing something light, use a light sticker.

"The stickers, as you know, contain tiny chips embedded in them. They will give us Strukul's location as long as the sticker is still attached."

He looked at them both again, sternly this time. "I caution you that you are not to interdict or attempt to capture the subject Silvio Strukul inside, or around the place of auction. It will be too dangerous. Strukul will likely have security with him, other buyers will have their own security, and the auctioneers will most certainly have theirs. Attempting to capture Strukul inside the venue will have unpredictable results."

This was the part she knew that Stark didn't like. They were supposed to tag Strukul, then follow him to wherever he went next and waylay him there. It made sense to Dubois, but Stark had questioned the logic again and again.

"If you can attach a sticker to the man," Jan said, "then we can follow him after the auction and possibly intercept him. If there is any mingling going on, and his security will allow it, just pass close to him and touch him. For obvious reasons, Agent Dubois has the best chance of pulling this off."

Jan looked at Stark. "No offense, Agent Stark, but you're not very pretty."

Stark smiled and shook his head. He looked like a man who was ready to get going. "None taken."

"One last thing," Jan said. "There are GPS devices sewn into your civilian clothes. This is how I will track your location if anything goes

127

awry or if you get split up. Whatever you do, try to continue to wear those clothes for as long as possible."

"Where are they?" Dubois said.

"There is one sewn into Agent Stark's boxer briefs. There's another sewn into your brassiere. We figured those would be the last things to come off."

The intercom came on again. "One minute. One minute to jump."

She looked at Stark. He got up, went to the door, and slid it open. Then he shrugged. "Ladies first."

She stood and crossed the open space. Now she was near the edge. The cold air was in her face. Beyond her was the underside of the wing and open sky. Below and behind her, and all around, a dizzying drop to the lights of the city. Her eyes caught on the tall white tower of the Martyrs' Memorial, and beyond that, the deep darkness of the Mediterranean Sea. Above her, she could see stars and wisps of cloud skidding by.

She felt like her breath had been taken away. She forced the air all the way out of her lungs, then took in a deep swallow of air. It felt almost like she was drowning.

She just needed to relax. There was nothing to this. On a static line jump, the parachute opened itself. She faced out the door. She was going soon.

For a second, an image appeared in her mind. She was very small, sitting on her father's lap, on the floor of a tiny plane, near an open door. It was daytime, the sky bright, nearly blinding, and below her was the vast expanse of Senegal. She was strapped to her father's chest. It was a tandem jump, one of her very first.

"Ready, my sweet thing?"

She looked at Stark.

"How are you feeling?" Stark shouted.

"Good!" she shouted. She gave the thumbs up signal again.

"Five seconds!" he said. "If the chute hasn't opened by then, cut it loose and deploy the reserve chute!"

She nodded. "I remember!"

Of course, she remembered.

Not for the first time, she realized how amazing this moment was. This was the moment when you put your life in God's hands.

The plane hit another stretch of turbulence. It bucked and shuddered around her.

Stark held her static line tight. It was attached to a hook on the wall of the plane. As soon as she jumped, he would let it out.

There was no sense doing a lot of analyzing here. There were three things to do:

1. Drop out of the plane and count down from five.
2. Wait until the chute opened.
3. Steer for the infrared strobe.

That was the whole sequence. Focus on these three things, but one at a time. After each task was done, move on to the next one.

Stark gestured at her helmet. "You might want to put down your infrared sight!"

She stopped. Oh yeah. That.

She put it down. It slipped in front of her left eye like one of those lenses they put in front of your eyes when you get an eye exam. She scanned the lights below her. She couldn't tell. There was so much going on out there.

No. Wait. There it was. It was still out ahead of them. They were approaching it. She could see it from here. It was incredible how bright this lens made it. That strobe was the brightest thing down there. A moment ago, it had been invisible. Everything else was a wash of greens and dark blues and black and oranges and pinks.

"Whoa!" she said. She had practiced with it, of course. But practice was one thing, going live was another.

"Incredible, right?"

She nodded. She lifted the lens for a moment, just to get her bearings back. Then she put it down again. She acclimated herself to how with one eye, the vision was normal, and how with the other, the strobe stood out against all other things.

"Whenever you're ready, girly girl."

Dubois took a deep breath. It was easier this time.

Okay. Okay.

"When you're ready," Stark said again. He said it more forcefully this time.

She took that to mean *Go Now.*

She stepped to the edge. She planted her right foot and turned back to face Stark. Behind him loomed Jan Bakker in his delicate glasses, his eyes wide with...something. Dubois dropped backwards into the void.

She was out the door.

She fell away. All of life was a rushing sensation.

5.

4.

3.

The plane was gone. The speed was insane and increasing every second. Between her feet, the lights were spinning.

Was she under control?

2.

She was falling very fast. The wind whistled in her ears.

1.

Her own reactions and motions seemed slow. The parachute wasn't opening. Maybe she should cut it loose and go for the reserve chute. Her hand reached behind her, looking for...

She felt, rather than saw, the chute flying out into the darkness above her. Then she was jerked violently, the jolt like a car crash, pulling her upper body backward, kicking her legs out in front of her.

Then she was riding in the darkness. The chute was open, and she was flying. Far below, everything came into focus. What she needed was right in front of her, and she tuned out the rest. She could easily see the strobe and around it, she could make out the outline of a flat, square surface, which was the top of the building.

She steered toward it, coming in at an angle, scanning for obstacles that might be on its surface. Closer...closer...it was coming quickly now.

Then it was there, just below her.

She touched down as lightly as she could, the sound of her feet making a THUMP on the tiled rooftop. Another jolt went up through her body. Then she was running across the surface, the chute billowing down behind her.

She made it.

She stopped, and looked back up at the dark sky, to see how Stark was doing, or if he had even come.

No worries. He was coming. A shadow emerged out of the darkness. Dubois focused on it and could make out Stark framed by the backdrop of his dark chute. He was nearly invisible up there, as she must have been. He came down, taking nearly the identical descent path Dubois had taken just seconds ago.

In another moment, Stark was on the roof. He was graceful for such a large man. He took a few running steps and stopped. His chute drifted down behind him. He grinned at her from inside his helmet and goggles. He lifted the infrared lens attachment away from his face.

She hadn't even noticed hers was still down. The world split between the normal view and a play of reds, purples, greens, and blacks had simply become the natural order of things for her. She lifted hers and everything went back to normal.

"Nice job, Dubois," Stark said. "I like the way you fly."

Dubois felt her heart racing, just a bit.

"I like the way you come down," she said. "You land like a ballerina."

Stark shrugged and headed for the strobe a few meters away. From this perspective, it was a simple silver canister, nothing remarkable about it at all.

"Maybe I missed my calling," he said.

* * *

The building was about six stories high.

Troy picked up the strobe, clicked it off, and scanned their surroundings.

They were high on a hillside overlooking the waterfront, maybe a mile away. He could smell the Mediterranean from here. The whitewashed buildings around this one were old and dilapidated, like much of this quarter of the city.

A nearby lot was a pile of rubble, as if a building there had simply collapsed. Next to that was the dome of a mosque. A narrow building nearby, taller and more modern than this one, looked like a stiff sea breeze would knock it over on top of the mosque. Nearly every flat in that building had the flicker of a TV set on inside.

"Do you think anyone saw us?" Dubois said.

Troy shook his head. "Doubt it. Everybody's watching television."

He handed her the strobe. "Can you hold that? We might need it again."

It was large in her tiny hand. "Where am I supposed to hold it?"

"You have a purse inside your jumpsuit."

"My gun is in there. It won't fit."

He shrugged. "Make it fit." He wasn't her superior. He knew that. But he did have a lot more experience than she did in situations like this one. He didn't want to argue. She had a purse as part of her costume. He didn't. Jan Bakker should have thought to make that part of their instructions. It was one thing to leave the jumpsuits behind. The strobe could come in handy.

He went to the low wall along the edge of the roof and followed it around to the front of the building. He leaned his head out just slightly. It was dark up here, and no one was likely to look up anyway, but you never knew.

Down on the narrow street, about a dozen SUVs and limousines were parked everywhere—on the sidewalks, two deep in the street itself. Maybe twenty men were milling around, a few of them with rifles slung over their shoulders. Men were going in and out of this building.

Troy looked up and down the block. At either end, sawhorses were set up to block traffic from entering. Each sawhorse had two men standing by it. The police were probably paid off to allow events like this to happen and to keep the local riff raff out. That was good. It made it all the more likely he and Dubois could simply blend in with the crowd.

Troy went back to Dubois. She was peeling down her jumpsuit, revealing a dark sequined mini-dress underneath it. The aforementioned purse and a pair of high-heeled shoes were clipped inside the jumpsuit.

"Sexy," he said.

"Stick to the job, Agent Stark."

He nodded. "This is definitely the place."

"Are the guests arriving?" she said.

"They're already here."

He peeled down his own jumpsuit, revealing the black three-piece suit beneath. His wingtip shoes were already on his feet—they were covered by thick neoprene booties to protect them during the jump. He had a small gun in an inside pocket—a Sig SAUER 1911 ultra-compact. Not sure what good it would do him with all the hired muscle around. The best thing to do was play this cool, like Jan said, and not use it at all.

Also inside his jumpsuit was the lock-breaking device. It was shaped like a small laser gun from a 1970s science fiction movie, with a pressurized CO_2 canister attached. It was for one time use only. He'd have to get it right the first time, or this was going to be a funny trip. For an instant, he pictured them being rescued by a maintenance man stepping out onto the roof for a smoke early tomorrow morning, after Strukul and his friends were long gone.

He stripped away his jumpsuit and tossed it aside. He stood up tall, ran his fingers through his hair, and turned to Dubois.

"How do I look?"

"Dashing," she said. "How about me?"

132

He shrugged and smiled. "I already told you."

They walked to the stairwell door together. It stood in the middle of the roof, sort of a poorly constructed concrete slab with a metal door embedded in it. The door was opened and closed by use of a silver handle. A locking mechanism ran through the face of the handle—if you had the key, you'd stick in the slot, and turn the handle.

Just for kicks, Troy gripped the handle and tried to turn it.

Dubois eyed him closely.

He shook his head. "No."

"Do you hear anything on the other side?"

"No. You?"

She shook her head. "No."

He took the lock breaker out. He used it the way Jan had demonstrated, pointing it like a gun directly into the lock. He held it with both hands to steady it. He squeezed the trigger—it took more effort than with a real gun. He pulled...pulled...kept the muzzle right on the lock...pulled.

KA-CHUNG!

The gun bucked in his hand. The CO_2 canister slid back along a rail. On the other side of the door, what sounded like a chunk of metal went bounding down the stairs. Troy looked at the handle. There was a hole where the lock had been. He could see right through it.

He tried the handle. It turned easily.

"Chalk one up for Jan," he said.

He went back and wrapped the used laser pistol in his discarded jumpsuit. There was nothing they could do about this stuff. They were just going to have to leave it all behind. He opened the door and they both peered inside. The stairwell was dark, but now they could hear chatter far below, like the sound of people at a cocktail party—polite conversation instead of raucous celebrating.

"Seems okay."

They were guests at this party, not interlopers, and the way to cement that status was to join the others as soon as possible. They moved quickly down the stairs, Troy leading, Dubois's small hand in his. They were a wealthy couple, English and French art dealers if anyone asked, here to see what they could scout out.

If push came to shove, they were really adventurers, hoping to start a clandestine business in stolen artwork on the continent. That was the fallback position. There was no position after that, except deny everything.

"Deny until you die," was an old slogan guys he used to know would throw around. But Troy had been to training at the CIA school on Camp Peary in Virginia. It was the place they called "The Farm."

He had seen the enhanced interrogation demonstrations and watched tough guys cave from waterboarding and electric shock in a matter of minutes. They were guys so tough they didn't even realize they couldn't stand up to torture. They had stood up to everything else, every form of physical punishment, their entire lives.

A few lasted two minutes. A minute and a half. One or two lasted longer.

A cover story was a ruse you tricked yourself with. It would work until it stopped working. After that, you'd be laid bare. Best not to mention this to Dubois.

They were passing through empty floors, the doors standing open, no lights in the hallways. This seemed like it had been a residential building at one time, but everyone was gone. It was possible they'd been moved out, so stolen art traffickers could use the basement. Nothing was ever out of the question.

They were one story above the ground floor. This was the moment.

"Deep breath," Dubois said, low.

"It's cool," Troy said. "It'll be fine."

Suddenly, a man was behind them. He just appeared out of one of the darkened flats. The flat had no door at all.

He barked something at them in a stern voice.

They both turned. The man had dark hair and a beard, neatly trimmed. He wore khaki pants and a dress shirt, with a light windbreaker type jacket. He was about four inches shorter than Troy and heavyset.

He said something else. He was speaking French. It meant nothing to Troy. His eyes were hard and intense.

Dubois said something back to the man. The man shook his head and smiled. "Slut," he said. Either he also spoke some English or slut was a universal term.

Troy didn't hesitate. His right hand snapped out, a hard punch to the man's jaw. The light in the guy's eyes dimmed. His mouth hung open, as if he was surprised. The thing he least expected to happen...had happened.

Troy punched him again, harder this time because he had an extra second to rear back. The punch came like a fast-moving freight train.

The light in the man's eyes went out completely now, and Troy guided him to the floor.

"What did he say to us?"

"He asked what we were doing up here. He said it was off limits."

Troy checked the man's jacket. Sure enough, the guy had a gun. It was small, a .22 caliber, some kind of no name street pistol. It was a piece of junk, but Troy took it anyway. The guy started to snore.

"What did you say to him?"

"I said we came up here to fool around. We couldn't help ourselves."

Troy shook his head. "That's all you could think of?"

"What would you have said?"

"That we were looking for a bathroom."

Dubois put a hand on her hip. "Well, whenever you learn a second language, feel free to have better responses than me."

She had a point.

"Listen, we gotta put this guy somewhere," Troy said.

CHAPTER TWENTY

11:15 pm Central European Time
Bar Nacht
Langstrasse
Zurich, Switzerland

"Well, well, well. We meet again."

Margaret Ainsley looked up to see a man standing over her table. She had eaten a cheeseburger and a salad, along with three heavy beers. She was beginning to feel sleepy, or maybe just drunk.

She had been here two hours already. The restaurant had started out crowded with families, who were now long gone. A younger drinking crowd had filled the tables and the bar area. It was dimly lit in here, which she supposed was the idea. It made it hard to tell who was who.

In another moment, if no one came, she was going to have to order dessert and coffee. The wait staff here were too polite to force her to leave, but it was clear they wanted the table.

She had nowhere to go. Her instructions were to come to this restaurant. A man here would know her. Of course she could leave, walk a few blocks and book her own hotel, but if she did that, she would lose contact. It might be hard to re-establish. The thing to do was simply wait. Or in other words, do nothing. If she had to give up this table, she would move to the bar and wait there until the place closed, if need be.

She had taken the train in from Berlin early this evening. Her bags were in a locker at the Zurich train station. She had a few toiletries she would need for the night, and the money the man in the The Wall nightclub had given her. And that was it.

Through the buzz of the beer, she was beginning to become concerned. She was very close, but she knew all along it could slip away at any moment. Perhaps they followed her to the nightclub last night and spotted her talking to that man. Maybe they abducted him as soon as he left the club, and they made him talk.

If that had happened, the best thing would be if they just abandoned her here.

But now this…man.

They were always men. She was one of the few women operating in this twilight world.

She looked at him. He was smiling. Gradually his face came into focus. The last time she had seen him, the last time she had made love to him, he'd had dark unkempt hair, a long dark beard, and brown eyes. Now he was clean shaven, with stylish dirty blonde hair reminiscent of a boy band pop star's hair, and blue eyes. But he still had the same angular jaw line, the same tall, ridiculously fit body, and the same glint of high good humor in those newly blue eyes.

When was the last time she saw him? It seemed like months. In fact, it was only six nights ago.

"Gray?" she said and smiled. "Gray."

He raised any eyebrow. He was holding a tall, narrow glass of beer in his hand. It had just been poured. "Gray? I don't know anyone by that name."

"In that case, what is your name?"

His smiled deepened. He seemed very relaxed. Of course, he hadn't been in Wintergarten. Wherever he had gone after Massachusetts, it must have been like a holiday for him.

"You can call me Thomas. Thomas T. Engine."

She nearly laughed. "What does that middle initial stand for, if you don't mind?"

"T is for Tank."

"Well, you're the little engine that could, I guess."

Now he shook his head and laughed. "I am that. Do you mind if I…" he gestured at the seat near her.

"Please," she said. "Why don't you join me?"

"Thank you. I will." He slid into the chair and immediately touched her knee. She didn't mind at all. It was an immense relief to see him. She felt like she could breathe again.

"What can I call you?" he said.

She shook her head. She had the Margaret Ainsley alias, but that wouldn't do. You didn't give your partners anything traceable, anything they could attach to anything else, no matter how transient. The police could do something with the name Margaret Ainsley. What certainly seemed to be a real passport had been issues in that name. That person was leaving behind them a trail, paper or digital or both.

"You know…" She burst out laughing. "I just haven't given a name much thought, to be honest. I don't know why. I guess I'm tired."

"Well," he said. "How does Princess sound? Princess Dye."

"Is that die as in dead, or dye as in…"

"The colors, of course. I wouldn't give you a name with bad luck attached."

She nodded. "I know you wouldn't. I know that about you."

He nodded in turn and seemed very satisfied. "Princess Dye it is, then. I made that up on the spot."

There was a long quiet moment where they just stared into each other's eyes. She picked up her beer and took a long sip, watching him over the rim of the glass. He did the same to her. All around them, she noticed the chatter and the laughter in the restaurant. In Europe, the restaurants always seemed to get louder and more energetic as the night wore on. In the United States, the place would be closed by now.

"We're in Switzerland," she said.

He nodded. "Yes, we are."

"Why are we here?"

"I think you already know," he said.

"Tell me."

"We're going to Geneva tomorrow. We'll meet the others there. I have a car. We're driving together. We're just a couple of young kids on a romantic hook up. Geneva is a lot more romantic than Zurich, wouldn't you say?"

She shook her head. "I don't know. I've never been there."

He held out his glass to her and she clinked it with her own.

"Trust me," he said. "It is."

"Is it…?"

"The big one?" he said. "Yes. It's the big one."

She took a small risk by saying the word out loud. But she had to know. She needed complete clarity. "CERN. And we're in on it?"

He shrugged and smiled. Then he blushed. "What you said. We did such a good job before, that we are most definitely in it. Was there ever any doubt?"

Her own thoughts turned dark for a moment. They seemed to turn that way on a dime these last twenty-four hours or so. She met his eyes again. "A lot of bad things have happened. I didn't mean for any of it to go like that."

In her mind, she watched Hy Wire burn, seemingly in slow motion. Again. In real life, she couldn't have seen him on fire for more than a second or two, but in her imagination, it went on and on.

"I know that," Gray said. She still thought of him as Gray. She would have to get used to him as Thomas. "Let's not talk about it tonight. Okay?"

She nodded. "I don't want to talk about it at all."

"Good," he said. "I don't, either."

"How does the big one look?"

He looked at her deeply. "I don't want to discuss it here, not in any detail. But the bit that I know so far, it looks very, very good. We have people inside, just like last time. We have items, let's say, that are already in place. We have our exit plans ready. I'll just say that we look unstoppable on this one, much like we were before. The children are going to be very sorry they played with things that God did not intend for them to play with. And they're going to be very sorry they underestimated our resolve."

The talk had gotten serious. There was a lot of pain associated with this, at least for her. She tried to keep it all in separate compartments because what else could she do? The cause was important, possibly the most important cause on Earth. But people had died, and she carried some of the blame for that. If she could save the world without killing anyone, she would do it. And of course there was that other thing, which she couldn't even hint at, not in his presence.

What would he do if he knew she was on more than one team? Would he try to kill her? She didn't think so. But he would be hurt, maybe to his core. And she didn't want to hurt him.

Of course, she didn't even know him. Maybe he was doing the same thing or worse. Maybe he was a CIA plant. It was impossible to know anything. You just put one foot in front of the other and confronted the next thing when you arrived there.

Instead of dwelling on these things, she decided to lighten the mood again. She found that with just a little effort, she could manage it. "So what do we do now, Thomas T. Engine?"

"We finish up these beers, and we go to my flat. I've been there a few days now, and it's very comfortable. How does that idea sound to you?"

She finished her beer in one long gulp and set down the glass. "It sounds like the best idea I've heard in a while."

CHAPTER TWENTY ONE

11:30 pm Algeria Standard Time (Central European Time)
The Casbah
Algiers, Algeria
North Africa

"Quite a scene," Troy said.

The basement bore no resemblance to the rest of the building. It was well below the surface level of the street. A narrow, curving, stone stairwell came down here from a suite of empty rooms just beyond the foyer upstairs. When he reached the bottom level, the place was nothing like Troy expected.

It was almost like some trick of physics. You would never expect that this venue was somehow concealed beneath the dilapidated tenement above. The basement was so extensive, it must be dug out below several of the buildings in the neighborhood. It had high ceilings, maybe two stories high. Troy peered up at it. It was tiled, the tiles in red and blue flower mosaic patterns. There were narrow windows up near the ceiling, which must be at street level, but they were blacked out.

A crystal chandelier hung from the ceiling in the middle of the room. It was lit up, its lights sparkling against the tiny jewels that were also part of it. It provided some light, but most of the light came from a series of standing lamps placed around the periphery.

The floor was covered in a deep pile red carpet. The curving walls, which seemed like they were carved out of wet cement, were painted some dark color Troy couldn't make out. There was a low stage of sorts up at the front of the room. You could step onto it by raising your foot about six inches. The place reminded Troy of an event room at some fading Atlantic City casino.

This was the Islamic world, but there were bars on wheels at either end of the room, each staffed with two bartenders, and other staff who continually disappeared back into the shadows, soon to reappear with more alcohol. The bars were doing a steady business.

The place was packed. Cigarette and cigar smoke hung heavily in the air. There was a buzz of conversation, and it was loud. The electricity of anticipation was in the air.

Some of the people were black-market types: European and Arab gangsters, both wearing the same uniforms—track suits and sneakers. Troy hated that look. He wouldn't be caught dead in a track suit, no matter the brand.

"If you ever catch me wearing a track suit," he said to Dubois. "Just shoot me."

She looked up at him. "What?" She couldn't hear. That was okay.

There were a few groups of men in flowing robes that Troy guessed were Arab princes, in from Saudi Arabia or Dubai. There were a handful of East Asians. There were also quite a few people who might be normal rich people from Europe, the United States, or maybe Australia. It was a diverse crowd of bargain hunters.

Troy scanned the crowd. He and Dubois were not calling any attention to themselves—they blended in fine. His eyes suddenly landed on Strukul. The subject was here after all, hiding in plain sight.

He looked more or less exactly like the photographs Troy and Dubois had committed to memory. He stood a bit under six feet, Troy guessed, and wore a gray suit nicely tailored to his body. He was deeply tanned, both from his genetics and from living on the coast. He was thick, but not too plump—just a guy in middle age putting on a few extra pounds. He probably said yes to a second and third glass of wine with dinner on a regular basis. A gold watch was loose on his wrist, and a thin gold chain was around his neck. He had curly salt and pepper hair, what Troy thought of as the Alexander the Great cut. His shoes were leather loafers.

There were two young women with him: thin, fashion model types in tight mini dresses. The fashion models clung to him, one to a side. There were two young men with him as well, also of a certain type. They were big, crew-cut bruisers, generic bodyguards with generic sports jackets not hiding the fact that they were carrying guns. The guns and their holsters made ridiculous bulges, almost as though each guy had grown a tumor in the exact same place. There were easily a dozen such men in this room.

Well, there he was. Silvio Strukul. Aging international playboy, and scion of a wealthy family. Publisher and businessman. Tax fugitive, also wanted for embezzlement and bank fraud to the tune of tens of millions of euros. He looked every bit of all of those things. What he didn't look like was a cult leader, radical environmentalist, and terrorist mastermind.

Troy studied Strukul's group without looking directly at them. Jan was right. There was no way to separate Strukul from his bodyguards and walk him out of this crowd. They were just going to have to put the trackers on him and see what developed. Maybe they could catch him on the way out of town. Maybe he was here on a yacht and planned to sail back to Albania.

"Do you see him?" Dubois said. "He's at about ten o'clock."

Beyond Strukul, another man appeared. He was a smallish man with dark cream skin, dressed in a white shirt, black pants, and black jacket. He was one of the staff members hovering around the bar to the left side of the room.

It was Alex. Now he was working for the smugglers, serving drinks to the thirsty auction buyers. How did this guy infiltrate everywhere?

"Oh yeah. I see him."

Up at the front, an Arab man in a three-piece suit stepped onto the stage.

Troy looked at Dubois. "It looks like they're about to start," he said. "Can I get you a drink?"

"Are you going to try to tag him?"

"Yeah. If I can't get there, then you go. Okay?"

She nodded. "Sure. Maybe we even tag him twice."

"Fine. What can I get you?"

"White wine, if they're serving that."

For a split second, a fantasy passed through Troy's mind. This wasn't an auction at all. It was a ruse to get a bunch of rich people into a room and spike their drinks. And Alex was a party to it.

He shook that away. It wasn't possible. There were too many teetotalers in here. Too much hired muscle that wouldn't take a drink until they got back to their hotel rooms later. Too many powerful enemies to make. The smugglers would spend the rest of their lives on the run.

Troy moved through the crowd, sliding this way and that, putting his hand on various people's backs to nudge them along. No one seemed to mind that much. They were all stuffed in here like it was a subway car at rush hour.

He had a dark sticker on one finger. It wasn't a perfect match for Strukul's gray suit, but neither were the light stickers. Leave it to Strukul to wear a suit that was neither light nor dark. Troy glided around the bodyguard to Strukul's left and slid in behind them. The bodyguard eyed Troy but didn't see anything he minded. Troy was dressed as fashionably as anyone in here, and more fashionably than most. What he didn't look like was a hired gunman.

He moved past Strukul and his fashion models. At the last second, he changed his mind and bumped into one of the girls. Her mini dress was dark, and she was traveling with Strukul. She turned and scowled at him.

He raised both hands. The sticker was gone, now attached to the girl. Even if that dress came off, it would probably land on the back seat of Strukul's limo, or on the floor of the master cabin aboard his yacht.

"Sorry, sweetie," Troy said. "Tight back here."

Her blank eyes said she didn't speak English.

Got one. Troy moved on to the bar. Up at the front, the man was saying something quietly into a microphone. The crowd began to quiet down. Troy couldn't make out what the man was saying. He was speaking French. It didn't really matter. Troy wasn't here for the auction.

He arrived at the bar. The timing was good. Alex was behind it, and at the moment, by himself.

"Don't I know you from somewhere?"

Alex shook his head and shrugged. "English. Don't speak."

Troy held up two fingers. *"Vin. Blanc."*

He was trying.

Alex suppressed a smile and nodded. He reached under the bar and came up with two glasses. He spoke three or four sentences in rapid fire French.

Troy just nodded.

Alex poured the wine and handed the glasses across.

"Careful," Alex muttered under his breath. It was low, but Troy could just hear it. Probably no one else could. Alex had that gift—he could speak and only be heard by the intended party. "A lot of shooters in here. And something bad is about to go down."

"Bad?" Troy said.

Alex shrugged. "Be cool. Walk out alive. It happens all the time."

"What is it?" Troy said, but Alex had already turned away and was fiddling with something in a chest on the floor.

143

Troy moved back through the crowd toward Dubois. Everyone's eyes were on the stage now. A new speaker had appeared at the microphone.

"Ladies and gentlemen," the man said in English. "Thank you for coming tonight. We have many rare and wonderful pieces for your consideration. Please note that all sales are final, and all settlements are in cash. Please also note we are under a time constraint this evening. Some individuals in our audience who are keen to bid on the most valuable item for sale must also leave soon. And the item in question is so priceless, so beautiful, so without peer, and also so illegal, that we must move it quickly. As a result, we will be auctioning that item first. Once it is gone, and its new owner takes possession, the rest of us will be able to relax, and take our time considering the other very valuable items available."

There was a growing buzz around the room. Something was going on here. A lot of people knew about it, including Alex, but Troy didn't.

"Does everyone who wants to bid on the first item have a bidding paddle?"

Troy reached Dubois and handed her a glass of wine.

"Did you tag him?" Dubois said.

"I tagged one of his mannequins."

She took a sip of the wine. "That makes sense. We can follow her to Paris while he goes to Istanbul."

"I'm so glad I married you," Troy said. "You make me happy."

A hush went through the crowd. Up at the front, two large man appeared, moving something onto the stage. The thing itself was behind a dark curtain.

"Our first item," the man on the stage said. The other man, the one who spoke French, said something into his microphone. They were going to auction it in English and French simultaneously.

"This special item is beyond beautiful. It moves my soul to offer this to you. Found in Belarus, brought here untouched, unsullied, and we guarantee that. You are the first to have this great prize. We will begin the bidding at half a million euros. Each new bid is worth ten thousand euros, unless specified by the bidder. Now, I present to you...Tatiana."

The curtain dropped. Standing there was what looked to be a nine- or ten-year-old girl. She was indeed very pretty, with long flowing blonde hair. Her eyes were blindfolded. She wore a silver dress and a garland of yellow flowers in her hair. Her hands were bound in front of her with what looked like a zip tie. There were silver slippers on her tiny feet.

There was suddenly a lot of ooohing and ahhhing. But beneath that, another sound went around the room. Troy couldn't say what it was. It sounded almost like a low animal growl.

"The blinder cannot be removed until after the sale, and she is taken away from the auction room. We are mindful of her emotional state. Note that her eyes are deep blue, like the waters of the Greek isles. They are very beautiful eyes, which will look up to you in awe and complete adoration."

Immediately a bidding paddle went up.

"We have a half million bid."

Another went up.

"Five hundred and ten. Now twenty. Thirty? No, fifty. Five hundred and fifty thousand euros."

Troy stared at the girl. She was shaking and swaying. A man stood behind here, steadying her with one large hand. He was like a puppeteer, keeping the puppet upright. From beneath the blindfold, tears were streaming down the girl's face.

"What in the hell?" Troy said.

"We are at six hundred thousand."

"Oh my God," Dubois said.

To Troy's right, one of the Arab princes raised his paddle.

"Six hundred and fifty. Increments are now fifty thousand."

"This is a joke, right?" Troy said.

Dubois put a hand on his wrist. "Stark…"

"It's not going to happen, lady. I can't allow it. Sorry."

She tried again. "Agent Stark."

They auctioned children in Iraq. They auctioned them in Afghanistan. Especially Afghanistan, where the children were the so-called "dancing boys" instead of girls. But they never auctioned anyone in the presence of Troy Stark. There was something about it. It cut through him like a rusty can. It cried out for revenge.

How did they even get this girl? Kidnap her? Buy her from someone else?

A bad memory flashed through his mind, and then was gone almost before it came. He had once killed eight men in a hookah lounge in Kabul for this very reason.

For an instant, he saw all of them dead in pools of blood on the floor, blank eyes staring up at their God, or at nothing, the dancing boy they were bidding on screaming and crying at the front of the room. The bids were a lot lower in that case.

It was a war crime. It was a massacre. Yes, it was. He got chewed out for it. They covered it up. He would do it again in a heartbeat.

Like now.

"Stark, we have our assignment. This isn't it."

He nodded. "I know. I apologize for that. But I don't let things like this stand. I suggest you start moving toward the exit. I'll give you ten seconds but get going right now. Good luck. I'll see you later."

"Seven hundred and fifty thousand euros. Amazing bidding. A breathtaking item. Tonight is the night. This is a once in a lifetime opportunity."

"Stark!" Dubois shouted. He could barely hear her over the din.

"Go. I mean that. It's about to get ugly in here."

She turned and stormed away from him. He could only imagine the report she was going to write after this. He watched Dubois go. She slipped between people, moving quickly towards the staircase.

"This is a goddess! This is Paradise on Earth!"

Troy turned back to the matter at hand. Dubois was a grown woman. He had told her what was going to happen. She needed to take herself out of harm's way. He began sliding through the crowd now, heading to the front.

"Eight hundred thousand! Do I have nine hundred?"

The stage was right in front of him. He squeezed between the last people. He glanced around, looking for the way out. It was bad. They were underground, and he couldn't kill everyone in here. There was one staircase to the surface, and the only windows were too high and too small to be of any use. There was that big chandelier, but he couldn't shoot it down with the gun that he had.

He spotted Alex by the bar, eyes wide, mouth open. He was watching Troy, seeing what was about to go down, and helpless to stop it. It was almost comical, seeing Alex that way. He was a man who was always ready, always one step ahead. But not this time. Okay. It was simple. Alex must know another way out. Troy would get the girl and make his way to Alex. That was the whole plan.

"Yes! Nine hundred thousand euros!"

The auctioneer enjoyed his job too much. The other man, the French speaker, was speaking in the same tone of enthusiasm and really, joy, but Troy had no idea what he was saying. That was going to save his life, the fact that Troy didn't understand him. For all he knew, the guy was saying, "Don't buy this girl! Repent your sins!"

Troy stepped onto the stage with them. Immediately, the large man behind the girl stepped to the front of her. That was okay. He was easily a foot taller than her.

Troy's gun appeared like magic. One second it was inside his jacket, the next second it was out and in his hand.

BANG!

He shot the big man in the head.

The guy barely had time to register a look of surprise. His head snapped back, and he dropped like a bundle of old clothes. Somewhere behind Troy, a woman screamed.

He turned to the man on the microphone, the auctioneer. The guy was well-dressed with a close-cropped beard. He was just staring, not moving at all. Unlike the big man, he did have time to be surprised. He had stopped at nine hundred thousand euros. He didn't seem to be looking for any more bids. For a guy with so much to say a moment ago, he was certainly quiet.

"Surprise," Troy said.

BANG!

And shot him in the face.

The guy went down with the microphone and the stand. There was a shriek of feedback when he hit the stage.

The French speaker was already gone.

Another guy, in a light blue tracksuit, ran and jumped onto the stage. He was ahead of himself. He was already here and didn't have his gun out yet. He made a move to pull it from inside his light jacket and didn't quite get it. His momentum carried him. He changed midstream and tried to tackle Troy instead.

He made a rush like a bull, head down. That was dumb.

BANG!

Troy shot him in the crown of his skull. He put his free hand on the guy's shoulder and pushed him down face-first. The guy was dead before he landed.

The girl was frozen in place. Troy went to her, scooped her up with his left arm, and threw her over his shoulder like a sack of rice. She was very light.

He looked out at the crowd. It was surging like a raging ocean—people on the floor, people falling, people rushing for the stairway, people climbing over each other. It seemed like everywhere, goons

147

were still on their feet, pulling guns. Tracksuit goons, sports jacket goons, a goon in white flowing robes.

Seconds had passed since Troy started shooting. Four, maybe five, at most.

He had the girl. She was worth a million euros. Were they going to shoot him and risk killing the girl?

Yes.

The guns were out now, all trained on the stage. Any second, bullets were going to chew him up. He had just killed himself and the girl.

DUH-DUH-DUH-DUH-DUH-DUH-DUH.

Seven guys hit the deck at once.

The shots came from Troy's right. He looked, and Alex was there with an AK-47. Alex paused, resighted, and let off another burst.

DUH-DUH-DUH-DUH-DUH.

Alex was shooting over everyone's heads, laying down suppressing fire. Troy had never seen Alex shoot at anyone before. Or even punch anyone. No, that wasn't true. He shot that pitbull with a tranquilizer dart.

Troy was already running toward him, stepping on the squirming bodies of people who had hit the deck. It was like the floor itself was alive and moving.

Alex had turned and was running back into the shadows, where the staff had been going to get the alcohol.

Troy followed him, sprinting now, bouncing from body to body, not even trying to stay down or protect himself. The thing to do was to move fast. If someone got a shot, then he was a dead man.

There was a door up ahead. It was a low door made of some heavy metal, with a combination lock built into it. It looked like the door to a safe. That wasn't good. A safe was not good. That would mean they were trapped down here.

Alex yanked open the door and held it open as Troy ducked and ran inside. The doorway was so low, he nearly scraped his head on the top of his.

Alex slammed the door shut behind them. A second later, and a second too late, a sound came like popcorn popping. Someone outside that door had recovered their composure and was firing at it.

Troy took a deep breath.

There was a tunnel here. It was long. There were a few overhead lights where they were near the door, along with some bar supplies—

cases of wine, cases of beer, bags of melting ice—piled up on the floor. Deeper, the lights ended, and the tunnel ran on into total darkness.

"You're such an idiot," Alex said. "You know that?"

"You knew that was gonna happen," Troy said. "You should have warned me straight out, instead of dropping cryptic hints."

Alex started moving into the dark, walking fast, the machine gun still cradled in his arms. Troy followed, keeping his head down. After a few moments of walking, his eyes started to adjust to the lack of light. The tunnel ran on and on, curving to the right.

"What is wrong with you?" Alex said. "I knew there was going to a human auction. I found that out today. I didn't know you were going to cause a bloodbath."

"What's wrong with YOU?" Troy said. "You gonna stand by and allow that to happen?"

"It happens every day, Stark. It'll happen again tomorrow, somewhere else. The world doesn't start and stop because you drop in."

"I killed three guys. They were all involved. I don't feel the least bit bad about that."

"You think no one got trampled to death back there?"

"Occupational hazard when you go to a human trafficking convention."

Troy shrugged. For the first time, he remembered he still had the girl on his shoulder. She was screaming now, absolutely screaming, and growing louder all the time. The sound of her shrieks echoed off the walls, up and down the tunnel. It was the soundtrack to a nightmare.

He tried to bounce her on his shoulder, like she was a baby. It was uncomfortable. She was a bouncing bag of rice. That wasn't going to work.

"Shhhhh. It's okay, baby. That's okay. We're going to get you home."

"How do you propose we do that?" Alex said.

"I don't know. We'll figure it out. Okay?"

Behind them, the light was fading away. But a new sound came. Men were shouting. The door back there was open. It was only a matter of time. Someone else had the code. Of course they did.

"Oh, man," Alex said. "If they open fire now, we are cooked."

They reached a place where the tunnel suddenly made a sharp left. That was good. It would provide some cover. Troy could hear their pursuers breathing back there. They weren't plunging ahead. They didn't want to get killed.

"Give me the gun," Troy said. "Take the girl."

"What?"

"Give me the gun and take the girl. Keep moving. I'll get rid of these guys."

Troy set the girl down on her feet. Her legs were like wet spaghetti. She nearly went straight to the ground.

"You have to carry her. She can't walk."

Alex said something to the girl. She blurted something out to him. He said something else, his voice soft and almost cooing like a pigeon. He handed Troy the gun, then lifted the girl's chin with his hand, still speaking softly. She nodded.

"What are you speaking?"

"Russian. She's from Belarus. They can speak Russian."

"Do you speak every language?"

"Just the important ones. You might try it."

He said something else to the girl.

"What are you saying?"

"I told her she's okay. She's safe, she just needs to be quiet and come with me. She understands. She's basically shell-shocked. She'll do whatever we say, pretty much."

Blah blah blah. Troy was barely listening. His ears were focused on the sounds coming from behind them.

"You have another magazine for this thing?"

Alex's hand appeared with another loaded banana clip.

"My man," Troy said. "Always prepared."

He popped out the half-empty magazine and slid in the full one. He slipped the half-empty in his front pants pocket. It hung there like a weight.

At this moment, he almost couldn't express in words how pleased he was to be partnered up with Alex. He hoped that was coming across clearly. The guy had his own form of magic. He was constantly pulling rabbits out of hats. Troy would have to apprentice Dubois to him if this other thing was ever going to work.

"You're a cold-blooded murderer, Stark."

Troy nodded. "I know. I know that. I try not to be, but sometimes there's nothing I can do. So just take the girl and go. Get her somewhere safe. Home, UNICEF, I don't know. Whatever you come up with is good. I'll see you around."

"You know the way out?" Alex said.

"No, but I assume there's an exit somewhere."

150

"There are a lot of exits, but you have to pick the right one."

Troy was getting frustrated with the conversation. "Just go, all right? Evaporate. It's gonna get hot here in another minute or less."

"Good luck," Alex said. A second later, he and the girl were gone.

Troy stood very still.

His whole body was listening, picking up the smallest hints from his environment. He heard Alex's footfalls for another moment, but then they were gone. Now he was alone. He took a deep, silent breath.

Back in combat.

The turn they had made was a few feet away. He got low and crept to the edge. There was a long, curving tunnel here, going back to the doorway he and Alex had entered through. He could hear the men in the tunnel. They were coming along, moving slowly, taking no risks, but whispering to each other. The whispering, all by itself, was a risk. It gave them away.

Their eyes must have adjusted to the dark by now. They weren't using flashlights. Troy glanced around the corner. No one there. They were further down the curve, out of his line of sight. They were coming at a snail's pace. He couldn't discount the idea that they knew this tunnel, knew this sharp turn was here.

Slowly, silently, he lowered himself to the ground. This tunnel was dusty and dirty, and if it hadn't been already, his suit was now ruined. He wriggled out into the tunnel like a worm. He lay on his left side, facing down the long, curving slope. This was the first time he had noticed there was any slope at all. He had been running on pure adrenaline before—he could have run straight up a mountainside and not noticed the incline.

He pointed the AK down the tunnel. His hands were firm. His breathing was deep and controlled. He was not in a hurry. He was not nervous. He could stay like this all night if he had to.

These guys were coming. And that meant they were bad guys. They knew the risks. They were willing to pay the price. Why? Because the girl was a valuable piece of merchandise, and they wanted her back? Because Troy had shot up their party? Because they were cops on the take?

It didn't matter. Coming up that tunnel revealed them for who they were. So, Troy watched and waited. Every second of delay, every second these guys were uncertain, bought Alex another second to get that girl out of here.

Suddenly, the men were on the move. They came running around the curve, racing towards him.

Troy couldn't say how many there were.

The two front men fired their guns.

BANG!

BANG!

BANG!

They screamed and shouted as they ran.

The sounds of gunfire and screams were deafening, the echoes multiplying them, bouncing up and down the length of the tunnel. The muzzle flashes were blinding. They kept firing. Chunks of stone and sprays of dirt fell on Troy from the wall above him.

He let them come. Closer, closer, four men, maybe five, all running right at him, shooting the walls.

DUH-DUH-DUH-DUH-DUH-DUH-DUH.

He sprayed them, hosed them down with gunfire. He let out a burst, paused half a beat, then let it rip again. His spray took them out at the legs and midsections. He kept firing, into their fallen bodies, and above them at anyone who might come up behind.

Then the magazine was spent. He had dumped all of it. Now he slithered back behind the sharp corner, a snake instead of a worm. He ejected the dead mag and slapped the half-empty one back in.

He rolled on his back, facing up at the corner, in case someone came around it. He lay there, his breath coming in harsh gasps.

"Come on," he whispered. "Come on, I'll kill you."

No one came.

After a long minute, his heartbeat and his breathing began to settle down. It slowed and slowed. He pushed himself to a sitting position, then slid along the wall to his feet. He glanced around the corner again.

It was hard to tell what was out there. It seemed like a solid mass on the ground maybe ten meters down the tunnel from here.

"Hey!" he said.

Nothing. No response. There wasn't a sound anywhere.

He crept around the corner, gun out, ready to shoot. He moved quickly to the dark mass. It was a pile of men. Five of them. None seemed to be moving.

None seemed to be faking it. Just a bunch of dead guys. He felt nothing about that. Corpses didn't upset him. There was nothing frightening about them. He had learned a long time ago that the dead don't bother you. It was the living you had to worry about.

He was done here. He had to go find a way out of this tunnel now. "Good night, guys."

* * *

"Where is he?" Jan Bakker said over the phone.

Agent Dubois shook her head. "I don't know. I'm not with him."

She was walking quickly away from the building where the auction had taken place. The phone was pressed to her ear. Behind her, people were still streaming out of there. She did not want to stay around in case anyone noticed she had been with Stark.

"Is he alive?"

"I don't know that either. There was a lot of shooting. He was the one who started it. I was already on my way up the stairs. He warned me to leave, told me he was going to do it. I don't see how he could have survived. There was no way out of that place. It's an enclosed space, underground."

"What happened?" Jan said.

"It was human trafficking. A girl was for sale. Stark took issue with it and decided to start shooting people."

Her entire body was shaking. She was worried she was about to do something she did not want to do. She felt like she was going to cry, and she couldn't allow that. She was a special agent. She was a grown woman. She was...

"Stark!" she shouted at the phone. In an instant, she realized she was about to say something about the mission. She couldn't do that, not over the telephone. So she stopped. Specific complaints about Troy Stark would have to wait. "He's crazy!" she said instead. "I hate him!"

"Okay, okay. Don't talk about it."

"Can you see my signal?" she said.

"We're pinpointing you. There are a lot of signals, a lot of interference. Give us another moment."

"I don't feel good about this, Jan. I am in a vulnerable position right now. Stark wasn't supposed to do that."

She was walking further away from the building. She was a woman, dressed to the nines, and walking at night in a dilapidated part of Algiers. Everyone who was at that auction came there in armored SUVs and limousines. No one was going to walk away from there. No one but her.

"Was the subject tagged?"

"A member of his entourage was."

"Good."

She kept walking, anything to get away from the gunmen in that building. But then, maybe that was wrong. Maybe she blew her cover even more by leaving. It was a suspicious act. What kind of Western woman would walk around Algiers at night by herself?

She was walking downhill along a narrow street. A forest of power lines crisscrossed above her head in what seemed like random patterns. She passed a building, its front doorway shaped like a minaret. Its façade looked pock-marked, as though someone shot it up with a machine gun. A group of young men hung around in the dim light given off by a yellow bulb above the open doorway. Their hard eyes followed her as she passed.

"We have you," Jan said. "We also have the subject, the entourage member."

"Where are you?" Dubois said.

"We are in a car to your west, heading to your position. You should find that you are walking downhill. Keep going in that direction. There will be a wide boulevard several streets below you. We will meet you there."

"Okay," she said.

"The entourage member is moving quickly to the east and north. They must be in a car. I think they may be going to the docks. I'm not sure yet."

As if Dubois were interested in that right now.

"We'll have to get some guidance about a possible interdiction, either on the water or to the east of the city if they keep going that way."

Dubois ignored talk of pulling the subjects over on the high seas. To ask them what? There was no evidence of them committing a crime. They were at an event where crimes were being committed, but that didn't implicate Silvio Strukul in any way. He could simply say he was there because he was curious. He went to an auction. He wasn't even sure what was for sale.

Unless Miquel was playing all the way outside the rules now, they had no grounds for questioning Strukul about anything.

"How soon until you get here?"

Dubois looked back. Behind her, a few of the young men had peeled away from the others and now were slowly following her down the street. The street itself was little more than a winding alleyway. A few of the buildings gave off a bit of light from windows above her head. A few were completely dark, the windows like blank dead eyes. It was an unpleasant neighborhood.

She still had her purse. She unclipped it and stuck her hand inside. She gripped the pistol inside the purse and slid the safety to OFF with her thumb. She was just a woman carrying a phone in one hand, and a purse in the other.

If those men came at her, if they so much as asked her an impolite question, she was going to make them very sorry. She could almost kill them for the mildly intimidating way they were following her. The threat was there. It was implied, but it was there nonetheless. And she could kill them for it. She had killed before.

That's what spending time with Troy Stark did. It drained you of empathy. It drained you of humanity. You were prepared to kill over a misunderstanding. Maybe the men weren't following her at all. Maybe they were walking home.

"We can be at your position in another twelve to fifteen minutes," Jan said.

"Oh," Dubois said. "That's just wonderful."

CHAPTER TWENTY TWO

November 18
2:45 am Central European Time
A flat
Zurich, Switzerland

"I need to tell you something," he said.

Here it comes.

Princess Dye lay on her back, her head propped up with pillows. She was drinking beer from a can. They were sharing it, the same way they had shared cigarettes in between bouts of making love.

It was dark in here, the way she liked it. There were streetlights outside, but he had drawn the shades, and barely a sliver of the light made it into the room. The window refused to close all the way, a crack at the bottom remained open, and it was chilly out. They were under a blanket, handmade from thick yarn. It was a beautiful blanket, deep blue in color, but it was not the warmest.

In another moment, she would have to press herself against him again for the body heat. She hoped he didn't ruin that with whatever he was about to say. Mr. Gray, Thomas T. Engine, whoever he was, wherever he came from, he was a very good man to press against.

"Okay," she said. "Tell me."

"I'm not sure how to do it."

"Just blurt it out," she said. "That's probably the best way."

She passed him the beer, and he nodded. Then he took a sip.

"All right," he said. "Here it is. I know what you're planning to do."

She froze. For what seemed like a long moment, but was probably only a few seconds, she couldn't move at all. Her heart may have stopped beating.

He couldn't know. It wasn't possible. If he knew…In her mind, she excused herself to the bathroom, went down the short hallway into the kitchen, and came back with a very sharp knife.

Then again, maybe he was talking about something else.

"You know what I'm planning to do," she said.

"Yes."

"I have no idea what you're talking about."

"Of course you do," he said. "During the operation, right near the beginning, you plan to slip away to a suite of offices tucked above and away from the main control room. What is in the offices is a secret, even from most of the people who work there. As a result, the high-level security protocols in place, say, for entering the particle accelerator, do not apply. The rooms are locked, but the locks should be relatively easy to defeat. Once inside that suite, you intend to steal computer files that are not stored on the facility's servers, along with paper files that are thought to be there."

"Buster, I think you've finally flipped your…"

"Then you plan to leave the facility while the crisis caused by the operation is still going on. You will use it as a cover story, if necessary, that you were a hostage who escaped. That's if anyone discovers you. If no one discovers you, the preferable outcome, you will simply disappear into the countryside, and turn on a tracking device so your handlers can find you."

She didn't say a thing.

"Please, call me Thomas, not Buster."

"You're wrong," she said. "But now I'm curious. What makes you think that you know this about me?"

She could kill him, she realized. If she had to do it, she could. She had come this far, and if he was some kind of policeman or infiltrator, she wasn't about to let him stop her. She certainly wasn't going to let him put her in prison.

It wouldn't be that hard. Men often fell asleep after sex. He was no exception.

"I've been assigned to accompany you and protect you," he said.

"You've been…"

"You can stop pretending," he said. "Yes, the same people who approached you also approached me. They are aware of us and what we're up to. Don't ask me how they know, but they do. A man gave you a device when you were in Berlin. The code to unlock it is the date John F. Kennedy was assassinated. If this wasn't true, how could I know that?"

It was as if all the air went out of her at once. Her head and shoulders sunk deep into the pillows. Her body became part of the mattress. She sighed. She was at the end. All of the secrecy, all of the sneaking around, and Thomas T. Engine here knew everything.

"Who are you?" she said. Her voice didn't shake, but there was a little choke of emotion deep in her throat. "FBI? CIA? Interpol? Who?"

He shook his head. In the deep darkness, she could somehow sense the movement without looking at him.

"None of those. I'm just a guy. I've been in the movement since I was a kid. Do you remember a giant Hummer dealership in San Diego that blew up and burned for two days about five years ago?"

"Vaguely," she said. "Yeah, I do."

"That was me."

"By yourself?"

"Me and one other guy."

"Who was he?" she said.

"Oh, man. He was a guy. Native American, maybe. That's what he said. He went south into Mexico. I don't know what became of him."

"So, you're American? I thought you were German or something like that."

He chuckled. It wasn't a full laugh. It even sounded a bit sad.

"I learned to put on an accent. It's an accent that sounds like English isn't my first language, but I'm doing my best to suppress that fact. It's a double misdirect. You think I'm a German who speaks English fluently. I'm actually an American who barely speaks ten words of German. I'm pretty good in Spanish, though. I studied it in high school."

She thought about that for a long moment.

"How did you come to join this group?"

"I didn't," he said. "I'm not a follower of this man who you probably think of as the leader. I've never even met him. I just have experience blowing things up. A guy came to me with an offer. Yeah, it included money, but it also included the chance to get in on something big and important. It seemed good at the time. Now I wonder."

Something about the way he spoke irritated her. He didn't even know Silvio. He was just doing all this for money. So when another group approached him, he apparently took their money too.

"You're a mercenary," she said.

He nodded and took another sip of the beer. "I guess I am. It didn't start out that way, but yeah. Anyway, so are you."

It hurt. The truth hurt. She had been shielding herself from this fact. Now there it was in front of her, plain as day.

"Who are they, do you think?"

"The people who hired us to steal the secrets?"

"Yes."

"At a guess? They're Russian intelligence. That's the best I can come up with. Something is going on at CERN, something very high-tech. They know it's happening; they probably even know what it is, but they don't know how to do it. The western world is racing out ahead of them. So they want it."

"What is it?" she said.

He shook his head. "I don't know. But that's not even the point I'm trying to make. The point is I think we should leave."

"Leave?"

"Yeah. I think tomorrow morning, when we're supposed to head to Geneva, we should just go somewhere else. Anywhere else. Maybe we should even leave now and get a head start."

"It's not possible," she said. "They'll kill us."

"Not if they can't find us."

She nearly laughed. This man was very good at any number of things. He had obviously been out on the edge for a long time. And yet, he was incredibly naïve. It was almost endearing but not quite.

"They know where we are," she said. "The tracking mechanism that I'm supposed to turn on after the operation? It's probably on right now. They probably had someone follow us to the bar, then follow us back here. Or they already knew where you were staying. It's too late to leave."

She wouldn't say this to him, but she had also come a long way for a very big payday. She was inches from crossing the finish line. Even if they didn't kill her, she'd be crazy to leave now.

Yeah. She was a mercenary, all right.

"Remember the man who called himself Purple Hays?" he said.

"Of course I remember him."

"Two nights ago, he passed through here. He came to see me. He was on his way to Geneva. He's in charge of the operation. Not our little secret part, he doesn't know about that, but the overall operation. It's similar, but bigger, than the one in Massachusetts. He said there are ten people in the cell, including us."

"That's good," Princess Dye said. And it was. Purple Hays was as professional as they came. He seemed to have been a soldier at one point, probably with combat experience. Nothing shook him. He moved from task to task without fear. If he was in charge, then the operation would go as planned, buying her even more time to...

"It's not good," Thomas said. "He and I went to a bar. We sat in a corner by ourselves. The place was crowded, and I don't think anyone could overhear us. But he got drunk and told me some things he shouldn't have."

"Uh oh," she said.

"Right."

"Should you tell me?"

"No. Suffice to say he's a bad person. He did bad things during the last operation. He did bad things before that operation. He's done a lot of bad things in a lot of places. Apparently, he does bad things even when it's not necessary. It doesn't upset him. He thinks it's funny. It upsets me because now I know this about him."

"And so he has a reason to…" she didn't finish the thought.

"Yes, he does. He's capable of causing a bloodbath during the operation itself. He told me he will shoot his way out if he has to. I think he'll do it even if he doesn't have to. I don't want to be part of that. I didn't want to be part of it before, and I don't want to be part of it again, but it keeps happening."

He paused for a long moment. "And, just by the way, the people who hired us…"

He trailed off and didn't finish the thought.

Have every reason to kill us as soon as we hand the materials over to them.

She didn't believe that. She *wouldn't* believe it. They had been paying her all along to keep moving up the line, to get closer and closer. If she pulled this off, the final job, they wouldn't just kill her. Why would they do that? If anything, they'd want to hire her again. She was a known quantity, who had proven she could do good work.

"I think we can thread the needle," she said.

He sighed. It almost sounded like a wheeze. "I was hoping you wouldn't say that."

"I believe it. We can make it out. We leave Purple Hays in the dust. That's the plan anyway. He does what he does. We do what we do. We get the materials, but we don't hand them over right away. We don't turn on the tracking device."

"I thought you said it was already on."

"I lied," she said. "It's not on. We keep it off, and make our way to a safe, neutral location. Once there, we turn it on. And we hand the materials over on our terms, in a crowded public place, in broad daylight."

She was thinking now. Her brain felt like it was on fire.

Suddenly, everything seemed more dangerous than ever before. But she was going to make it through.

For a moment, she wished she could talk to Silvio about this, her mentor, her lover, the man who had sent her down this path. She needed his advice and his wisdom. He would probably laugh when she told him of the predicament.

"I knew you would betray me," he would say.

"Do you hate me?"

She could almost see him there, smiling in the dark. "No. My beautiful girl, don't you know? I love you."

Then he explained to her exactly how to survive the operation, how to escape with the secret materials, and how to get paid by the Russians without getting killed. He told her all of it, and he wasn't angry with her. On the contrary, he treated her with complete compassion and understanding.

He knew. She realized that now. Of course he did. He knew she was doing this. He had known all along. And it didn't bother him one bit. He knew what she would do before she did. He loved her and wanted her to succeed. He wanted her to become her best self. He had told her that often when they were together.

He was the greatest man she had ever known. No, he was more than a man. She took a deep breath. She wasn't afraid. Everything was going to be fine.

"I'm sure it's going to work out," she said now. She pressed herself up against Thomas again and felt his heat. It felt very good. This wouldn't bother Silvio, either. He had already told her it was fine. He had set it up this way so she wouldn't be lonely.

"Just stay close to me," she said.

Silvio was watching over her. He would protect her and help her.

He had that power.

CHAPTER TWENTY THREE

6:15 am Central European Time
Adriatic Coast
Albania

"You're so stupid. Did you know that?"

Silvio Strukul stood on the white stone patio behind his house. The house was built on a rocky outcropping high above the water. It was designed to capture a sweeping southern exposure, facing down the coastline, but also out to sea, to the west, as far as the eye could see. In front of him, the sun was just up and beginning its daily journey across the pale blue sky.

From here, there was a wide stone staircase down to the pool deck. From there, one could follow a narrow stairwell cut into the cliffs, all the way down to a small sandy beach. The beach only existed at low tide. Some of the young people ventured down there, but Silvio rarely did.

As a practical matter, the way the property was situated meant you could view the sunrise, bask in the sun by the pool all day long, and then watch the sun set in spectacular colors in the evening. It was one of the most breathtaking views he had ever seen, and it was his.

Well, not entirely his. He did have his sponsors. Once in a while, they reminded him who really owned everything. They sent messengers to make it perfectly clear. Messengers like these men standing behind him right now.

Silvio turned to face them. The leader was Viktor, a thin man in slacks, loafers, and a green Polo shirt. Silvio had dealt with him before. He was perfectly bald, with a beak of a nose and the narrow eyes, not so much of a bird of prey, but of a clever bird, like a crow—a bird that ate dead things. He had a bit of a strange little potbelly, although his arms and shoulders were muscular. Alcohol caused that belly, vodka most likely. These Russians were renowned for the amount they drank.

The two men with him were younger and bigger. They both had the same haircut, which was to say close-cropped at the sides with a little bit of fur at the top. They were dressed in a manner similar to their boss, but they also wore sports jackets, one beige and one dark blue. Those jackets were a problem. If not for the jackets, these three men could be out for a pleasant holiday, motoring along the Albanian coast.

Jackets tended to hide guns.

"Okay," Silvio said. "I suppose I deserve it. So tell me."

They didn't like him leaving this compound, the Russians. Thinking back, if he had known it would mean being a prisoner in his own home, he may never have gotten involved with them. It was a lovely home, and there were always lovely young ladies here with him, the true believers, but he was trapped. A beautiful prison cell was still a prison cell. And with partners like this, there was no escape.

He sighed. There was no escape anyway. He was under indictment in six countries. In Italy, he had already been convicted in absentia. If he went home, it would be to a real jail cell. He was fifty-four years old. These days, he felt every minute of it and more. He had lived in luxury his entire life. There was no going back. There was no paying his debt to civil society and starting over.

"We know you were in Algiers last night," Viktor said.

Silvio nodded. Of course they knew. "Yes. I went for an art auction. It did not turn out as I imagined."

Viktor offered a wan smile. "No. I suppose not."

"But I'm back here and unharmed. No one in my group was injured. We left as soon as the shooting started."

He was still processing what had happened. A beautiful little girl had been for sale. This was not something Silvio desired, but he recognized that there were men who did, and they were willing to pay for the pleasure. For some reason, in this instance, the bidding had gone out of control. Hundreds of thousands of euros for one girl? It was unprecedented, at least in Silvio's experience. Then, just like that, a man walked up to the stage and started killing people.

An aggrieved bidder who couldn't keep up with the rising price? The child's father? Who could say?

It was chaos escaping from there.

His bodyguards, who were not bodyguards in any real sense, but were just young men trying to become members of the community here, had fled without attempting to rescue Silvio. Silvio himself had dragged his two young followers, Katie and Beatrice, up the stairs and out of the building.

He had left the young men in Algiers out of spite. He didn't even bring them to the airfield. They were not followers of his. They didn't

163

believe. They were worse than useless. They had been hovering nearby because Silvio was rich, owned this impossible home, and always had beautiful young women with him.

If confronted with these Russians, they would simply fold up and blow away on a stiff breeze.

"No one knew I was there," he said.

Viktor shook his head slowly. "On the contrary. You were followed there. One of the people in your entourage seems to have been tagged with a tracking device. We were able to follow it and watch. Someone else was too."

"A tracking device?"

"Yes. It's still here in the house. It went live at the site of the auction just before the violence broke out. Of course we knew you were there already. We're not stupid. Do you think we're stupid?"

Silvio shook his head. "No. Of course not."

"Then why do you keep trying to fool us?"

"I don't. I never do."

"In any event," Viktor said, waving that line of questioning away. "We knew you were there, and so did someone else. They're watching you. They're following you."

"Who is it?" Silvio said. He honestly had no idea.

Viktor shrugged. "The Americans, maybe. The Germans, the European police. We don't know. It doesn't matter. You're under suspicion. We can't have that. You know a great deal about everything that has happened, and everything that's going to happen. It makes you a weak link in the chain."

Silvio felt a knot turn in his stomach. Russian spies telling him he was a weak link was not something he wanted to hear, not in the early morning, or really any time. He was glad he hadn't eaten anything yet.

Holy mother of God. He wished he'd never become involved with them. The attacks, the deaths…it was too much.

All of it was just a buildup, a misdirection, a ruse. This was how dangerous these people were. They were willing to blow things up, instigate protests and riots, and kill innocent people, simply to create a cover story for something else.

The Russians were excluded from the particle accelerator work at CERN. They, the Chinese, and the Iranians. All of them had been left out. That was bad enough. The Israelis were full members, even though they weren't a European country. This was appalling to the Iranians, of course, but even more so to the Russians. Russia was part of Europe. It was an insult.

But insults went on all the time in international politics. There was more. A rumor had gone around that a weapon was being developed. They were already creating particle beams with massive energy. A secret group within a group at CERN, scientists with the highest security clearances, were studying a new technology. If fully realized, it would permanently upset the balance of power.

"Peanut butter waffles," Silvio said.

"I'm afraid so," Viktor said.

Repeated references in English to "peanut butter waffles" had been detected in communications coming from CERN. It made no sense. But then there were nonsensical references being made in French, as well. "Agence France Press," the famous French news syndicate distributed around the world.

The Russians had discerned, or perhaps simply decided, that "peanut butter waffles" was a veiled reference to "particle beam weapons." When combined with the French translation *Armes Faisceau de Particules*, it became clear to them what was meant by Agence France Press as well.

Someone at CERN was building, or had already built, a particle beam weapon. If true, it would, of course, be destabilizing. A powerful directed energy beam, weaponized, and traveling at nearly the speed of light. There would be no way to defend against such a thing.

Personally, Silvio didn't believe it existed. The Russians didn't care what he believed. If it was there, they wanted the schema so they could build their own. At the very least, they wanted to know if it was real or not.

They had used him, and his community, as a front. It was his own fault. If he had not made himself vulnerable with his financial…peccadilloes, then none of this would have happened.

"What do you want to do?" Silvio said. It occurred to him now, and caused him some relief to realize, that they hadn't come to kill him. If they had, he'd already be dead. They wouldn't have bothered engaging in this conversation.

Viktor shrugged. "As far as everyone is concerned, this little cult of yours has been money well spent."

"It's not a cult," Silvio said. "It's a community of believers."

Viktor raised a hand, palm outward. His hands were oddly large compared to his body. It was as if a digital artist had superimposed the hands of a bigger man on his frame.

"The young ladies all seem to believe that you're God, or a god, or something like that. I don't know how or why they came to believe that, and obviously I don't agree with them."

The men behind him giggled like schoolboys. All this time, Silvio had been staring right at them and almost forget they were. Until now, they had been standing as still, and as silently, as statues.

"In my mind, that's a cult," Viktor said. "You can call it a community. I don't care what it is. But I also need to tell you this. A decision has been handed down. It's time to pull the plug out from the wall. The community is over."

Silvio felt a sharp jolt, like a stabbing, in his side. He stared at Viktor. This is what he had been afraid of all along. He had partnered with them to save his own skin, but also to help build this community. And when you partnered with people like this...

Terrible things could happen.

He shook his head. "No. It's too soon."

Slowly, Viktor took a cigarette from a slim metal case that was in the breast pocket of his shirt. He slid the case back where he found it, then pulled a lighter from his pants pocket. He popped the smoke in his mouth, lit it, and inhaled deeply

"You say that as if you have a choice in the matter."

He took another long drag.

"Believe me, Silvio, we didn't want to take this route, but now you've forced our hand. We can't let you jeopardize this project. And this isn't the only project in which we're involved. There's a lot going on, much more than you know. This is the wrong time for scrutiny. You've already shown we can't trust you."

Silvio barely heard most of what Viktor said.

He wished he hadn't gone to Algiers. He wished he could go back in time and undo it. And now...he wished he could stop time right in this moment. He didn't want Viktor to say another word.

"The community has to end."

Silvio shook his head. "I won't allow it. We're building something here, something important."

Viktor laughed. "You won't allow what? You're not building anything. You work for us. It's best if you remember that. We're moving you to a dacha outside Sochi, on the Black Sea. Don't worry, it's very nice. It doesn't quite compare with this place, but you'll survive. And we can keep a better eye on you there."

"And my people?"

Viktor shook his head. "You have no people."

The men behind him giggled again. They were like children.

Viktor raised his arms. He turned in a grand sweep, taking in the house, the pool, the cliffs, and the surrounding grounds. "Where are your people now? Bad men have come to take you away. Yet no one races to save you."

What was Silvio supposed to say? They were young people, and they tended to sleep late. His girls especially rarely roused themselves before 11 am. His people, the members of his community…were mostly lazy.

"They liked you for your money. I suppose they didn't know you had none. And I suppose they'll wander off now and find another rich man with no money."

Silvio shook his head. He couldn't seem to find any words.

"My people," he said at last, "are the ones carrying out your mission."

Viktor nodded. "Some of them, yes."

"The most important one," Silvio said.

"She isn't your person," Viktor said. "She betrayed you. We dangled the money in front of her, and she betrayed you."

Silvio thought about that. His best, his truest, believer was a gifted athlete and fearless warrior on behalf of the planet. She had loved him deeply, fiercely. It was not to too extravagant to say that she had worshipped him. And he had favored her for a time, among all of his women.

But he had given her to this project because of her many abilities. She was an extraordinary woman. What she didn't know was that he had given her away to them. The Russians coming to her, and hiring her as a double agent of sorts, was always part of the plan. And she had fallen for it. She had taken the money. She had agreed to become their operative.

"I think," Viktor said. "She was always with you for the money. There was nothing else."

How dare this man say these things to him? How dare he? But of course Silvio knew the answer. He drew his power from the people lurking behind him. *Those people…*

"No, it was love," Silvio said.

The men behind Viktor didn't giggle or even smile this time. Perhaps they were thinking of the women in their own lives.

"She took the money from us. She lies to you whenever you speak to her. She lies to everyone. She takes other lovers, from among the operatives and activists. She will risk her life and do everything possible to deliver the materials we request, so she can receive the final payment. She is a mercenary."

"Still, I know her. It was love."

Viktor shrugged. "Leave it at that, then. It was love."

He took another deep inhale, then pitched the cigarette away onto the stone tiles.

"Are you ready to go?"

No. He was not ready. He was not going to leave here, not without his followers. He didn't want to lose this community. He was God to these people. He could do anything he wanted with them. He could probably even kill them—kill them without lifting a finger. They would kill themselves, just because he asked.

That sort of power was amazing. It was...everything. Silvio couldn't let it go. He wasn't ready.

"You have to give me some time," he said. It was all he could think of.

Viktor shook his head, dismissing the idea. "Time is something you don't have."

"I won't go. I'll scream, and everyone will come running. Are you going to drag me away, in front of my people, as they witness it?"

"No," Viktor said. "I am allowed wide discretion for action. My friend, the dacha on the Black Sea was my idea. I thought of it because I like you."

Silvio shook his head violently. He was emphatic. Suddenly, he felt like a child about to throw a tantrum. "I'm not going. I'm not going to some threadbare villa in Sochi, surrounded by fat, drunk, Russian holiday makers. I'm not doing it. Don't make me raise my voice."

He pointed at them. "Everyone will see you. All my people will come."

Viktor shrugged. "I'm sorry you feel that way. In that case, *da svidaniya.*"

The Russian phrase for goodbye. It must have been a signal to the two men Viktor was with. They both stepped up as one, each removing a pistol from under their jackets. Silvio saw, to his dismay, that the guns had large silencers fitted to their barrels. The silencers were nearly larger than the guns themselves.

"No!" he nearly shouted but didn't.

The men pointed and fired in one motion. The guns made sounds, but the sounds weren't much. Silvio barely heard them, and he was standing right here.

An instant later, he was on his back on the stone tiles, staring upwards at the pale blue sky. He had no memory of falling to the ground. Viktor appeared in his line of sight, looking down. The two gunmen loomed behind him.

The three men stared down at Silvio. The bright day seemed to frame their heads in halos, like Christian icons of the medieval period. They were holy men, come to witness the birth of the King of Kings.

Silvio thought they must have fired three times each. That seemed like the right number. He remembered now, the stinging feeling, and the way he jerked as the bullets pierced his body.

It was an odd sensation, being here on the stonework. He could feel that he was badly damaged and probably dying. But it didn't hurt.

He tried to speak, but his throat wouldn't work.

"What should we do with him?" one of the big men said.

Viktor's face was blank, without emotion. "Feed him to the sharks."

CHAPTER TWENTY FOUR

7:05 am Central European Time
Elvissa Harbour
Ibiza Town
Island of Ibiza, Spain

"Honey, I'm home."

The seagulls were calling, and the sun was already bright. Troy piloted the big dark boat slowly through the No Wake zone around the harbor of Ibiza Town. The boat was a powerboat, shaped like a wedge, but not as long and narrow as the go-fast boats Troy was used to in the United States. At the stern, there were three powerful engines. He could hear their rumble beneath the water. The boat itself only had four seats. Troy had stood at the wheel all night.

He had taken the boat from a private dock along the waterfront in Algiers. It had been squeezed in among a line of old fishing boats. Fishing boats were nice, if you liked to fish. Troy wasn't against fishing, as pastimes went. But fishing wasn't on his itinerary. Instead, he had made a nighttime run across the Mediterranean.

Ahead of him were the whitewashed buildings of the Old Town, climbing the steep hillsides to an old brown church tower looming over the harbor at the top. Around him were moored sailboats and motorboats. Behind him, closer to the mouth of the harbor, were a few giant mega-yachts of the masters of the universe, whoever they were.

He was dressed in his boxer briefs, a t-shirt, and bare feet. His clothes were pasted to his skin. They had been soaked in the night and were just beginning to dry. He had stuffed his suit and shoes, along with his fake passport, his cash, and his phone, into one of the storage lockers along the stern. He had dumped the AK-47 and the other guns into the sea somewhere about halfway across. He was hoping the GPS unit sewn in his underwear was still functioning after the night he'd had.

He had run into a line of squalls, not unexpected, in the open sea. The Mediterranean didn't look all that daunting on a map, but there was a lot of water out there. It had its reputation, he supposed. A lot of less-than-seaworthy immigrant boats went down trying to make the trek.

He had a good boat. It was well-maintained, gassed up, and fast. For all intents and purposes, he didn't exist, and that was how he wanted it.

Troy sighed. At least during the storms, he hadn't had to scan the skies for aircraft or the path behind him for signs of pursuit. For long periods, he was alone in the dark, the wind, and the rain.

For a moment, he flashed back to it. The deck was slick under his feet and the boat lurched up and down like a cowboy riding a bucking bronco. The waves were gigantic, marching in a line off into the distance. Each ride up the face of a giant wave brought the certainty of a plunge down the other side.

Ahead and to his right there had been a light show in the distance. Heavy dark clouds, and just behind them, lightning, like the world's greatest laser rock-n-roll show. The lightning was too far away to hear the thunder. He gazed out at the black water, the massive waves all around him, throwing up white foam, surging like so many giant, hungry beasts.

It was good. That lightning was to the north and east, and he was moving to the north and west. The worst of it had already passed. And riding the storm meant he had to stay alert. There wasn't really time to think.

He pulled the boat up to a transient dock with a couple of slots available and killed the engines. It was November, so the place wasn't as crowded as it would be in the summer or early fall. Someone—the harbor master's office, passport control, or maybe Spanish customs—was going to want him to check in.

He wasn't going to do that. He figured he'd just leave the boat here, go into the public restroom they must have around this place, and put the suit back on. Then he would just…call someone?

Whoever he might call was bound to be plenty irritated with him right now.

Well, he had some cash. Maybe he should just assume his false identity and live here. He'd been here once before, years ago, and it was nice. Kind of a crazy party scene in the summer, but this time of year it should be fine.

Maybe the call he made should be to Aliz Willems.

"Where are you now?" she would say.

"Ibiza."

"Ibiza? What are you doing there?"

"I decided to retire. Want to come down?"

"Ibiza is one of my favorite places. Of course I want to come down."

He hopped onto the dock and tied off the boat. It was as natural to him as tying his shoes. The early morning sun felt...he could barely find a word for it. Beautiful. It felt beautiful. The smells came to him— the salt in the air, some hint of fish and the wrack along the tide line. He loved it. It made him want to dive in and go for a swim across the harbor. Just a long open water swim like back in SEAL training in Coronado, California. Well, maybe not *that* long.

New smells came to him on the breeze. Somewhere, there was fresh coffee and eggs and those long, deep-fried dough things dipped in sugar that the Spanish liked.

Breakfast. That's what he would do. He was going to put the suit on and go have breakfast at an outdoor café. Heck, he was in Spain. In time, later today even, he could make his way back to Madrid. Just turn up at the office as if nothing out of the ordinary had happened.

"Nice boat," someone said. "Where did you get it?"

Troy looked up. Standing about twenty feet away along the dock, leaning on a post, was big Jan Bakker, his arms folded in front of him, his ever-present thin-framed glasses softening his otherwise imposing features. He looked ready for the workday, in slacks, shoes, and a dress shirt. He didn't seem angry. He seemed like he might smile, as if something was funny to him.

"Oh, this old thing?" Troy said. "I found it. No one was using it, so I figured...you know. It would be okay if I borrowed it."

"It was quite a trip you made across the water, considering the storms. We lost touch with your beacon for quite a while, though I always assumed you'd turn up again."

Troy shrugged. "It felt like old times."

"An hour ago, it became clear to me you were making for Ibiza, so we came."

"Who are we?"

"Myself, Agent Dubois, and the pilot."

"How's Dubois doing? She okay?"

"She is very, very irritated."

Troy nodded. "Understandable, given the circumstances."

"Miquel is concerned," Jan said.

"I'll explain it to him."

Troy stepped into the boat, got his suit, and came back onto the dock. He carried the suit, shoes, and everything else in a bundle. He

172

and Jan walked down the dock toward a small parking lot at the end. A black sedan was parked there on the blacktop.

"The plane is waiting at the airport. We're returning to Geneva at once. Miquel has brought on an intelligence consultant, and now he's more convinced than ever that the ultimate target is CERN."

"A consultant, huh?"

Jan nodded. "Yes."

"How do you feel about that?"

It seemed like an odd move by Miquel, and probably not a response to Troy going cowboy during a slave auction in North Africa. Jan Bakker was supposed to be one of the best data analysts and overall intelligence agents in Europe. That's what everybody said. Why jump on another horse now?

Jan shrugged. "I do my job. I'm curious to learn what the new information is, if any. Other than that, I have no opinion."

They reached the parking lot. The smell of food cooking was much stronger here and was coming from the lowest street level along the waterfront. Troy could see a few people sitting out at tables in front of a cafe.

"Any time for breakfast?" Troy said. "I've been up all night without a bite to eat."

"You might remember," Jan said. "We have a coffee maker, some bottles of water, and pre-wrapped sandwiches on the plane. Also cookies."

"I remember," Troy said. "All too well."

The passenger seat of the sedan opened, and Dubois stepped out. She wore a dark blue jumpsuit, belted at the waist, and black boots. She had sunglasses on, and her thick, curly hair was up high with a red sash holding it in place.

She took the sunglasses off and put them on top of the car.

Her eyes were hard.

Troy tried to think of something funny, or maybe even flippant, to say. She had gotten out, as he had known she would. She'd had a jump start that a lot of people didn't have, including Troy himself. He had given her the time to escape. And now she seemed fine—angry yes, but not injured and none the worse for wear.

She walked slowly toward him.

"Agent Dubois," Troy said. "Good morning. Glad to see you're..."

"Where is the girl?"

"The girl is fine," Troy said, although he had no way of knowing that for certain. He had given her to Alex, and Alex had...disappeared. Troy took it on faith that wherever Alex went, if he escaped, he did the right thing.

"What does that mean?"

Troy shrugged. "It means she's with friendlies. She's safe."

"You lost her," Dubois said. It wasn't a question.

"No. I handed her to someone I trust."

Troy could feel the rage coming off Dubois in waves. Her body seemed to have a current of electricity flowing through it. She was trembling.

Adrenaline. Fight or flight. She was ramping up. She raised her arms.

"Who do you trust in Algiers? Who do you even know there? How did you get out of that basement alive? What are you not telling us?"

Troy was suddenly mindful that his feet were bare and his arms were full of clothes. He looked at Jan. The big man stood idly by, as if none of this was his concern. Back in the SEALs, guys got into scraps from time to time. Troy wouldn't expect that to be the case here in El Grupo, at least not between himself and Dubois.

"Dubois, don't get any ideas. It's not going to go the way you..."

She stepped forward and drove a right-hand punch directly into his face. It was a nice shot and his head snapped back.

"Dubois..."

She didn't stop, not for a second. She delivered a side kick to his midsection, catching him in the ribs on his left side. Her boot was heavy, and he felt it connect. If he wasn't careful, another shot like that was going to break his ribs.

"Dubois!"

"You nearly got me killed!"

A left hand came around and he ducked this one, only to catch a right-hand uppercut to his face again. He staggered backwards. She tagged him that time.

He dropped his bundle of clothes on the blacktop and bounced backwards, out of her reach. She kicked the suit, knocking the wallet sliding several feet through the parking lot. A handful of Euro bills made a mini tornado on the sea breeze.

Troy took a right-handed boxer's stance now. He was aware of how crazy it looked, a big man in his underwear and bare feet, squaring up with a tiny woman with a foot of Afro piled on top of her head and dressed like a Marxist guerrilla. In a parking lot at the local marina. And all before breakfast.

"Dubois, I swear to God. I'll knock you out if I have to."

"You almost got me killed," she said again.

He shook his head. "No I didn't. I gave you time to run. I almost got myself killed. But it was for a good cause, and I would do it again without hesitating."

She had a small holster on her belt. She reached inside and pulled the gun. It was a pistol, one of these small Nano-type guns. Troy didn't know the make or how many rounds it was holding. It must be European.

She pointed it right at him.

"Dubois," Jan said now. "That's taking it a little too…"

She ignored him.

"Last night," she said. "Last week. Every time we go on an operation, every time we leave the office, you almost get me killed. Don't you know that? I don't want to die, Stark. I'm not you. I'm not one of your special forces buddies. I didn't take an oath to die for America. I'm not from America! You watch too many American movies!"

Troy put his hands down. Okay. Okay, he got it.

"I'm sorry, Dubois. I am."

He meant it. He did. For the first time, he saw it from her perspective. Only now, it began to dawn on him.

"I understand. Shoot me, if you have to. If that'll make it…"

She threw the gun at him. He wasn't expecting it, but it came right at his mid-section, and he caught it. He even felt bad about that. He really was that guy. She threw the gun at him, and he caught it. She could have thrown a bomb at him, and he would have grabbed it in midair and tossed it in the ocean. He was gifted for starters, and he was about as well-trained as a human being could be. It was easy to overlook this.

Too easy.

"That's what you want!" she screamed. "You want to die. But I don't. And I'm so afraid that you're going to get me killed."

It was clear, Troy thought, that he didn't want to die. Far from it. But he didn't mention that now. It was the wrong time.

Jan stepped between them. His giant back hid Dubois from Troy's view.

"I hate you," he heard her say.

175

The remark pierced him like a spear. He stood, in an early morning parking lot, with the beautiful sea behind him, and the picturesque island village rising above him, impaled by Dubois's anger.

He didn't know where they went from here. It was him. He knew that. He had been drummed out of the Navy. Now he lived in some nether region in between worlds. He was a bad fit with the Europeans, and the Americans wouldn't offer him a straight job. They only wanted him so he could spy on the Europeans.

His closest partner, the person most similar to him in any of this work, was a ghost, a man who turned up unannounced and disappeared just as suddenly, and who wouldn't reveal his own name. And Troy had been put in this awkward place by his former commanding officer, someone who supposedly liked and respected him.

Troy was a hard person. He knew that about himself. He was trying to be a good person, but there were all these walls between him and other people. He had been out on the edge for a long time. He often forgot that the people around him had very little experience with the edge and didn't want to go there. It just slipped his mind.

Dubois was right. Given enough time, he was going to get her killed.

Troy sighed.

Maybe Miquel would do everyone a favor today and fire him.

CHAPTER TWENTY FIVE

3:05 pm Central European Time
Suisse Extended Stay Suites
Geneva Airport
Meyrin, Switzerland

"Goodness no," Miquel said. "Out of the question. I'm not going to fire you."

Troy stood and watched him but didn't respond. Miquel was wearing a blue dress shirt and slacks, along with leather work boots. He was drinking something hot from a white ceramic cup.

"I'm not going to accept your resignation either, if that's what you think."

They were in a suite of rooms in a nondescript airport hotel. Miquel must think of this as the command center. It had one bedroom, with two queen beds. It had a living room that currently had three laptops set across the long coffee table, with a bunch of other electronic equipment, and thick wires snaking along the floor. A fourth monitor was set on a table over in the corner. A fifth monitor, not attached to anything yet, was lying on its side on one of the beds in the bedroom.

Jan Bakker was here, with a headset on and carrying a long device that almost resembled one of the elongated dusters that housekeeping staff use to reach ceiling fans and along the tops of tall windows. He swiped along edges and under tables and under surfaces with that, while simultaneously watching a digital readout he held in his other hand. He was sweeping the place for listening devices.

He had apparently taken the large flat panel TV set off its mount, and then pulled the TV itself apart. Its hard plastic shell and various internal components were lying on the floor. He had done the same to a couple of lamps.

He had placed a small white noise machine on the floor near the door to the hallway: one in the living room and one in the bedroom. The low hum of static filled the place. It was a little bit distracting to talk over it.

177

Miquel gestured at the kitchen counter. There was a cheap coffee machine on top of it, the clear glass container filled halfway by dark liquid. "There's hot coffee if you want some. I just made it a little while ago."

"What about Dubois?"

Miquel shrugged. "She can have some, if she wants."

Troy's shoulders slumped.

"There will be plenty of food. I'm having them deliver enough to get us through the first day or two. I figured we'll camp out here for the duration and monitor the situation."

Miquel had moved hotels. They were nowhere near the water now. Instead, they were just three kilometers from the CERN campus and one kilometer from the airport. Miquel had scored an MH-6 helicopter for the occasion.

It was the chopper that Troy thought of as the "Little Bird," or the "Killer Egg," beloved by special operators and commandos. Interpol had acquired a few that were leftovers from United States NATO operations in Kosovo.

A typical Little Bird would be armed to the teeth with an M-134 minigun, Hydra rockets, and Hellfire or Stinger missiles. This one was apparently outfitted with no weapons at all. But it could put the group down anywhere on either of the CERN campuses within minutes. The chopper was currently parked at a small helipad owned by a private aviation company on a back lot of the airport. The pilot was on call. They could get to the pad by car from here in about two minutes.

It was a good set up. Jan would fly a low-elevation drone from here, and also had access to spy satellites. Meanwhile, Troy—and he supposed Dubois—could go anywhere in the area of operations very quickly. It made sense that the chopper was unarmed, since if they did go up, they'd be flying in an area heavily populated with civilians. They hadn't talked about personal weapons yet, but Troy assumed that conversation was coming.

"You know that's not what I mean," he said. "Dubois said she hates me."

Miquel shook his head. "She doesn't hate you. I've known Agent Dubois nearly her entire career. She's angry with you. She's worried about what you're going to do next. And she doesn't trust you right now."

Troy waited. He got it. He deserved this.

"I don't blame her," Miquel said. "You went on a surveillance mission together. Instead, you risked her life and yours. In the process, you killed several people and created an international incident. We are very lucky that no one has pointed a finger at us. I would not like to have El Grupo taken away from me so soon. You also lost the opportunity to engage the subject, which was why you went there in the first place."

"Do you know why I did all this?" Troy said.

Miquel nodded. "Of course I know why. But please consider. Had you engaged the subject, perhaps questioned him closely, we might know more about this upcoming attack, if it exists. It might even have been called off. We don't know. If my instinct is correct, many people could die in the next day or two, all for the..."

"The life of one little girl," Troy said.

"You lost sight of the bigger picture."

Troy nodded. "And I would do it again. You're talking about maybes, possibilities, things we don't know. I know that the girl escaped."

"Which is another question that arises," Miquel said. "Where is she now?"

"She's with friends," Troy said.

Here it comes.

"A mystery inside a mystery," Miquel said. "Agent Dubois, Agent Bakker..."

Troy glanced at Jan Bakker, who had finished his room sweep, and was now sitting at the three laptops in the living room, moving his attention from one to the next in a delicate ballet that only he understood. He was still acting as though this conversation wasn't taking place. He still had the headset on. Maybe that meant he couldn't hear the conversation. Or maybe he was amplifying it and piping it directly into his skull.

He was speaking in a low voice into the microphone. Troy couldn't hear what he was saying.

Miquel barely skipped a beat. "Agent Dubois, Agent Bakker, and myself are all interested to know how you made friends so quickly in a city like Algiers, in the middle of the night, during an emergency."

"You hired me," Troy said. "You know I was SEAL Team Three."

Miquel nodded. "With operations in Southwest Asia, yes. Or what many would call the Middle East. Tours of duty in Afghanistan, Iraq, and Syria. Other classified tours, assignments and loans to other

179

organizations that were not made available to me during the hiring process."

Troy nearly laughed. There was barely any hiring process. Miquel wanted him, and Miquel hired him. He didn't ask many questions.

"Algeria is in North Africa, not the Middle East," Miquel said.

Troy shrugged. "I operated throughout what you might call the Islamic world. And even beyond that. I have friends in a lot of places. I rescued the girl and brought her to some people I trust. She's safe now."

He had no idea if that was true or not. He hadn't seen or heard from Alex. He hadn't dared to call Missing Persons in New York, not with Jan Bakker hovering nearby. Troy didn't know what Alex did with the girl, or if he even made it out.

"I gave Dubois the chance to leave," he said. "She left. She's safe too. After it was all over, I came back to Europe and reconnected with the team as soon as I could, by the means that were available to me. That's the whole story. It's really that simple."

"I believe you," Miquel said. "But I think you're going to have earn Agent Dubois's trust back."

"That's going to be hard," Troy said. "Especially if we're paired together, riding a helicopter into the middle of a terrorist attack."

"I know," Miquel said and nodded. "Which is why we'll have a somewhat different arrangement on this operation, if it comes to that. I picture the helicopter as a roving operations command. I'll be in charge of it, in direct contact with Agent Bakker, who will be here. You and Agent Dubois will be with me, depending on circumstances."

"And who will I partner with, if not Dubois?"

He was half-expecting Miquel to say, "You will operate on your own." Troy would have welcomed that. Miquel had been right when he concocted that silly exercise before Troy left for the United States. These guys weren't special operators. They weren't what Miquel would call commandos, even if Miquel himself had been one when he was young. These were the police. They were well-trained and very smart. They were a pleasure to work with, generally speaking. And Troy was going to get one of them killed.

"There will be three of you, which will give Agent Dubois the option not to follow you, depending on your actions. You can call her free-floating. Meanwhile, you're going to partner with Agent Gallo."

"Agent Gallo?"

"Well," Miquel said. "Señor Gallo. He isn't a true agent of ours."

180

"Is this the consultant I heard about?"

"Yes." Miquel turned to Jan Bakker. "Jan, can you please ask Mr. Gallo to come in?"

Jan didn't stop what he was doing. "Of course." He pressed a button on a vertical touch screen in front of him, and a phone call window came up. Jan murmured something into his headset, then hit a red button to end the call.

"He's coming."

"Who is he?" Troy said.

"He's an American," Miquel said. "I don't know if you will like him, but I think you will understand each other. I've known him from when I was a young policeman. He was an American intelligence agent in the old days. I was undercover on the streets of Bilbao, pretending to be a drug dealer. He was pretending to be an international smuggler. We were trying to crack a gang of Basque separatists who were funding their bombs with the cocaine trade. Those seem like quaint times now."

"Then he's CIA," Troy said.

"He's self-employed."

Troy didn't know what he was expecting when they told him Miquel was bringing on a consultant. He supposed he figured it would be a young German guy in a suit and wearing glasses, who would lecture Troy on police brutality and the rights of the accused. What he didn't expect was ex-CIA. He didn't know if he liked that idea or not. But one thing was sure, Miquel was full of surprises.

"Well, this should be..."

He turned toward the door, and the man was already standing there. Physically, he made an impression. He had a white beard framing his face and a shock of white hair on top of his head. He was wearing polarized sunglasses, even though he was indoors.

He stood about six feet tall and was very tan, with broad shoulders and big arms. He wore a colorful flower-patterned button-up shirt tight to his big upper body, with the top two buttons unbuttoned. There was some kind of medallion hanging there.

His sleeves were rolled about halfway up his veiny forearms. Wrapped around his right arm was some kind of razor wire tattoo that came just past his elbow. There was a gold watch on his wrist, hanging loose.

The guy looked a movie director, which is to say, he looked ridiculous.

He came all the way into the room and let the door close slowly behind him.

"What should it be, Troy?" he said.

Troy shook his head and smiled. "It should be one for the time capsule."

"Troy Stark, meet Carlo Gallo."

Gallo raised a strong hand. "Carl. Please. My parents called me Carlo, but Carlo Gallo? It doesn't go. For some reason, Miquel insists on calling me that."

Troy held out a hand and the two men shook.

"I've heard a lot about you, Troy. And read a lot."

Troy nearly sighed but contained himself. Already, the guy was at it. They were always this way, the freelancers. They had been inside, and they still had friends inside. They had a million contacts. They wanted you to know that. Classified paperwork got legs, walked out the door, and somehow found its way into their hands.

"You've seen my files, I guess."

Gallo shrugged. "I was Special Operations Group for ten years. You know how that goes. If someone has worked for SOG, I've probably seen the file. Metal shop? That's quite an assignment. They only take the baddest of the bad. You're an impressive guy, Stark. You step in sheep dip from time to time, but I don't have anything against that. You might say I've done the same."

Troy shook his head. He was taking a disliking to this guy immediately. If Gallo was hoping to endear himself, this wasn't the way to go about it.

"See, it's already wrong. You don't announce that you were SOG. You don't tell me you know I was SOG once upon a time. Who does that? It's a not a social club. You're not supposed to acknowledge that it exists. This other thing? Metal shop? I haven't heard that term since the seventh grade."

Troy looked at Miquel. "Who is this guy, really?"

"He's who he says he is."

Troy shook his head. He turned back to Gallo. "Why didn't you just stay with the agency? You could have walked off with a nice pension at the end. A guy your age, you'd probably be retired now."

Gallo shrugged and smiled. "Why didn't you stay with the Navy?"

That slowed Troy down a step.

"Okay. Point taken."

"I go where the money is," Gallo said. "I run my business out of Amsterdam. There's a lot of money in Amsterdam. There's a lot of money in Europe, and Amsterdam is right smack in the middle of it."

"Why are you with us, in that case? If you're about money?"

"Miquel and I are old friends. I'm sure he told you that. He asked me to jump on board."

"And you're coming in? If we go?"

Gallo patted his flat stomach. "Of course I am. I stay in shape for a reason."

"I am thinking that you and Carlo could be partners for this operation," Miquel said. "Just one time. We'll see how it goes. Agent Dubois has concerns, as we talked about, and I respect those. Carlo doesn't have the same concerns."

"We haven't done any training together," Troy said.

Gallo laughed. "I have a feeling that we'll be on the same page in the playbook pretty quickly."

"It's not supposed to be an open book," Troy said.

Gallo slowly removed his sunglasses. "You have a lot to learn, Stark," he said. "You just entered private life. You're not government-issue anymore. You can say anything you want out here. Guys who were in Delta Force are writing books now. They're not supposed to admit Delta exists, but they do, and they do it in public. Guys who were on Top Secret JSOC infiltration and assassination teams are writing books."

"And that's okay with you?" Troy said.

Gallo shook his head. "I don't even know myself. Not really, I guess. Look, don't listen to me. Half the time I just prattle on, and it makes no sense. I must have early-onset dementia."

He glanced at the kitchen counter. "Hey, is that coffee fresh? I'm dying for a cup."

"Help yourself," Troy said. "I just made it."

Gallo nodded. "Good man."

He went about getting a white ceramic cup out of the cabinet and poured himself some of the coffee. It didn't look like great coffee. In fact, it looked like an oil slick. Troy and Miquel watched him while he worked. Troy looked at Miquel. Miquel had a sort of half-smile on his face. He seemed to think this guy's performance was funny. Or maybe he was just remembering old times.

"The way I see it," Gallo said. "You got big problems."

"We do? Does that include you?"

Gallo shrugged. "Sure. I'll own it with you. I'm on the payroll now. For now. We got big problems. This operation is like looking for a needle in a haystack."

He paused. There wasn't much to his coffee making. He took the oil slick black, so he just poured it into the cup, and he was ready. He shook his head.

"No, that's not right. It's like a game of whack-a-mole at the carnival. There's no way of telling if the terrorists are going to hit here or not. But I do think Miquel is right, and they are going to hit here."

Troy nearly smiled again. It was the consultant's job to agree with the boss. The boss was paying him because he thought a terrorist attack was coming. So, as a matter of course, Gallo was going to think the same thing.

"But if they do, who's to say they're going to hit the Large Hadron Collider? Why would they? It's the hardest thing to hit in the whole place. It's the hardest thing to reach. Why not hit one of the gatherings or parties during the event? Why not hit one of the smaller inventions, one with a lot of radioactive material stored up? There are over a dozen high-tech gizmos here, and at least twenty separate projects. There are at least two highly secret projects with military applications. Why not hit those, if you know what they are? Why not wait until the hubbub dies down and hit two weeks from now?"

He paused, and Troy jumped in.

"Secret projects with military applications."

Troy looked at Jan. Jan was still immersed in his computers and digital readouts. This was the first anyone had mentioned secret projects.

Gallo scratched his face near his white beard. "Yeah. At least two. Don't ask me what they are because I don't know. What I do know is there's traffic of encrypted messages going out of here, to the United States Department of Defense, in particular the Defense Advanced Research Projects Agency and the Defense Intelligence Agency. That's been going on for years. Whatever they're doing, the Yankee doodles are keeping an eye on it."

"You know they're sending information to the feds, but you don't know what it is," Troy said.

Gallo nodded. "That's right."

Troy didn't like that, either. The United States had its own high-tech research. It had entire industries, universities, and government

184

agencies devoted to it. It didn't really need CERN. Also, CERN was far from a top-secret facility.

"The terrorists are supposed to be environmentalists," Troy said. "That's the assumption we've been going with. The enviros don't like modern technology. They don't like scientists playing Frankenstein."

Gallo shook his head. "I don't think that's it. I can't be sure at this stage, but my gut tells me no."

"Do tell." Again, Troy didn't like this. He didn't like Gallo's style. He also didn't love the unsettled feeling that came when some guy walked in at random and claimed to know things nobody else knew.

"Have you ever been around environmentalists?" Gallo said. "I mean the ones that blow things up. I used to do surveillance on them. They aren't good at what they do, generally speaking. They get lucky here and there, but you can't expect them to consistently pull it off. They don't usually have any military training. They hate the military. They have no resources. The people themselves are eccentrics. Getting them all rowing in the same direction is like herding a thousand cats. Also, they don't want to hurt anyone. In all the so-called green scare attacks I saw going back twenty years, no one, not one person, was killed. It was rare that anyone even got hurt."

He paused and shook his head. "If this was really environmentalists, I wouldn't be concerned about it. And I am concerned."

"In that case, what is it?"

Gallo shrugged. "I don't know. Did you notice any countries that do high-tech research conspicuously missing from the CERN members list?"

"Sure, lots of them. Russia, China, Japan, Iran, South Korea, South Africa. And that's just for starters."

Gallo nodded. "Right. Leave off Japan for now since CERN scientists likely share information with them willingly. Leave off South Africa and South Korea because they're small potatoes."

"Okay, so Russia, China, and Iran."

"Right. Leave off Iran because they're a pariah state. Almost nobody wants to deal with them. But then you've got China and Russia, two world powers, locked out of some of the highest tech projects on Earth. Dismissed. They can't like that. I think we know for a fact that they don't. And if there's military applications…"

He didn't bother to finish the sentence.

"I think you see my point."

"Is this the consultant?" a voice said.

Troy looked toward the door and Dubois was standing there. She had slipped in silently and unnoticed. She was already dressed in a black jumpsuit, ready for action. It was the middle of the afternoon. Troy supposed she liked to get a head start on things.

She looked great, as always. The jumpsuit was tight to her body. Her hair was subdued by a black bandana. She had big black boots on. She would be in her urban guerrilla fighter style, except for one thing—the black jumpsuit said INTERPOL in white letters across the front of it.

It was pretty snazzy. Troy didn't dare say a word about it. Miquel must have broken the piggy bank and sprung for new outfits. Thankfully, he went with INTERPOL instead of ERRIU.

Gallo's eyes lit up at the sight of Dubois. "Well, well, well. What kind of exotic creature do we have here? Yes, I am the consultant."

Dubois's dark eyes shifted from Gallo to Troy and back again.

"So, you'll be the one Agent Stark gets killed, instead of me?"

"I will die for you, little lady."

Dubois nodded. "Thank you. I'm too young to die. But you look like you're the perfect age."

CHAPTER TWENTY SIX

3:45 pm Central European Time
An old sewer works
Geneva, Switzerland

"Killing people will not help us."

The man who once called himself Purple Hays was speaking. His name was Scott Free now. When she knew him before, it seemed like he had an accent from somewhere, maybe Eastern Europe. There was a vague hint of a vampire voice to him, like Transylvania. Now he had no accent of any kind. It wasn't even the Midwest of the United States. He was the man from nowhere.

"Necessary murders are one thing," he said. "Frivolous murders are quite another."

Princess Dye watched him. He was a big man, with medium length dirty-blonde hair. Not long ago, he had been bald. He couldn't have grown the hair in this short time. It must be a wig, but it was a convincing one.

The scar that had marked his face was gone. He had tattoos of anchors on the backs of his hands. The tattoos were very noticeable and would probably be gone tomorrow. So would the hair and the dark eyes.

The eyes cut like lasers. His big hands, and really his whole body, moved when he talked, almost as though he couldn't stop them. He seemed to have explosive energy in that body, just barely contained. She could picture him as a younger man, playing rugby or some other violent contact sport, blasting through men who were just like him.

He had always seemed big, but now he seemed like a giant. She looked at his feet. Naturally, he was wearing platform shoes. They were probably adding two or three inches to his height.

She could almost picture how he would look tomorrow afternoon. Tall, but not gigantic. Blue-eyed, bald, with a visible scar but no visible tattoos. Perhaps he would have a beard. She could see him hanging out at an ex-patriot pub in the south of France or the south of Spain, affecting an English accent and acting as though he had always been there. Would it be enough? She supposed that was his problem.

He was addressing them in some sort of underground tunnel system. This was a large open space made of brick at the confluence of five tunnels. The tunnels were below them, and some dark, fetid water trickled through them. Everything was dirty, muddy, or caked in grease.

Somewhere nearby was the sound of water rushing. It sounded like a lot of water. There were several metal wheels mounted on the walls, with pegs protruding from them that seemed like hand grips. Princess Dye guessed that at some point in the past, men came down here and opened and closed water tunnels by hand. Maybe they still did.

There were ten people at the meeting. Princess Dye was the only woman. Oil Derek from the Massachusetts operation was here. He was calling himself Izzy Bad. He had brown dreadlocks now. She couldn't seem to remember what his hair had been like before. There had always been something nondescript about him. He rarely spoke during their time in Massachusetts. He didn't want you to remember him. When those dreadlocks were gone, he would evaporate into just about any crowd.

Marcus Aurelius was also here. Princess Dye hadn't talked to him and had just barely acknowledged him. She didn't know what he was calling himself now. He looked much the same as the last time she had seen him. He was a fool, and as far as she was concerned, his operation had been a disaster.

The group had coalesced here, after entering the sewer system at different points, so as not to call attention to themselves. Thomas had known the way to this spot, and Princess Dye had simply followed along with him.

"We're not here to hurt anybody," Scott Free said. "On the contrary. We're here to save them. We can't completely destroy the target, but we can do massive damage to it, and we can call the world's attention to its dangers. But bear in mind. Every hostage is precious. Not only are they someone's mother, father, sister, child, or lover, they're also our ticket out of here. We're all going to walk away from this, and we're going to do it the same way the hostages do."

Princess Dye glanced at Thomas. She would love to know what was going on in his mind right now. Last night, he had wanted to leave, at least partially, because he thought Scott Free was a madman and a gleeful killer.

He sounded nothing like that now. He displayed complete confident in himself, in this team, and in the plan they were about to carry out. Why shouldn't he? The last operation had gone off as smoothly as

188

possible. No one got caught. The enemy facility had been utterly destroyed. Some people had died, but they were ones who were complicit in the operation of the facility.

"Where are my runners?" Scott said.

Princess Dye raised her hand, so did Thomas and Izzy. They stood close together. They were a team. They had pulled off a thing of beauty once before. They were assigned to carry out nearly the exact same task on this job.

"You guys are rock stars," Scott said. "Okay? Rock stars. That's nearly all I have to say." He seemed like he was on the verge of saying something more specific about the previous operation but stopped himself. "Move fast. Faster than you've ever moved before. But be meticulous. The rest of us, my people here, will be holding down the fort. We're going into action at precisely 6:45. When you guys turn up, we all know it'll be time to leave. So give us an extra minute or two. You do that by moving fast."

He raised one big finger, a pointer. He was either a natural born leader, or he practiced this stuff in front of a mirror.

"But be meticulous. There's no sense going fast and not having it work." Now he raised his hands in the air, almost as if in supplication. "If it works, we will all walk away. If it doesn't, they're waiting for us."

Compartmentalize.

The word occurred to her again. Princess Dye didn't know what Izzy Bad was going to be doing after they planted the charges, but she and Thomas had an appointment in another part of the building. They were going to have to move very fast, even faster than Scott Free suggested. They were just never going to show up at the main event.

She felt odd about that. It was a betrayal. But there were betrayals on top of betrayals now. She had also betrayed Silvio.

If Scott was the crazy murderer that Thomas believed him to be, then he was betraying Silvio too. Silvio wanted to create a better world. It was his passion, the reason he had come here in the first place.

"Are there any questions?" Scott said now.

He looked around at the group, meeting each set of eyes.

"Don't hold your tongue, then wish you hadn't."

Again, he waited.

"No? Good. Let's do it. We can't know what the future will bring, but I hope I will see you and work with you again one day. And I hope the spirit of the natural world guides you and protects you."

189

Princess Dye smiled. He was laying it on thick now. This wasn't his personality at all. The last time she had known him, he was a stern taskmaster.

Everyone changed, all the time. People in this movement changed at warp speed. They were constantly shifting, moving, disappearing, and turning up somewhere else, looking and acting different.

Sometimes, it exhausted her. At that flat in Brooklyn and at that flat in Berlin, she had felt dead inside, empty, and completely alone. But now, here, among these people, on the move, and about to make it happen one more time...

She loved it.

She could almost forget that she was playing for two teams at once.

"Let's go," she said to Thomas and Izzy. "Let's hit it."

CHAPTER TWENTY SEVEN

6:15 pm Central European Time
8th Floor, Center 42
CERN
Meyrin, Switzerland

"You people can go to hell."

The white-haired man sat at his desk in an unkempt office piled high with papers, several stories above the black-tie opening gala that was slowly gathering force on the main floor. His name was Oleg Karolyi, and the very large handgun he normally kept in the top drawer of his desk was in his right hand. The gun was a Smith & Wesson .44 Magnum Model 29 revolver. It was loaded with six bullets, though he would probably only need one.

In his left hand was a shot glass half full of vodka. The bottle sat on a pile of notebooks in front of him. In one sudden movement, he tilted his head back and poured the vodka down his throat. The delightful burn came to him like a line of fire along his throat and into his belly.

God. That was good.

Below him, he could hear the strains of background music—the organization had hired a cellist and piano player for the check-in period. He could hear the hum of people talking as the crowd accumulated.

Oh, the important people! They were pushing at the frontiers of science! They were lighting our way through the darkness. Right now, they must be sipping wine, eating cheese, and chatting together in a polyglot of languages about the wonderful progress they were making. They were very pleased with themselves.

The overall event, the Triumph of Knowledge, was an insult. If they had been trying to humiliate and further break the spirit of a broken old man, they couldn't do a better job than they had done.

For many years, Oleg had been the lead researcher on a dismal failure of a project that once seemed to hold so much promise. Indeed, you might even say he was the only researcher left. Everyone from his generation had retired or died. Younger people had moved on to other ideas with better funding and better opportunities to step into the

191

limelight. The romance of laboring anonymously and secretly no longer held much allure. Oleg had defected to the West from the Soviet Union decades ago, in an era when nearly everything that mattered was done in secret. He was highly esteemed in those days. It was a coup to steal him away from the communists!

Had he just thought that younger people had moved on to other ideas with better funding? It wasn't quite true, was it? No. They had moved on to better ideas in general. The idea that Oleg had spent his entire adult life on had turned out to be a colossal waste of time, money, his own personal energies, his enthusiasm, optimism, youth, and then his middle age. All slowly drained away.

The famous American inventor Edison was said to have once remarked after one of thousands of botched attempts to perfect the incandescent light bulb, "I have not failed ten thousand times. I've successfully found ten thousand ways that will not work."

This quote was almost certainly spurious, a capitalist old wives' tale spawned to convince mediocre American minds that anyone could become a great captain of industry if they only tried hard and long enough.

But it was applicable to Oleg's life, if only in an ironic way. For long years, he had discovered, over and over again, countless ways not to make a particle beam weapon. He supposed it was his own fault. If he searched his heart, he could see that he already knew it was impossible, given the limitations of human understanding twenty years ago. He should have moved on then. But he had already invested twenty years at that point.

He could scream. Forty years had been squandered. It was too much to accept. Even allowing himself to think about it was too much. He would slam the door of his mind shut if he could.

It wasn't that a particle beam weapon was impossible. That wasn't accurate. Given current technologies, particle beams as we understood them had to run along a pre-existing track. They ran particle beams in the various accelerators here at CERN night and day. That problem was solved in the 1950s.

But what good was it? A particle beam weapon implied that there was no track to guide it. If you were to fire a particle beam at a naval destroyer in the ocean, the enemy navy wasn't going to stand idly by for years while you spent millions of dollars constructing an accelerator up to the side of their precious ship.

His life's work was a bust. It was a disaster. He still dutifully sent encrypted reports to the American military intelligence agencies that sponsored his work here, but he knew what they thought of him. He was an embarrassment. He was a Cold War relic. His budget was a rounding error. If anyone spoke of him at all, it was probably to make a joke by the water cooler. He was a laughingstock.

They were waiting for him to die, and then they would close the book on yet another stupid episode in the history of American-Soviet relations. Remember how they were going to race each other across the solar system, claiming and colonizing the outer planets? Remember how they were going to defeat each other using remote viewing and other psychic phenomena? Remember the mobile nuclear missiles on truck beds along the line of contact? Remember how the Americans were hiding the bodies of four crashed aliens from outer space and were learning to use captured alien technologies?

Oleg's efforts belonged to that silly and dangerous era. He was inventing a space age weapon for a space age that never arrived. It was a curiosity, an artifact of another time. He could be a man in a wax museum, except there was no reason to celebrate him in a museum because his ideas didn't work.

Sometime in the past two years (he didn't remember exactly when—the vodka had begun to cloud his thinking), he had taken to sending encrypted emails out into the world, hinting there had been a breakthrough in the study of particle beam weapons. It was the adolescent vandal in him coming to the fore.

He sent the emails to dummy civilian email accounts he had created himself. He received them off-campus, sometimes at his own home, masking the whereabouts of the accounts using a VPN. It was a rudimentary, off-the-shelf security setup with encryption that any intelligence agency should easily break. But no one did. That was because no one cared. No one was monitoring his activities. He was well and truly forgotten.

Below him, the sounds of the gala continued to rise up through the building. It was like a gathering storm that would blow his house down. He was thinking very seriously about ruining their party by shooting himself in the head.

The giant handgun was absurdly powerful, a leftover from his days of being enamored with everything American. One shot under the chin should blast a catastrophic hole up through his brain and out the top of his skull. A bit more vodka and he might have the courage to go through with it.

In front of him on the desk was a piece of paper with a scribbled note on it. Before today, he had thought long and hard about what such a note should entail, but today, nothing would come to him. The words on that paper were the best he could do:

Messy, isn't it?

He giggled quietly. If nothing else, perhaps people would remember and respect him for his sense of humor.

CHAPTER TWENTY EIGHT

6:20 pm Central European Time
The Antimatter Factory
The Antiproton Decelerator
CERN
Meyrin, Switzerland

"These clothes are too much," Princess Dye said.

The other two didn't respond to her.

It was a cool evening, and might become a cold night, but she was wearing three layers of clothes, not counting her underwear. She had a white lab coat on top with a lightweight black jumpsuit underneath.

Beneath the jumpsuit were the black pants and white dress shirt of the catering staff. Beneath that was a wrinkle-free shimmering blue dress, mostly bunched around her waist, that if necessary, would indicate she was an invited guest to the gala.

She could change identities at a moment's notice. In fact, the three of them had entered the campus dressed as caterers and driving a catering van. Where the identities as caterers had come from, and how they passed muster with the guard at the gate, wasn't her department.

The science clothes were in the back of the van, piled behind the cakes, pies, and other dessert goodies they were supposedly bringing in for the event. But they weren't going to the event.

Right now, there was a heavy backpack over her shoulder, filled with explosive charges. Both Thomas and Izzy Bad were carrying similar backpacks. They were ready to make a mighty big bang.

The three of them stood near a small, one-story concrete outbuilding on a grassy knoll. There was a large tree overhead. The night was already dark, and they almost seemed like the shadows of the tree's branches.

As they watched, a man in a dark sweatshirt, his hood pulled up to hide his face, walked toward them. He didn't acknowledge or even look at them. Instead he went straight to the concrete pillbox. A card reader stood on one spindly leg next to the metal door to the building.

The man went to the card reader and flashed a white employee card in front of it. Then he grasped the door handle, turned it, and pushed the door open. A second later, and without a word, he turned and walked back the way he had come.

Thomas darted to the door and caught it before it closed. He turned, looked at her and Izzy, and smiled. "Masks up," he said. "We're in."

He pulled the black bandana from around his throat, up over the lower parts of his face, and then finally over his nose. He tightened it around the back of his head.

Princess Dye glanced past him into the building. This was a utility entrance. The doorway opened to an iron stairwell that went nowhere but down. The stairwell was lit with weak overhead lights.

She pulled her balaclava up over her face.

She, Thomas, and Izzy were now three sets of eyes staring at each other.

"Ready?" Thomas said. "Almost the same exact thing as before."

Princess Dye nodded. "Ready."

"Ready," Izzy said.

"This is for all the marbles," Thomas said.

He turned and went down the stairs, Princess Dye just two steps behind him, and Izzy right on her heels.

CHAPTER TWENTY NINE

6:25 pm Central European Time
Suisse Extended Stay Suites
Geneva Airport
Meyrin, Switzerland

"What are you doing, Jan?"

They were all in various parts of the hotel suite. Troy was lounging on a flower-patterned easy chair, the chair kicked all the way back like a dentist's chair, the footrest and the headrest extended. He was tired, nearly exhausted, after the night he'd had.

These guys had slept last night, at least a little bit. He hadn't.

Troy was wearing the new Interpol jumpsuit that Miquel had conjured. It had a base layer of super-light dragon skin armor, fit his body well, and had pockets galore. There was a vest that went with it that he hadn't put on yet. The vest had plate inserts for added protection. The suit also came with a helmet with radio functionality inside of it. That hadn't been tested yet in the field.

His boots were on. His gun, a standard-issue Glock 19 was sitting on the little table at his elbow. That was the best Miquel could get authorization for them to carry. It was a very good gun, but it meant they were going in light.

He was sipping a can of cold Rock Star Zero he'd found in the refrigerator. They must sell them around here somewhere. It had two cups of coffee worth of caffeine in it, along with a massive dose of vitamin B for energy. He didn't want to get caught napping. Everyone was dressed and ready for action. They could get called any minute, or they could spend the entire weekend hanging around and never do anything.

There wasn't a real good reason for the terrorists to hit tonight. Tomorrow was the big demonstration of the Large Hadron Collider. Tomorrow was when the most visiting dignitaries would be on campus, the most media, and even a couple of Nobel Prize winners. Tonight was just the welcome.

Jan's workstation had morphed into seven monitors in a row on two long tables, four of which were laptops. There were two other sets of keyboards. There was an additional server under the table, and three other smaller black devices with red and green LED lights. Wires snaked to three different surge protectors, taking up nearly every wall socket in the room.

"I'm monitoring the environment for anomalies," Jan said. His broad back was to Troy, and his hands moved from keyboard to keyboard as images flitted across each screen, changing every few seconds. He was wearing the same headset with earphones and extended microphone he'd been wearing earlier.

"I've been doing this for much of the day. I was trying to do it in Geneva, hoping to catch the terrorist group gathering, but, of course, the city is too big for discrepancies to stand out."

"As a practical matter," Carl Gallo said, "they probably know someone is doing what you're doing, and they've taken steps to stay invisible to you."

Gallo was sprawled out on a couch with a pile of pillows under his head, and his black boots up on a new coffee table.

Jan nodded his big bald head. "Yes. In the city, they can do that. Once they emerge on the CERN campus, if they do, I will spot them."

Troy watched the screens. There was a curving underground tunnel, with a super collider running along it. In the right-hand corner were the letters LHC. There were people in matching black pants and white shirts setting up inside an event space, getting ready for tonight's opening party. Center 42, it said in the corner of the screen. There was an aerial shot of the campus, cars flowing along and people moving like ants, the sun fading to the west over the curving horizon line. There was a ground-level shot taken at one of the entry gates, as two guards checked the credentials of people in a line of cars snaking from the roadway.

More views popped up, staying for several seconds, then disappeared again. Jan's hands moved like those of a piano player, from keyboard to keyboard. His head swiveled side to side, eyes bouncing from one screen to the next.

Troy glanced into the nearest bedroom. Dubois was in there, sitting on the bed, disarming dummy versions of the explosives used in the Massachusetts attack. They were flat circular charges, roughly the size and shape of hockey pucks. There was adhesive backing on each one.

They were essentially containers holding small round bricks of C4, with a chemical accelerant in a glass ampule to ignite the C4. The accelerant was protected inside a tiny steel box. To arm the charge, the terrorist needed only to twist it open, which slid one wall of the steel box away, exposing the ampule. Then the terrorist could stick it to a wall or other surface and move on.

By planting one every twenty or thirty meters, you were creating a daisy chain where each new explosion ignited the next one in line. To disarm it, a person had to peel the charge off whatever surface it was stuck to, then carefully twist the device closed again, making sure the tiny steel box shut firmly and completely. Dubois was practicing this, again and again, getting it into her motor memory.

Troy and Dubois had barely spoken.

"I'm still here because I'm a professional," she had told him, in the few words she had been willing to share. "But please know that I resent you compromising missions and putting my life in danger on a whim."

It was hardly a whim, he had almost said but didn't.

"I respect that," he'd said instead. "And I promise I'm going to do better."

Troy didn't know how he was supposed to make good on that promise. The bad thing that he had done, he would do again.

"How did you get that underground collider footage?" he said now to Jan. "Did they authorize that?"

Jan shook his head. "Unfortunately, no. I've had to take extraordinary measures to gain access to as many of the video feeds on campus as I can."

Troy glanced at Miquel, who was in the other bedroom. He was sitting on a bed in there, murmuring to someone on a cell phone.

"You hacked it," Gallo said. "You hacked the CERN security footage?"

Jan shrugged. "In a word, yes. I had no choice. It would have taken days or weeks to gain access to their security system, and there was no guarantee that they would even comply with my request. They're certainly under no mandate to do so. And we need the data now. It's best for everyone that we have it. Miquel agreed with me on this. He said he would manage any concerns with CERN if they catch us at it."

"Do you have the entry codes, the names on the ID cards, all that stuff?" Troy said.

"Of course. The footage wouldn't be much good by itself, would it? It's too easy to misinterpret. I decided I should just take everything."

199

"Well, so much for their cutting-edge security system."

Jan nodded. "So it would seem."

Troy took a sip of his Rock Star. He was going to have to sleep at some point, maybe tonight after the first gala was over. But just because the party ended didn't mean the danger did. The attack in Massachusetts took place in the middle of the night when no one was around.

The Rock Star didn't seem to be helping. Troy felt that if he closed his eyes right now, he would drift off. He looked at Jan again. Jan seemed fresh and alert.

Troy should just let go for a bit. If something happened, he was right here. They could wake him up.

He took a deep breath. Okay. His eyelids fluttered down. He was sitting across from Aliz Willems in the outdoor Madrid restaurant again, the jet fireplace a few feet to his right, casting a warm glow on his face.

"I have something," Jan said. He said it calmly, dispassionately, as if having something was the same as not having anything.

"What is it?" Gallo said.

"Three people. They appear to be two men and a woman. They're wearing lab smocks and black masks. They're carrying backpacks. They entered the facility for the Antiproton Decelerator through a utility entrance, not the main entrance. One identity card swiped, three people entered."

Gallo was already on his feet, moving in behind Jan to watch the screen.

Troy moved his chair into the upright position, eyes blinking. He grunted. He had been ten seconds from fast asleep.

He looked at the screen. It showed a wide angle view of what looked like a large concrete warehouse or loading dock. It was brightly lit. A thick yellow stripe ran along the ground. Banks of machines stood in a row. It was hard to say what they were. Iron stairs with no-slip runners climbed two stories to another platform with a yellow metal fence around it. Across the way there was a similar blue-caged platform.

A crimson and white Harvard flag hung from one wall. Words that had no meaning to him were painted on the walls. ATRAP. ALPHA. ASACUSA.

As he watched, three people in lab coats and masks came down the stairs in a single file line. They seemed to be the only people present. They went below the camera's view for a moment, then re-emerged,

200

following the thick yellow line on the floor. They moved off into the near distance, walking between two more high platforms.

"Follow the yellow brick road," Jan said.

"Where is that?" Gallo said.

Jan's left hand moved an inch, and an interactive map of the campus appeared on the screen just to his right. In a few seconds, the map zoomed in on AD—Antiproton Decelerator. A blue line extended from it to the giant ring of the Large Hadron Collider, and the smaller ring of the Super Proton Synchrotron, about a quarter of a mile away. It connected to the two rings where the rings themselves seemed to meet.

An orange line extended from the AD toward a large building closer to the entrance of the campus. Jan zoomed in on that building. CENTER 42. A stack of names appeared next to the title. AWARE Experiment. ACOG Experiment. LINEAR Accelerator Research. Niels Bohr Event Center. Others.

"That's a problem," Jan said. "The lines mean there are tunnels present from one facility to the other. The Niels Bohr Event Center is where the opening event is, starting right now. These people are either going to the Large Hadron Collider or to the opening event. Neither one seems good."

Troy pulled himself to his feet. The Rock Star hadn't done much, but he felt that old surge of adrenaline.

Dubois walked in from the other room. "Are we on?"

"Looks like it. Maybe."

Another video image came up. In the right corner, it said: LINEAR Accelerator. It showed a narrow tunnel, and the three people moving along it.

"They're on their way to Center 42," Jan said. "That's where the party is."

"How far apart are the buildings?" Gallo said.

"About four hundred meters. Can someone alert Miquel that..."

But Miquel was already in the room. He appeared there watching the three people on video as if he was conjured from out of a mist.

"How did they get in?" he said.

Jan pulled up a data screen. "It was an entry by someone named Alain Drury, 41-year-old accelerator technician. It's a breach of security."

"I'll bet Alain Drury is dead," Miquel said. "Good work, Jan. Please alert CERN security and tell them where the breach is. Alert the local fire departments. Alert civil defense in Switzerland and France and let them know we may need radiation decontamination. Alert Center 42 and tell them to evacuate the party immediately. But first, alert the helicopter and tell the pilot to start up. We'll be at the pad in three minutes."

Jan's hands were moving fast now. A phone call came up on one of the screens. It went from red to green. Then Jan was murmuring into his headset.

"Are we sure of all this?" Troy said. His brain was riddled with cobwebs. He blinked again. To tell all those people that this was the attack, with so little information to go on... *Three people are inside a tunnel! Alert civil defense!*

It seemed like a risk. Miquel could become the boy who cried wolf.

"I'm sure," Miquel said, and handed Troy his helmet. "Let's move, guys."

Troy shrugged. "Well, if you're sure, then I am too."

He picked up his gun off the table. He glanced at Dubois. Their eyes met for a second. Troy couldn't tell what was in those eyes. He hated the thought that someone, a teammate, wouldn't want to ride with him.

That the person was Dubois made it even harder.

But there was no time for that now. He had to shrug that off.

"Rock and roll," he said.

CHAPTER THIRTY

6:35 pm Central European Time
The Skies Above CERN
Approaching the Antimatter Factory
Meyrin, Switzerland

The pilot mumbled something to Miquel, who was sitting next to him.

"ETA thirty seconds," Miquel said.

Troy glanced out the open bay door to his left. The large office building Center 42 was lit up in light blue for the gala. The parking lot over there was full. People milled around outside the building. A larger crowd must already be inside. The event was supposed to begin at 6:30.

Nothing had started happening over there yet. There were no fire trucks, and no police cars. There were no sirens. No one was running. If Jan had sent out the alert, and Troy was sure he had, no one was taking it too seriously just yet.

No one but us.

The chopper was flying low and moving fast. Many of the offices in the buildings here were lit, probably with people working late. The campus roadways and paths were lit dimly. Ahead, in the near distance, beyond the edge of the campus, were the dark low mountains of France.

Troy was fully awake now. The fear, the adrenaline, that rush of excitement, had hit his veins like a drug. He felt alive and alert.

THIS was the feeling.

It wasn't just like a drug. It was a drug. And he was addicted to it.

He turned to the others. They were helmeted, visors up. Dubois was in the middle, shoulder to shoulder with Troy. Gallo was on the far side. Their eyes were on Troy. Gallo's were sharp, but relaxed. Dubois's were open and nervous.

The old instructions came to him of their own accord.

"Fast rope, we go over the falls. You've both done this before. Do it clean and crisp. Gallo, you and me first. Dubois, two seconds after we hit."

He paused. "Roger?"

"Roger."

Dubois spoke a second later, slightly hesitant. This wasn't second nature to her. And it was happening in her third language. Troy understood that. Even so:

"Roger," she said.

"Jan, can you hear me?"

"Loud and clear."

"How's that access coming?"

Jan was hacking the door lock to the utility entrance. Troy wanted to go in a side door, so they didn't get tangled up with campus guards or local cops.

"I've got it ready. I will pop it on your command."

"Good man." Troy looked across Dubois at Gallo. "Gallo, hit the ground, get out of Dubois's way. She's coming out your door. Be ready to lay down covering fire if need be. We'll move to the building fast and spread out."

Gallo nodded and smiled. "Textbook."

"Textbook, buddy," Troy said. "It's gotta be that way."

"Roger that."

They shouldn't need any covering fire. They shouldn't need to spread out. But the idea was to do it right. You could never know.

"The subjects have moved down the tunnel," Jan said. "I no longer have a visual on them. I cannot seem to find one. There's a camera on at the experimental area beneath Center 42, but they haven't reached there yet."

"Copy," Troy said.

He took a deep breath. They were about to drop into a tunnel loaded with bombs.

Nasty business.

"Don't go anywhere," Troy said. "We're gonna need you."

"I'm right here," Jan said.

The pilot said something to Miquel. An odd feeling passed through Troy, just for a split second. He couldn't understand the pilot. They needed to fix that. Troy had to have a chopper pilot who spoke English. Seconds counted.

The chopper was slowing to a hover.

"We are on the target," Miquel said. "Disembark when ready."

"Ready?" Troy said.

"Ready."

"Ready"

Troy nodded. "Go!" he shouted. "Go! Go! Go!"

A thick rope despensed from a pulley system extending outwards on either side of the helicopter. The chopper was in a low hover over a grassy knoll near a small outbuilding. There was a stand of trees obscuring the view back toward Center 42.

Troy scrambled left, out over the exterior bench, and went over the side. A second later, maybe two, he touched down onto the grass. He dropped the rope and looked around, getting his bearings. Gallo hit at the same second, then ducked away from the chopper. Two seconds later Dubois hit.

Troy caught a glimpse of the chopper circling up and out. Then he was running downhill toward the small building, twenty yards to Dubois's left. Gallo was already at the building.

"Jan! Pop that door!"

Ahead, Gallo reached for the handle and pulled the door open. Beautiful. The timing was perfect. Gallo must be everything he claimed to be. He was moving fast, and he was sharp, alert, and aware. He was exceptionally fit for an old man.

Troy reached the door one second behind Dubois. Then the three of them were in an iron stairwell, overhead lights shining a dim and sickly yellow. Gallo was down on the first landing, pistol in one hand.

Troy let the door shut and lock behind him.

"How's it look?" he said.

"Clear," Gallo said, dead serious. He was watching the stairs below him. The mocking clown act from earlier was gone, evaporated. Troy liked that.

"Let's move," he said.

Gallo took the point. He dropped down the stairs, taking it one landing at a time, turning, gun up, ready to fire. Dubois and Troy followed, guns also up, no sound but boots hammering on the ironwork. In this way, they dropped ten stories beneath the surface. At the bottom, there was a heavy door. They stopped for a breath, then Gallo opened it.

They came out into the cavernous space they had seen on the video camera in the hotel room just a few minutes before. They were out on the yellow-caged metal platform, two stories above the floor of the shop. The ceiling towered above them. The space was loud with the hum of computers, air pumps and purifiers, and other machinery. To their right, a giant metal turbine spun slowly inside a mesh cage at the mouth of a large tunnel. That hadn't been on the video monitor.

Across the way was the red and white Harvard banner hanging on a gray concrete wall. There were also the words painted on the walls that were meaningless to Troy.

ATRAP. ALPHA. ASACUSA.

"See anyone?" Troy said. "Anyone at all?"

"Negative," Gallo said.

Dubois shook her head. "No."

"Jan, can you hear me?" Troy said to his helmet.

He waited. Nothing came back but dead air. The helmet radios didn't work down here. Of course, that made sense. The only radios that did were probably connected to antennae or signal accelerators controlled by CERN.

"All right, we're deaf and dumb down here."

"Not a surprise," Gallo said.

"At least we're not blind," Dubois said.

Troy nodded. "True."

Below them was the thick yellow stripe painted on the cement floor. It wound its way around the outside of three areas of equipment inside a sort of octagon. At the far side of the open space, it ran alongside a large metal tube and entered a tunnel. There was an arrow painted on the floor right at the entrance.

Words were stenciled in black next to the arrow.

LINEAR ACCELERATOR.

AWARE.

ACOG.

CENTER 42.

"That's the way," Troy said.

If the bad guys were planting bombs down here, that's where they would be.

"Ready? Let's hit it."

He took the point now, Gallo spacing a few steps behind him, and Dubois after that. They reached the concrete floor, and followed the yellow line around the edge, moving quickly now. The tunnel was up ahead. It looked like the mouth of a monster or maybe the business end of a gun. There was going to be no way to spread out in there.

"Drop back twenty meters," Troy shouted. "Be ready to hit the deck and return fire."

"Roger," Gallo said.

He stepped into the tunnel, running now, gun out in a two-handed grip, the big tube to his left. The ceiling was maybe a mere foot above

206

his head. Troy was instantly claustrophobic in here. A guy with an automatic weapon could cut them to shreds.

The tunnel curved gently to the right. They passed through doorways that almost seemed to mark off separate rooms, but the tube continued on, endless and eternal.

"Use that curve to your advantage," he said. "Be ready for me to catch some arrows out here."

He was running, his breath loud in his ears. He could hear Gallo several steps behind him. Beyond that, sound was lost in the hum of machinery.

Must be 200 meters in now. They were halfway there. No sign of anyone. The curve made it impossible to see the end.

"Stark!"

It was Dubois's voice.

Troy stopped and pressed himself against the wall, giving anyone ahead of them nothing easy to hit. Behind him, Gallo and Dubois did the same. They all stood tall, plastered like statues. He looked back at Dubois.

She gestured at the tube with her chin.

"Look at it. The charges."

There they were. He had been running right past them. They were gray disks, nearly the same color as the accelerator itself, and roughly the same size as hockey pucks. They were very similar to the toys Dubois had been playing with back at the hotel.

"Nice catch," he said. "How far back do they go?"

"They just started. The first one is back behind me, maybe ten or twenty meters."

Troy sighed. It was ugly. If the charges were placed, that meant they were armed. Someone ahead of them could light up a bomb right now, and the chain reaction would come up the tunnel way too fast for them to escape it. They would get incinerated by a fireball barreling along like a locomotive. The four technicians in Massachusetts had died in exactly this way.

"Can you disarm them?"

Dubois nodded. "I think so."

She holstered her gun, stepped across the gap, seized a charge, and peeled it away from the accelerator. She grunted and winced as she pulled it free. Troy didn't love that, but nothing happened. Dubois returned to the wall and pressed her back against it. It was good situational awareness. Troy did like that.

She studied the device in her hands. Then she spun her hands, her left hand moving away from her body, her right hand turning toward her. Troy imagined he could hear an audible CLICK just below the hum of machines.

She stared down at it. "It's closed," she said. "So yes, I can disarm them."

She placed it on the floor at her feet.

"How do you feel about moving along the tunnel, and doing that to every charge you encounter?" Troy said.

"That's why I came," Dubois said.

Gallo nodded. "Good girl."

Troy nearly laughed. Gallo should write a book. *How to Not Win Over Agent Dubois.*

Troy looked at him. "You ready?"

Now Gallo was smiling. He loved it. You could see it in his eyes. They were on fire. "You bet."

"Let's go get these guys," Troy said.

CHAPTER THIRTY ONE

6:43 pm Central European Time
Niels Bohr Event Center
Ground Floor, Center 42
CERN
Meyrin, Switzerland

"Yes, it's quite nice," Adelina Jomo said. "It's a wonderful facility. So modern. I am very impressed." She gestured up at the soaring ceiling of the event center, several stories above their heads, as if that would explain everything.

Adelina was seventy-four years old. She was standing in the growing crowd with two excited young scientists who were visiting fellows here at CERN. They were all three drinking wine and eating cheese on bread. There was a trio of musicians not far from them, but Adelina could no longer hear them over the buzz of conversation.

In her time as an United Nations observer, Adelina had learned to make meaningless small talk. In fact, she could make it in several languages.

She spoke Portuguese, of course, as it was the official language of her home country, Guinea-Bissau. And she spoke the Portuguese-Creole that although unofficial, was the West African nation's dominant language. She was mostly fluent in English, since she spent much of her time in New York City. She also spoke some French, Spanish, and German to varying degrees.

And she spoke Russian. She didn't speak it as well as she once did mostly because of lack of practice. When she was a young woman, she had been sent to the Soviet Union to train as a nurse. The Soviets supported the successful independence movement of Guinea-Bissau against the Portuguese colonizers, and the revolution needed nurses to tend to the wounded.

Oh, yes. The free people of Guinea-Bissau remembered their true friends. There were white oppressors in this world, and there were white liberators, who stood with the people trying to cast off their chains. Adelina knew who was who.

She supposed she might not be the right person for an UN observer role in Europe. The wealth here, and the resources, were astonishing. Often, they seemed like wasted resources. And as naturally as night follows day, the Europeans treated their continent and their institutions as a club. Only the right people need apply.

It wasn't lost on her that the Portuguese colonizers of Africa were members of the CERN club. So were the Italians, and the English, and the French, and the Dutch, and the Belgians, each with their own cruel history of African exploitation. The Russians—the allies and liberators of Africa—were not. Nor were the Cubans. No African nations were members. She wasn't expecting any speech tonight about the great scientific partnership between Africa and Europe. There was no such partnership.

As an UN observer, she had witnessed violent elections in South Sudan. She had watched as the bodies of thousands of Rwandan genocide victims were unearthed, including many children, their tiny bodies hacked apart with machetes. She had taken rape accounts in the shanty towns of South Africa. To her, this was the important work.

Now, in her elder years, she attended art openings in Paris, cultural festivals in Scotland and Austria, and even this celebration of science and progress in Switzerland. Perhaps she was sent to these events as a reward for her many years of service. Or maybe it was because her employers thought she no longer had the energy for the more difficult jobs.

She wasn't sure. What she did know was that she increasingly looked upon the Europeans with disdain. They had too much when so many in other parts of the world had little or nothing. Worse, the Europeans were always well pleased with themselves. Seventy-five years after their most recent devastating war, and a mere thirty years after the end of their partition, it was as if they had never known division, deprivation, and hunger.

If her employers told her she was going to the war-torn Congo to open an Ebola clinic, it would almost seem a relief from stultifying conversations about how wonderful everything was.

"Did you say you're from Papua New Guinea?" the young woman in front of her said. The woman was an American, so Adelina could forgive the geography.

"Guinea-Bissau," she said, giving the young lady a bright smile, showing her that no offense was taken. "Papua New Guinea is in the South Pacific, near Australia. Guinea-Bissau is on the west coast of

Africa, just across from the Cape Verde islands. In fact, we used to be the same country. My mother was from Cape Verde."

The young woman returned the smile. "Duh," she said. "Excuse my ignorance. Map reading has never been my strong point."

"Yes," Adelina nearly said but didn't.

Never mind pointing out small, obscure countries on a map. It was her experience that many Americans could not stand in front of an atlas of the world and point out their present location. She would never say this though, not to this woman, and not to anyone. Her job was diplomatic above all.

"And what is your area of study?" she said instead.

As she said it, something happened behind the woman and the young man with her. Perhaps ten meters away, a very tall man loomed over the crowd. He was a giant, and he wore the white shirt and black paints Adelina associated with the catering staff. He was pushing a cart with all manner of finger foods on it, moving slowly through the dense forest of guests.

But then he reached underneath it and came out with a gun. It was a rifle of the type Adelina associated with her days in the Guinea-Bissau liberation movement. The fighters in those days used AK-47s, a gift from the Soviets.

This could be one of those or something similar. An automatic weapon.

The man seemed to move in slow motion. A few people around him noticed the gun, and scrambled to get away from him, eyes wide and mouths hanging open. They seemed to move in slow motion too. The man pointed the gun at the ceiling several stories above and began to fire.

DUH-DUH-DUH-DUH-DUH-DUH.

The young woman's smile died. Her shoulders flinched. She and the young man were spinning now, in slow motion, to look at where the shooting was coming from.

A young man in a tan security or police uniform came pushing through the crowd from the right. He moved as though he was running underwater. He shoved people out of his way. He had a pistol in his hand.

The big man took his gun down. He saw the newcomer now, security or policeman. He pointed the rifle and…

DUH-DUH-DUH-DUH.

He fired a short burst. The guard jittered and spasmed as the bullets passed through him. He fell forward, still running toward the big man.

"Get down!" someone shouted. "Get down!"

Another man, also in a white shirt and black pants, appeared with a long gun. He was pushing people to the floor.

Yet another such man appeared. He was firing into the air.

DUH-DUH-DUH-DUH-DUH.

They were shouting in several languages now, all some version of "Get on the floor!"

Adelina had wrestled with arthritis for years. Some days, it seemed to have her in its death grip. But it didn't matter. She hurled her body toward the ground, falling as one with dozens of other people all around her.

As she fell, her eyes were on the very big man.

He approached a guest from behind, an older man with thick glasses, pointed the gun, and fired it once.

BOOM.

The man's head snapped backward, and the glasses flew through the air. A spray of blood blew outward, and the man fell lifelessly to the floor.

Then Adelina was on the floor herself.

He shot that man without a word of warning.

Her whole body was shivering. Her heart pounded in her chest, the blood roaring inside her skull. If she could tunnel through the floor, she would.

CHAPTER THIRTY TWO

6:46 pm Central European Time
The Skies Near CERN
The Border of France and Switzerland

"Miquel?"

Jan's voice echoed inside his headset.

They had lost contact with Stark, Gallo, and Dubois several minutes ago. The helicopter was circling just outside the perimeter of the CERN Meyrin campus, as Miquel had assured his superiors he would do when it was not necessary to fly above it. His job was as much an attempt to avoid stepping on toes, as it was an attempt to stop horrible crimes before they happened.

They were passing over a small mountain village in France, the place a tidy grid of well-lit streets surrounded by dark hillsides.

Live and learn. Live and learn.

He had lived a long time already. He should have anticipated the problem with the radio. He didn't need to learn these lessons over and over again. His team was underground and out of touch when a terrorist attack might be looming. It was not the worst feeling in the world (Atocha was the worst feeling), but it was bad.

"Yes. Jan?"

"I am witnessing an attack inside the Niels Bohr Event Center as we speak. Men, they seem to be catering staff, have presented high-caliber automatic weapons. Shots fired, multiple casualties. They are forcing all the guests to the floor."

Miquel's heart skipped. "When did it start?"

"Now. Less than a minute ago."

Oh God. It was a two-pronged attack. At least two. Something worse could be in the offing.

Miquel nudged the pilot. "Return to campus," he said in Spanish, shouting to be heard over the loud chop of the helicopter. "The building called Center 42."

The pilot changed direction, banking hard to the right.

"How many casualties?"

213

"Impossible to say."

In the distance, Miquel saw the sirens of approaching emergency vehicles, converging on one spot. Now they were coming, when it was too late.

"How many gunmen?"

There was a pause while Jan calculated. "By my count, six, maybe seven."

"How many people are inside the venue?"

Jan answered immediately. "At a guess, three hundred."

The chopper was flying fast, crossing the campus. They would reach the building in a few seconds.

He saw the woman again, the same white blouse and brown leather jacket. Her hair in the same tight bun, her face made up, her eyes open and staring. She lay on the ruined platform at the Atocha train station, gone below the waist, nothing there except a tangle of bloody gore.

Miquel's hands balled into fists. He had known this attack was coming, known it in his very bones. They had come here days early, they had toured the campus, he had spoken to his superiors, and still it happened anyway. Everyone had listened to him, and everyone had been very polite, but they hadn't taken him seriously. His superiors had given him a helicopter and just an extra bit of leash. They didn't care what he did, as long as it didn't reflect poorly on them.

He had been right all along, and it didn't matter.

Below them, at Center 42, a dozen emergency vehicles had either arrived or were seconds away. Police units were setting up a perimeter around the building. Civilians who had been outside the building were streaming away from it.

"Shall we land?" the pilot said.

Miquel shook his head. "No. It will make no difference."

"We hover, right here, and we wait for our team to re-emerge."

He paused. His heart was racing, and his breath was catching in his throat.

"Jan?"

"Yes, Miquel."

"Can you see our team?"

"Yes. They just reappeared on camera."

"What are they doing?"

CHAPTER THIRTY THREE

6:50 pm Central European Time
Beneath Center 42
CERN
Meyrin, Switzerland

The bad guys were RIGHT THERE.

Troy burst out of the long tunnel, running hard. His gun was up and in front of him, in the two-handed grip. Suddenly, he was in another huge concrete bunker. There were giant machines, banks of computers, air pumps, and platforms. It was similar to the place he had just left. A person could be forgiven for confusing the two.

Troy had no time to absorb it all because the terrorists were right in front of him.

"Freeze!" he screamed. "Freeze! Get down on the floor!"

He had no idea what language they spoke. He used the only one he knew.

One of them, a man with a black bandana on his face, was crouched on the floor, fidgeting with some sort of control device. The two others, a man and a woman, were on a steel platform maybe half a story above the main floor. There was a metal door behind them that the man was holding open.

The woman wore a mask, but she had short hair, and it was blonde, nearly white. Troy marked that. The second man was…hard to say.

He was a man, tall, also with a mask on.

Behind Troy, Gallo emerged from the tunnel. Troy felt him there but didn't turn to look. Then he saw him from the corner of his eye. Gallo moved left, separating them as a target, and triangulating fire. Good man.

"Don't you move a muscle!" Troy shouted.

Suddenly, the man and woman on the platform darted through the door and slammed it shut behind them.

Okay. That was okay. He had this one.

The crouched man was frozen. Troy and Gallo slowly walked toward him from different angles. Troy could see what the guy had in front of him now. It was another charge, this one larger than the others and rectangular. It had a timer with a digital readout on the front.

"Put those hands where I can see them."

The couched man pivoted and rolled onto his back. He turned and there was a gun in his hand. He had to make a choice, Gallo or Troy. He chose to go for Troy.

"Gun!"

BANG!

The shot rang out, and the sound echoed off the cement floors and cinderblock walls of the vast open space. The guy's head jerked, there was a spray of blood from an exit wound at the back of his skull, and then he lay sprawled on the floor, not moving at all.

The kill shot was instant, and the guy was dead before he knew what hit him. A pool of blood began to appear like an angelic halo around his head. He didn't move at all. His body didn't even twitch.

Gallo had taken him out. The guy hadn't given him much choice.

Troy approached the body. Gallo did the same. "Don't touch him, in case he booby-trapped himself."

Troy looked at the digital readout on the explosive device. 08:15:21, timing to one hundredth of a second, and counting down. Troy blinked, and it was at 08:11:34.

"Eight minutes," Gallo said.

"I see that. You wouldn't know how to disarm this thing, would you?"

Gallo shook his head. "Not my specialty."

The last two hundred meters through the tunnel had been completely seeded with the explosive charges. This bomb here was going to set them all off.

08:04.01.

"We gotta get Dubois," Troy said. "And we gotta get those people above our heads out of there."

"You get Dubois," Gallo said. "I'll go upstairs."

No sooner had Troy nodded, than he was running back the way he had just coming. His last glimpse of Gallo was the man leaping up to the platform the man and woman had just been on, taking the stairs two at a time.

Troy ran up the tunnel, gasping, nearly shrieking for air. He ran and ran, his gun still in his right hand, all but forgotten now. The tube of the collider ran along beside him. These machines! What were they even for?

Dubois was just ahead now, down on one knee, focused on the tube, pulling a charge away from it. She looked up when she heard him coming.

"How's it going? I heard the shot fired."

"Gallo killed one of them. The other two took off. Look, never mind these charges. It's too late to disarm these things. We have to go."

"I'm making good progress," Dubois said.

She turned back to the task at hand.

"Dubois! The main bomb is in the control room up ahead. It's on a timer. There's about seven minutes left. We have to get out of this tunnel, or we're gonna get cooked. And we have to go upstairs and evacuate that event, or a lot of people are going to die."

Dubois looked up at him, her eyes wide. "Seven minutes?"

"Yeah. Less than that. The more we stay here talking, the more it counts down. And we have to go past it to get the event. So come on, okay?"

Then Dubois was on her feet, and they were running down the tunnel, right toward the bomb. They exited the tunnel and passed the bomb on a dead run.

Troy glanced at the timer. 6:23:14.

They charged onto the metal platform, Troy in the lead, Dubois one step behind. Troy pushed through the doorway, half-expecting to find Gallo here with the terrorists.

He wasn't. There was nobody here.

It was an empty foyer with a bank of two elevators. There was no button to summon an elevator. There was a simple card reader embedded in the wall next to each elevator. Neither he nor Dubois had an ID card that they could swipe.

"Oh, God. We can't take the elevator."

Troy looked to his right. Another doorway was there. A sign on the wall next to it had the zig-zag pattern that indicates stairwells. He walked over, turned the handle, and opened the door. At least this thing was unlocked.

He gazed up the iron stairwell. The first landing was just above his head. Then there was a turn and a new set of stairs coming back this way. At a guess, it was ten stories up to the ground floor. The only blessing was that they didn't seem to have more than twenty stairs per story. But it was still a long way.

Dubois stood next to him now.

217

Troy had been running back and forth like a madman, and he was winded. They had to go ten stories in six minutes. He could almost cry in frustration.

He hoped that Gallo had made it to the event center by now and was already clearing the place out.

"What are we waiting for?" Dubois said.

Troy raised a hand in front of himself, as though he was offering a tray of food.

"Ladies first," he said.

A second later, Dubois was pounding up the stairs in front of him.

CHAPTER THIRTY FOUR

6:54 pm Central European Time
8th Floor, Center 42
CERN
Meyrin, Switzerland

"Oh God, oh God, oh God."

Princess Dye repeated this under her breath as they raced up the stairs. She was half a story below Thomas, pushing herself as fast she could to keep up with him. She was only half aware she was speaking, until she reached the top step.

Thomas was there, at the door to the hallway. He raised both hands. "Shhhhhhh," he said, his voice very low. "It's okay."

"I think they killed Izzy," she said. "They had their guns on him. You heard that gunshot, right? I think they shot him."

Thomas nodded. Princess Dye was realizing, maybe for the first time, that Thomas was a rock. He seemed completely calm. "I know," he said. "I think so too. It's okay. There's nothing we can do about that."

His chest was heaving as he caught his breath. She followed his lead and let herself breathe. The lab coat over the catering costume, which covered dress pants and a dress shirt, were weighing on her. The face mask made it hard to get any oxygen. She was wearing too many clothes. She felt like she needed to rip them all off.

Her body was overheating, from the excitement and the terror, and from running through the tunnel and up all those stairs. And yes, from seeing her friend die just a few steps behind her. Izzy Bad. She shook her head. Oil Derek. Who was he really? They had lived together for weeks at the lake house, and she had never really come to know him. Now he was dead.

This job was too rushed! They had spent all that time preparing for the Massachusetts operation. Here, they had all just come together last night and today, had a few words of instruction, and off they went.

They were all professionals, she supposed, but...

She shook her head.

Thomas was watching her. "Are you ready?" he said, his voice barely above a whisper. "We need to keep moving. This place is going to blow up. Those cops can't stop it."

She nodded. "I know. I'm ready."

"Good," he said.

She pulled the mask down for a second, stood closer to him and kissed him on the cheek. "For luck," she said.

Now was not the time to catch feelings, but Izzy had shaken her badly. Seeing Hy Wire go up in flames had been horrible, but she didn't know him at all. Even though she had never connected with Izzy, he felt like family.

Thomas nodded. "Okay. Let's go. In and out in three minutes."

He opened the door. They went out into the hallway. She glanced down at the screen on her navigation device. Everything was on this little toy. The office they were targeting was just up the hall here and around the corner. She led the way.

Once there, it would hopefully be a simple matter to gain access and find the…She stopped. The door was just ahead. She had a photo of it on the device. An ordinary wooden door from an earlier time, with a window of frosted glass. The number 808 was just below the window. It looked like the door to a classroom when she was a child in public school. There were important files in there, files worth killing and dying for, and just any old door would do to protect them.

A light was on behind the frosted glass.

She stopped. Thomas stood next to her. She glanced up at him. He pulled down the bandana that served as his mask. He mouthed the words instead of speaking them.

"Is that it?"

She nodded.

He reached inside his own lab coat and came out with a small pistol. The gun didn't look like much. She shook her head. Until this moment, she hadn't known he was even carrying a gun. But nothing could surprise her anymore.

He shrugged and moved toward the door. She followed behind him, close but not too close. He put his free hand on the metal latch that opened the door. It moved just a bit. He turned to her, his eyes wide. They were bloodshot eyes, and she felt like she could almost trace the lines of red that ran all through them.

"It's open," he mouthed.

She had nothing to say to that. This was the place. The door was open, and a light was on. It was as if the gods were inviting them to come and meet with destiny. If someone was in there, they would just have to deal with it.

If she had to, she would encourage Thomas to kill whoever they found. She had come a long way. She was too close to have it unravel now.

Thomas pushed down the latch and shoved the door open. He burst into the room. She followed, just a second or two behind him.

An old man was here. His hair was bright white. He was sitting at a desk that was almost impossibly messy. She got a sense of papers piled high everywhere she looked. She got a sense of old soda cans. She saw a bottle of clear fluid. A word on the label jumped out at her:

VODKA.

The man turned around in his chair—it was the kind of chair that spun. He was holding a gun in his hand. The gun was huge!

Her heart…

"Drop the gun!" Thomas shouted. "Drop it!"

He was pointing his gun directly at the man.

"What do you…" the old man began. His face was lined and weathered. His eyes were deep set, as though the man's face itself was a mask.

"Drop it!" Thomas screamed.

Then he fired.

BANG! BANG!

The old man fired. BOOOM!

It was one shot, incredibly deep and loud. Princess Dye dropped to the floor, covering her ears. Her ears were ringing. She almost couldn't hear herself screaming over the sound of them.

She rolled into a ball for a long moment, trying to quiet herself. But them she found herself crying. Her eyes were tightly shut. Before she opened them, a thought flowing lazily across her mind.

Why did he shoot?

Princess Dye opened her eyes. Thomas was lying just across from her. She could almost reach out and touch him. His eyes were open, but they were the blank eyes of a mannequin. He was already dead.

Blood was pooling underneath him. His dingy white lab coat was being stained dark red. It was a lot of blood. She could see from here that he had been hit in the chest. The bullet from that big gun must have gone through his heart.

She groaned.

After Izzy died, just in the last several minutes, she had decided to think of him as family. She couldn't allow herself to think of Thomas at all. She turned away and decided not to even look at him again. He had made his choices. She had made hers.

She climbed to her feet. The old man was still in his chair, slumped over. She approached him carefully, but then realized it didn't matter. There was a small hole just to the side of his forehead. Blood was running out of there. Thomas had popped a bullet in this old man's skull.

"Why did he do it?" she said out loud.

If Thomas hadn't fired the gun, they probably could have…she didn't know what. Maybe they could have convinced the old man to drop his gun. But then, maybe they couldn't. Even in death, he was still holding it. It was a giant monster of a thing, its barrel the longest handgun barrel she thought she had ever seen.

Gingerly, she took the gun out of the man's hand. The man offered no resistance. He was past caring. The gun was very heavy.

She took the navigation device out. There were photos of some of the things she needed to look for, along with descriptions of others, and possible locations in the office of everything. She had read through the descriptions in the past two days. They made it clear that if she was in doubt about the importance of something, err on the side of including it.

There was a lot to take. She'd better get started.

Behind the old man on the desk was a piece of white paper with a handwritten note on it. She gazed at the paper, taking a long moment to understand what was written there. The man's handwriting was chicken scratch. But then finally, the words came together for her.

Messy, isn't it?

She stared at the old man, blood now flowing in a rivulet from his skull, down part of his face, and then dripping into his lap. Then she glanced back at Thomas, lying on the floor with wide dead eyes, seemingly in shock at the news that he could die. There was blood pooling all around him now.

"Yeah," she said. "It is."

Then she went to work.

CHAPTER THIRTY FIVE

6:59 pm Central European Time
Niels Bohr Event Center
Ground Floor, Center 42
CERN
Meyrin, Switzerland

"We're here. Okay, we're here."

Troy could hear Dubois gasping as she repeated herself. They had climbed the stairs at a sprint, never slowing down, not for one second.

They had reached the ground floor of the building. They left the iron underground stairwell and came out into some kind of lobby area. They had returned to the surface of the Earth, and that meant floors of polished stone, bright colors, and decorations on the walls. They were in a hallway with framed photographs of famous people, scientists probably. Troy didn't even look at them.

Across the way, there were two double doors. To the right of the doors, words were stenciled in an elegant block script.

Niels Bohr Event Center.

"We have to hurry," Troy said, his voice a harsh rasp, and then they were running again. His lungs were burning. The doors were ten feet away. He accelerated towards them, several feet ahead of Dubois now. He was going to burst through them, and just start screaming at everyone. He was going to scream the one word known to get people moving.

FIRE!

Five feet from the doors, he saw that they were locked. He could see the bolt in the gap between them. It didn't matter. He was going through them, no matter what.

Faster.

He accelerated again, going for the last bit of energy he had. Everything, his whole being, it didn't matter if it was all gone. Those doors were going down.

BOOOM!

223

He launched himself into the doors like a missile, throwing his shoulder at them. The lock broke apart and one of the doors came off its mount. For a moment, the door was hanging sideways, and he was tangled in it. He shoved it savagely, pushing it aside, and stumbled into the large event hall.

The ceiling of the place soared above his head.

That was the only thing that made sense. He didn't understand what he was looking at. Everyone, hundreds of people, were lying on the floor. It was like a carpet of humanity, all the way across the venue.

No. There were a handful of people standing. The catering people were on their feet. They seemed like the statues of Easter Island, the way they stood out. One was standing right here, by the door.

The guy was holding an AK-47. What a crazy weapon to have. He turned it, butt forward, and rammed Troy in the face with it.

Troy's head snapped back, and then he was on the floor too.

His gun. He had a gun in his hand. But then the guy with the rifle loomed above him, pointing it at his head. The guy stepped on Troy's wrist.

"Let go of that gun or I'm going to unload this thing into your face."

Then Dubois was there, right behind Troy's head.

"I'll blow your head off," she said.

Her two hands, with her 9mm appeared there, inches from the guy's head.

"Hey!" someone screamed. "Hey! You drop that goddamn gun or I'm going to kill you both."

Troy looked at the direction the voice was coming from. A very large man was advancing with another rifle. He was stepping over, and on top of, the bodies on the floor. People squirmed like eels to get out of his way.

The guy was big. There was something about him. He moved fluidly and decisively. His voice was commanding. He had seen combat before. He had led troops before. They had gone to upstate New York to find a similar big man, the man who led the Massachusetts attack.

There was nothing Dubois could do. The big man had the drop on her. She dropped her gun and it clattered to the floor.

Troy fixed his gaze on the man who had clubbed him in the face. If Troy lived through this, he was going to have a nasty welt there. And that's if he was lucky. If he was unlucky, the guy had broken some of his facial bones.

The guy still had the AK-47 pointed at Troy's head.

"Buddy," Troy said. "This place is about to blow up. You do you realize that, don't you?"

CHAPTER THIRTY SIX

7:00 pm Central European Time
8th Floor, Center 42
CERN
Meyrin, Switzerland

"Hello," a male voice said. "What are you carrying there?"

Princess Dye looked up.

She had emerged from the office just a few seconds ago. She had been marching down the darkened hallway, so intent on getting out of here that she nearly walked right into a man who was blocking her way.

She stopped and stared at him in the gloom. He was a broad man with big shoulders. He was older, his hair and beard neat but entirely white. His face was all hard lines and shadows. His eyes were like the eyes of a hawk.

He wore a black jumpsuit with the word INTERPOL across the chest in white. Was he one of the policemen from the tunnel? She couldn't say. She had escaped from there so quickly that she hadn't stopped to absorb what anyone looked like.

It was very quiet here in the hallway. She could hear sounds from all the way downstairs, screams, shouts, but they seemed very far away.

"Nothing," she said, and immediately grasped how silly that was. "I'm not carrying anything." But she had a big canvas satchel over her shoulder. She had found the bag in the office, and now it was stuffed with paperwork and computer disks. She had taken everything that seemed remotely important and put it in this bag.

More obviously ridiculous was the giant gun in her right hand.

The man smiled. He was vibrant, alive, full of pent-up energy, like a coiled snake getting ready to strike. He was nothing like the old man who had just died in the office. Maybe he was younger than that man. It was hard for her to say. Most older people looked the same to her. Silvio Strukul was a notable exception.

"Nothing?" There was a hint of mocking in his voice. "I doubt very much that you would come all this way and take all these risks, for nothing. I don't think you'd climb eighteen stories at warp speed and from deep underground, for nothing. You have something there, all right. I want you to give it to me."

"I work here," she said.

He shook his head. "No. You don't."

Okay, she didn't have time for this. She couldn't allow this cop to arrest her. He was right about one thing. She had come too far for that.

She raised the gun and pointed it directly at his chest. Aim for the center mass. That was one of the few things she knew about gunplay.

"Sir, if you'll excuse me. I have somewhere to be."

"Kendra, I know you won't shoot me. You're a good girl. Anyway, I'm wearing body armor under these clothes. Look at me, Kendra. I have a gun too."

The comment stopped her in her tracks. It wasn't the gun, which she now noticed in his right hand. It was that he knew her name. How could that be? If he knew who she was, that meant she had much bigger problems than she thought.

There was a trail of dead people behind her.

"But Kendra, look at what I'm going to do. I'm going to put my gun down on the floor." Slowly, he bent and did exactly what he said he would. He placed his gun on the polished floor. Then he stood tall again.

"All I want is the information you have there. I know it must be very valuable. We're all curious about what it might contain. Give it to me, and I'll let you go. You can walk out of here a free woman. No one has to know anything."

She took a deep breath.

He had her there for a second. But now she felt her composure coming back and her resolve. This wasn't an arrest. It was a stick-up. He probably wasn't even a cop. He had followed her here because she knew where the secrets were kept, and he didn't.

"I don't know who you think you're talking to. But I don't have time for it."

"Kendra Johns. You grew up outside Chicago, in a nice suburb. You have two sisters, a mom, and a dad. Well, your dad died a few years ago. You were a standout volleyball player in high school, then played at Michigan, though you were more of a..."

Suddenly, the whole building shook. It was violent, everything swaying from side to side. For a second, she though the pace might crack apart. The tremor came from far below, below the party where

227

people were being held hostage, from below the earth, from hell. A long, rolling BOOOOM followed it.

The explosions had started. Another one like that might take the place down. A series of them happened, one right after another. She couldn't make sense of the sound. The building was still trembling. Down the hall, a chunk of masonry came loose from the ceiling and fell to the floor like a bomb.

The people at the gala were screaming now. Shrieking, in a panic. That could only mean one thing. At least they were still alive.

Kendra. She was Kendra. She really was. And this man knew that. How he knew it didn't matter. He knew it, and he was in the way. She had to get past him.

So, she shot him.

BOOM!

The giant gun bucked in her hand.

The bullet must have hit the man chest high. He staggered backwards.

She gripped the gun with both hands now. There was no other way to control it. Control it? The recoil was like riding a bucking bronco.

She pulled the trigger again.

BOOM!

The sound echoed up and down the hallway. She was going to drive herself deaf.

BOOM!

The gun was an animal. Not a bronco. An elephant.

The man was still on his feet.

BOOM!

He stumbled backwards and fell to his knees. She didn't know how many more times she could pull this trigger. She could barely hold the gun up anymore.

BOOM!

He snapped backwards and fell to the floor. His head bonked off the stone, or the concrete, linoleum, whatever it was.

She walked over and stood above him. He wasn't dead. Maybe he wasn't even that badly injured. He was writhing on the floor, gripping his chest, and gasping for air. His face was bleeding. There was a big gash across the side of it. There was blood all over the floor, spreading outward in a pool.

That last bullet must have grazed his head on the way down. The rest of them must have been absorbed by the body armor under his clothes. Neat. It had saved his life.

But not for long.

"You're a bad girl," he said, between gasps. "Oh God, that hurt."

He seemed to be in agony. She should put him out of his misery.

"I can't believe you shot me."

She put two hands on the gun, pointed it at his head, and pulled the trigger one last time.

Click.

"Ah man," he gasped. "Don't kill me. Come on. It's not very sporting."

He rolled over onto his stomach.

"Unh," he said. "Oh baby."

It was strange how a man she had just shot several times could still seem to be mocking her.

She aimed at the back of his head and pulled the trigger again. Click.

That was it. The gun was empty. She hadn't counted her bullets, not that she knew how many were in there in the first place.

She tossed the gun away and it clattered along the hallway. She looked behind her. She could go pick up his gun and kill him with that. But he probably had all kinds of other weapons and tricks up his sleeve. In the time it took her to get his gun and figure out how to use it…

Something blew up far below them and the building shook again. If possible, this one was worse than before. She steadied herself with one hand on the wall. The walls themselves were starting to crack.

Down in the event center, the hostages screamed again. They sounded like they were riding a roller coaster down there. The building must be on fire by now. Who knew what kinds of chemicals and radiation were about to be set loose? She had to go.

"It's your lucky day," she said to the man.

She stepped over him and continued to the stairwell.

CHAPTER THIRTY SEVEN

7:03 pm Central European Time
Niels Bohr Event Center
Ground Floor, Center 42
CERN
Meyrin, Switzerland

"Get out! Out! Out!"

The catering staff were dragging people to their feet now, pushing them toward the doors. The event center was shaped like a circle or a ring, with double sets of doors all along the edges. The doors were open now, as if by magic, and terrified hostages were streaming out into the night.

More and more came. Bottlenecks developed at the doorways.

From deep below, there was the sound of another explosion came. The sound was muffled, whatever it was must be farther down the tunnel, but the floor beneath Troy shook. Machines were blowing up down there. The fire that was raging underground must be like something from the depths of hell.

The man with the gun pointed at Troy stumbled off balance. He turned to look at the people running away. He seemed ready to do the same.

He had stepped on Troy's wrist, but he hadn't taken the gun. Troy reached and picked it up. The guy turned back just in time to see the gun in Troy's hand. He moved to renew his aim at Troy's head with the AK-47.

BANG!

Too late. Troy shot him in the face. The man's head snapped back, and he fell right where he had stood. He landed on someone's back and then rolled onto the floor. Troy stayed low and crawled for the guy's gun. It was time for an upgrade.

They're releasing the hostages. Hundreds of them.

Of course they were. And they were dressed as caterers. Maybe some were dressed as guests. The terrorists were simply going to walk out of here and disappear into the night.

He picked up the AK and holstered his own gun. He checked the magazine. It was a thirty-round banana mag, and it was full. The guy hadn't fired his weapon. And then he had died. Troy shrugged. That was okay. He should never have been here. Play stupid games, win stupid prizes.

Dubois was here on the floor. She crawled to him. She still had her helmet on. It occurred to Troy that he did too. They were on the surface now. The internal radio should work again.

A man tripped over Dubois, fell, then got up again. People were falling all over each other.

"Dubois, get out of here! Take some of these people with you. This place is gonna be an inferno in a minute."

"I know," she said. "What are you going to do?"

The building hadn't caved in from the explosions, and the fire hadn't reached here yet. That didn't mean it wasn't going to. Either way, he wasn't ready to leave. The guy with the AK had rung Troy's bell, and something like that might impact decision making, but all in all, he felt clear-headed.

"The terrorists are planning to blend in with the crowd. I can't allow that."

He looked across the room. The big man was there, probably thirty meters away. When the explosions began, he had instantly moved on from Dubois. He had slung his rifle over his back. Troy watched as the guy picked a woman up off the floor and shoved her toward one of the open doorways.

Then he stood over a man, pulled a pistol from his belt, and shot the man in the head. The man's head and body jerked, and he lay still. The shot echoed in the chaos of the giant hall. A few people near the dead man flinched. A woman screamed, but there was a lot of screaming going on.

Why did he do that?

That settled it. Troy looked at Dubois. "Get out of here. Get these people out."

"How?" Dubois said. "How am I supposed to get them out?"

Troy scanned the room. There was a long line of curtains two stories high along the far, curving wall. Troy pointed at it.

"I'll bet that's windows behind those curtains. Smash them. Obliterate them, and then Pied Piper out that way. Come on, Dubois."

He pushed himself to his feet. He brought the gun up, but he didn't have a clear shot. There were too many people between here and there. He started moving, the big man straight ahead of him.

He stepped over people who were still on the ground. People shoved past him, their eyes widening with terror when they saw the gun in his hands. Who was he kidding? He couldn't open fire with an AK-47 in this crowd.

A hand fell on his shoulder. He turned, and Dubois was there, moving step for step with him. "Give me that gun," she said.

He nodded and handed it over to her.

"It's heavy," he said.

She shook her head and cracked a ghost of a smile. Then she took off at a sprint.

Okay, this was better.

Now Troy started to run, bouncing off people, coming at the target from the side and a little bit behind. The big man pulled another woman to her feet and shoved her. Then he stood over another man. He raised the pistol again, as a balding middle-aged man in a suit cowered at his feet.

He's killing men.

Was there something more noble about that?

No.

Troy was at a full sprint now. To his left, one of the walls was on fire. The fire had climbed ten stories, maybe up the stairwell, an elevator shaft, or an air shaft, and now it was here. That was bad.

People were screaming again, trying to get away from it. The entire crowd surging like a herd of mindless animals. The doorways were plugged with people. If someone didn't get another exit open soon, a lot of people were going to die.

Not just any exit. A big exit. A gaping hole.

The big man pointed the gun down at the man on the floor and said something to him. Troy could clearly see the smile on the big man's face. He was killing for the pleasure of it. He was killing because he liked it, and he thought he was going to kill whoever he wanted and then walk out of here.

He was five feet away and Troy was coming fast.

At the last second, the man saw Troy out of the corner of his eye.

BAM!

232

Troy hit him just above the knees, knocking the pistol from his hand in the same move. Troy put his shoulder to the man's legs and bulled him across the floor. The man was strong and didn't go down.

They crashed into a party guest and all three went down in a heap. The guest squirmed away.

Troy climbed on top of the big man. The man's hands tried to push Troy off. Troy clamped one hand on the guy's throat, his grip like a talon, then he reared back and punched the guy in the face.

POW!

He did it again.

POW!

He would punch this guy's face back through his skull.

He reared back.

Now the guy had a knife. He shoved it at Troy's chest but hit the Kevlar plate there. His knife hand slid along Troy's body. He swung it, dragging it across Troy's face.

"Ow!"

The guy cut his face.

BAM!

Troy punched the guy again. The guy's head bounced off the floor. The guy moved the knife like a piston now, thrusting and pulling back, thrusting and pulling back, trying to stab anything. Troy tried to catch that arm.

He sliced Troy's hand. He got under the dragon skin somehow and sliced Troy's upper arm.

Troy pulled his pistol.

The big man grabbed Troy's gun hand and bent it away. If Troy pulled the trigger now, he would hit a bystander.

The knife stabbed again. Troy grunted. He couldn't let this guy keep cutting him.

He threw the gun away, pushed his hands to the floor, and leapt backwards onto his feet. Now he was up. The big man was on his back, moving like a spider. He held the knife out in front.

Troy sidestepped and kicked the man in the head.

The guy threw the knife at Troy, but Troy batted it away. It was a ploy to by time. The big man rolled onto his side and tried to pull the AK-47 that was slung over his back. He gripped it and pulled, pulled…

It didn't work.

Troy raised a boot and stomped on the guy's head. Then he did it again.

And again.

That was enough.

Troy kneeled down and unslung the AK from the big man's back. He patted the guy down, reached inside his caterer's jacket, and pulled out what he knew he would find—an extra magazine for the gun.

"Thanks," he said to the dead man.

Troy's hands were covered in blood. One of his sleeves was shredded. He was tired now. It was time to go.

Just then, an automatic weapon opened up nearby.

DUH-DUH-DUH-DUH-DUH-DUH.

Troy looked up. Across the room from him, Dubois had found some way to pull back the curtain. Sure enough, there were tall windows behind it. During daytime, those windows probably gave a nice view of the campus.

She had just given them a burst from her AK. The safety glass or plastic or whatever it was shattered and came down in a rain of tiny pellets.

She moved along it, and fired again, spraying it.

DUH-DUH-DUH-DUH-DUH.

More glass showered down. She moved again and gave it another burst. The windows were wide open now.

She turned and shouted something in French. Troy couldn't hear it. He wouldn't have known what it was anyway.

People hardly needed to be told. In an instant, the crowds were moving toward the windows and flowing outside.

The entire left wall of the place was on fire now, reaching high above their heads. Troy stood and shuffled toward the broken windows with the crowd.

CHAPTER THIRTY EIGHT

7:15 pm Central European Time
Outside of Center 42
CERN
Meyrin, Switzerland

"Look what I found," Dubois said.

Troy was sprawled on the ground, leaning against a tree maybe fifty meters outside the line of control set up by the emergency services. His AK-47 lay alongside him, along with his helmet.

Dubois and Gallo walked toward him. Neither one of them seemed to have their helmets anymore.

Beyond Dubois and Gallo, in the distance, the tall steel and glass Center 42 was engulfed in flames, lighting up the night. Farther away, the building that was connected to Center 42 by the underground tunnel was also on fire. Dozens of fire trucks, police cars, armored cars, and ambulances were here, lights flashing and sirens whooping.

Behind Troy, maybe a quarter of a mile in the other direction, they were setting up a field hospital under tents to triage the injured. Car traffic was shut down. People streamed away from the campus on foot like a Biblical exodus, refugees from some horrible act of God.

"What happened to you?" Troy said to Gallo.

Gallo shrugged. "I got shot."

That didn't really answer Troy's question, or at least not in the way he meant it. But yes, Gallo's face was covered in blood. He was holding what might have once been a white towel to the left side of it. Now it was a red towel.

"In the head?"

Gallo nodded. "Yeah."

"I guess it didn't hit anything important," Troy said.

Behind them, maybe twenty meters away, an event guest walked by. It was a young woman, and she moved as if she was sleepwalking. That made sense. Nearly everyone here was in shock. If he was honest with himself, Troy might also be in shock. He didn't like to think of it that way, but what else would you call this daze?

"Loss of blood, maybe."

"I'm sorry?" Dubois said.

Troy shook his head. "Just rambling to myself."

He looked at the woman again. She was very attractive, wearing a shimmering blue mini dress. She had short hair, like a bob cut, blonde to the point that it was almost white. She was moving away now, carrying a canvas satchel of some kind.

Troy looked at her shoes. They weren't shoes at all. They were a pair of black sneakers. The sneakers were nondescript with no markings of any kind.

Troy bet she could run pretty fast in those sneakers.

"I'm taking him to the triage tents," Dubois said. "I'll be back for you in a minute."

Troy nodded. "Okay." There was no sense arguing.

Once Dubois and Gallo were gone, he took a deep breath, and pushed himself to his feet one last time. It was like rolling a boulder up a mountain. He picked up the rifle. Maybe he would take a little walk and satisfy a curiosity that he had.

* * *

Kendra walked across a low, rolling hill.

She had turned on the transponder. Let them find her. She couldn't think of anything else to do. Anyway, she had the documents, so there was no reason to kill her. She probably had more than they needed.

She crossed a campus roadway choked with abandoned cars. Traffic had come to a dead stop, and people had simply gotten out and walked. Some were running. They were all moving along the roadway, which must head to a gate and away from this burning apocalypse.

She wasn't interested in that. She didn't want to go with these people. There was a large open area over here on the other side of the road, maybe some kind of soccer pitch, or track and field venue. Why they would have sports fields at a science facility…eh, she didn't even want to think about it.

She climbed a few concrete steps to the field. It was wide open in front of her. She was tired, more tired than she ever remembered being. Thomas was dead. Izzy was dead. That old man in the office, whoever he had been, was dead. There must be more people dead in the explosions and the fire. Hy Wire was dead. Remember him? At least four people had died in Massachusetts and maybe more. The guards had never turned up, as far as she knew.

All this death had wiped her out.

She had ditched both the lab clothes and the catering uniform. It was a cold night, and she was barely dressed now, but it didn't matter. She could picture herself walking out into the middle of this field, lying down, and sleeping until the Russians, or whoever they were, came and found her.

She would use the bag with the secret documents as a pillow.

She was out in the middle of the field now. Above her head, she could hear the WHUMP of an approaching helicopter. She looked up, and for the first time, she noticed there were a lot of helicopters in the sky.

Of course there were. A disaster had taken place. She could see lights in the sky ringing this entire area. They seemed to move in a line like ants.

And here was one now, lights very bright, coming down to land on her head. It put her in a spotlight. Wind from the rotor blades whipped all around her.

The helicopter touched down. It was a sleek black one, very nice looking. She had flown in helicopters before with Silvio. It wouldn't surprise her at all if Silvio had sent this one for her.

But that wouldn't make sense, would it? Because Silvio wasn't supposed to know anything about…

She approached the helicopter, ducking under the rotors, although she was hardly tall enough to have to worry about that.

A door to the passenger cabin slid open. She climbed up and inside. The helicopter was modern and new. It was designed for comfort. There were four bucket seats, two facing backwards, two facing forwards. A young, bulky man sat in one of the rear facing seats. He had a machine gun on his lap.

Facing forward was an older man, maybe middle-aged, who was perfectly bald. He had a nose like a beak and dark piercing eyes. He wore a form fitting, long-sleeved shirt. He looked strong, though he had a small potbelly.

The pilot must be in another compartment at the front.

She sat next to the older man. He was clearly the one in charge.

"My name is Viktor," he said. "What shall I call you?"

Kendra shook her head. She wasn't in the mood to play the name game. "Anything you want."

The helicopter was already lifting off again.

She gestured at the younger man across from her. She would guess he was in his mid-twenties. He was big, and his eyes were hard and flat. He looked like he had all the intelligence of a farm animal.

"He won't need that gun," Kendra said. "I'm not going to hurt you guys."

* * *

"Miquel, are you on here?" Troy said. He'd had to switch the radio inside his helmet on and off a couple of times to get it to work again. He stood at the edge of the ballfield, watching the passenger helicopter take off into the night.

"Yes," came the voice. "Stark?"

"Yeah."

"How are you?"

"I'm alive."

"How are Dubois and Gallo?"

"Also alive."

For a moment, Miquel sounded like a tire that had just been slashed. All the air went out of him at once.

"Where are you right now?" Troy said.

"We're in a holding pattern at the edge of the campus."

"Listen, do you see chopper taking off from an athletic field on the campus? Right now, it's not a hundred feet in the air yet, but it's climbing."

There was a pause.

"We see it."

"Those are bad guys. One of the terrorists who blew this place up just boarded that thing and is getting away. Do you mind coming down and getting me, so we can remedy that? I'm on the same field."

"We can be there in one minute."

"I'll turn on my light."

Troy had a small LED light as part of his kit that was super bright. He took it out, turned it on, and pointed it at the sky. It wasn't long before the chopper was coming down. It hovered a foot above the ground, he jogged to it, and climbed onto the exterior bench. Then it took off again.

Miquel poked his head out. "Do you want to come in?"

They were still talking inside their helmets.

238

Troy shook his head. "I'm good out here."

Miquel gestured at the AK-47. "Where did you get that?"

Troy patted it. "Somebody gave it to me."

The world fell away below them. They moved higher and higher. Behind them, fire climbed into the sky. Ahead was the darkness of the countryside.

Troy belted in and leaned back on the bench, the gun across his lap. He looked to his left. Out ahead, he could see the lights of the other chopper. The lights were coming closer, right in front of his eyes. This was a combat helicopter, with a top speed of 175 miles per hour. Whoever those people were, and whatever they were flying, they weren't going to outrun it. And that meant they were going to do something stupid.

Closer...closer...

As if on cue, the other chopper slowed down drastically. Then someone over there opened up with a machine gun. Troy saw the muzzle flashes. Bullets whined around him. One made a THUNK as it hit metal. He flinched.

"Mmmm."

"Stark? You okay?"

He nodded. "Yeah. I'm fine. Just a little aggravated. They're plucking my last nerve here. See if you can pull almost even with this guy, can you? Just behind him and to his left."

"All right."

They were zooming now. Troy got the sense of a dark forest zipping by below him. They were pulling even with the other chopper now. The chopper was taking shape against the black night behind it. This was the dangerous moment. They were close now. Too close.

The door was open over there. A man leaned out the side. Troy imagined he could see the snout of the man's gun poking out.

Troy aimed with the AK. He let it rip.

DUH-DUH-DUH-DUH-DUH-DUH.

The gun bucked in his hands. It felt good and right. He caught the line of the tail and strafed along it. Sparks flew. A burst of flame licked out at the very end.

He paused, keyed on the doorway, and fired off another burst for good measure.

DUH-DUH-DUH-DUH-DUH.

The guy in the open doorway ducked back before he could fire. The other chopper sped up and veered away sharply to the right.

"Tail rotor," Troy said. "I hit the tail rotor. He's gonna lose it."

The Little Bird veered sharply to the left and began a steep ascent. Troy sat back, staring up now at the dark sky above him. Whoever this pilot was, he was good. He knew what it meant when a tail rotor went, and he was getting away from it.

Below them and across a wide distance now, the other helicopter began to spin. Its forward movement had stopped. It circled slowly around and around, the spin gaining speed. Then it dropped down into the darkness and disappeared.

Troy held his breath. A moment later, far below, the chopper reappeared when it burst into flame. It blew outward in orange and red against a black canvas.

Thin tendrils of fire reached away from the blazing center like tentacles.

"Beautiful," Troy said, and meant it.

"We better go down and take a look," Miquel said. "See if there are survivors."

CHAPTER THIRTY NINE

Time Unknown
A hillside
The French countryside

She lay on her back in the darkness, staring up at the sky.

Somewhere nearby, the helicopter was on fire. She could see the orange flow of it in the corner of her eye, hear the crackling of the flames, and feel the heat on her face. It was like a giant bonfire on an autumn night. It was burning with intense energy. They used to call a fire like that a "rager." It was nice to think of it that way.

She must have been thrown clear of it in the crash. That was the only way to explain why she was here, and it was over there. She didn't know if anyone else had survived. She doubted it. She seemed to survive everything, again and again, while the people around her died.

Probably not this time, though.

She wasn't in pain. Outside of the heat from the fire warming her cheeks, she couldn't feel anything at all. She couldn't move. She couldn't get up and keep moving away from this disaster. She couldn't even turn her head to look at the downed helicopter. She couldn't breathe very well, either. There was something building up in her throat, some kind of fluid. She felt like she had to puke.

She remembered, just a few moments ago, the helicopter spinning, moving at dizzying speed. The bald man, Viktor, had been shouting orders at the pilot. He had been speaking Russian or some other Slavic language. His shouts were guttural barks. She didn't understand a word of it.

Somewhere in the helicopter, an alarm was sounding. Beep, beep, beep, beep, beep. It wasn't even very loud. They spun faster and faster, and they dropped out of the sky. There was an instant of nothing, just perfect spinning, terrible and horrible like it was never going to end.

Then there was darkness. And now this.

A man was standing over her now. No. There were two men. One was a big man and broad. The other was smaller, maybe older. She stared at them. They were both wearing those black jumpsuits. They both had the word INTERPOL across their chests.

Good Lord. More cops.

"Who are you?" the smaller man said. He spoke English with an accent.

She tried to speak, and found that with effort, she could manage it. "My name is Kendra."

"What were you doing here?"

"Nothing."

It sounded like the croak of a frog. It was the truest thing she ever said. She had done nothing here. She had accomplished nothing. A lot of people had died. The secrets, whatever they were, were on fire inside the helicopter.

And now?

Things got very dark for a long moment. The two men above her were no longer there.

There was a lake in Wisconsin where they used to go in the summers when she was a child. She was very small and had just learned to swim. She stood on the dock behind the old house where they stayed.

Her father, who she loved very much, was in the water. He was a funny man who wore his glasses all the time, even when he went swimming.

For an instant, the image was frozen. There was the water of the giant lake, the greenery all along the coastline, and the vast spread of pale blue sky above her.

"Come on, Kendra," her father said. He waved her on.

She looked at him. She stepped up to the edge of the dock. She was a little bit afraid because the water seemed so dark.

"Come on, sweetie," he said. "You can do it. Jump."

There was nothing left to do.

She   jumped.

CHAPTER FORTY

November 19
1:05 am Central European Time
Centre Medical de Geneva
Geneva, Switzerland

The night was cold, and Troy didn't have a jacket with him.

He came out of the Emergency Department doors expecting to a hail a taxi back to the hotel. It was brightly lit out here, and the driveway was a small circle where ambulances could pull in. This was a small hospital on the outskirts of the city. They had done a steady business earlier tonight, taking many of the less demanding cases from the disaster.

Inside, they had x-rayed him, cleaned and disinfected his wounds, stitched and bandaged them up, and given him some pills for the pain. They told him he would be tired the next couple of days and to keep an eye out for infections.

He had a hairline crack in one of his facial bones. It was swelling up, and it was going to get worse. Also, the big guy had managed to cut him six times, three in his left arm, two in his right, and one on his lower right cheek just above the jaw. Troy was lucky. None of the major arteries or veins had been nicked. He could have been sliced to ribbons. As it was, the stitches would probably leave scars. He already had more scars than he needed.

"Eh," he said to no one or maybe to the cold night. "It builds character."

Gallo was still inside. They had taken him into surgery. He had absorbed a shot to the face with a large caliber weapon, which mostly grazed him, but it did rip the flesh up, and it did hit his cheekbone. The bones there had fractured, and there were some tiny metal fragments embedded in there that had to come out. Then the whole mess had to be sewn back up again.

Gallo was lucky he wasn't dead. It was quite a showing for a guy who was just out here doing a favor for an old friend.

243

Troy felt bad for him, he supposed. He was a jerk and a showoff, but he was our jerk and showoff. Before they took him in to surgery, he was being a little mysterious about how he sustained his injuries. Clearly someone had plugged him, not just once, but several times. When they took his second skin off, his upper body was bruised from shots to the torso. Whoever shot at him was shooting to kill.

"Need a ride?" someone said.

Troy looked up. Off to the right, there was a black sedan. Agent Dubois was leaning on it. She had changed her clothes to jeans, boots, and a leather jacket. Her hair was up again, held in place by a red sash.

She'd saved a lot of people, and she had come through the whole thing unscathed. Troy imagined she'd gone back to the hotel, took a nice hot shower, changed into comfortable clothes, had a bite to eat, and was now back here. To do what, rub it in?

"What happened to Miquel's SUV?"

She smiled. "That's a dad car. I'm not a dad."

Troy shook his head and smiled as he walked toward her. "No, you aren't."

He expected her to go around to the driver's side, but she didn't. Instead, she stayed right where she was, leaning on the car. Her arms were folded. She stared at him, her eyes hard. Maybe there was the smallest hint of a softening in her face. Maybe there wasn't.

"Were we a team tonight or what?" Troy said.

She nodded. "We were. I wouldn't be here to pick you up if we weren't."

"Are we buddies again?"

She sighed. Now she did push off the car and stood straight. "I don't know if I'd go that far. But we are teammates." She went around to the driver's side.

"You saved a lot of people tonight, Dubois."

She nodded. "Thank you for recognizing that. I couldn't have done it without you."

There was still plenty of tension between them, he supposed. It would take work to get the two of them consistently on the same page. Troy was going to have to learn to flex a bit and make space for someone who was not like him. But maybe things had improved a small amount. He wasn't sure, so he might as well test these good feelings and find out if they were real.

"See?" he said. "I'm not all bad."

Dubois shook her head. "No. Not one hundred percent bad."

Troy nodded. "Right. More like seventy-five percent."

She shrugged. "Eighty."

She slid into the driver's seat. A moment later, the lock popped open on Troy's side. Then the window powered down. She stared at him through the open window.

"Are you going to get in or what?"

He nodded and climbed slowly into the car for the ride back to the hotel.

CHAPTER FORTY ONE

November 24
10:15 pm Central European Time
A flat
La Latina
Madrid, Spain

"How's the pain?"

Earlier today, Troy had ordered from a food service for lunch. He was doing that a lot these days, while he was recuperating. It wasn't that he couldn't walk or carry home groceries, it was that he just didn't feel like it. He was being lazy.

When the delivery guy showed up at his door, it was Alex. Of course it was. Alex had a gift for masquerading as service industry people. He was always some bartender, or hotel or food service guy. He always had the keys, and he tended to let himself in.

Troy shrugged. "It hurts."

"Yeah, well," Alex said. "I guess that's what pain does."

Troy was sitting in a chair in his small living room. Alex was standing on the gleaming hardwood floor, framed by the daylight from the window behind him. Troy had the place just the way he liked, which was to say sparse. Largely undecorated. Not too much furniture.

Alex had put the bag of food down on the coffee table. He had also put down a bouquet of about a dozen yellow flowers. The flowers were just emerging from their bulbs. Troy hadn't ordered any flowers.

"I'll set these up in water in a minute," Alex said. "They come with this nutrient miracle grow stuff nowadays. It makes them pop like fireworks. Really nice. They'll lighten the mood in here for sure."

"The mood is pretty light," Troy said.

Alex stared at him. "Is it?"

Troy decided to change the subject. "I noticed you weren't at CERN for the big event."

Alex shook his head. "I can't be everywhere at once. And you left me with a situation to clean up."

"How is the girl?"

"She's good, man." He nodded. "She's good. If you must know…"

"I risked my life and killed a bunch of people."

"Yeah," Alex said. "You did. I'll grant you that. We brought her to London first, just to get her out of Algeria. Did a little bit of digging, but it didn't take much. She had been abducted off the street in Belarus ten days before the auction. That was the whole game. Some human traffickers spotted a pretty little girl, waited until she was alone, and took her. Kidnapping is a viable business in some of these former communist countries. A lot of times it's for ransom, but in this case, it was to sell her."

"And the upshot?" Troy said.

"She's with her family. We did a little checking, and they had nothing to do with her abduction. So, we gave her back to them. The family is poor, and the girl is probably traumatized, but at least she has a chance at life again."

Troy nodded. "Good."

"Yeah," Alex said. "It is."

He paused. He almost seemed hesitant to speak. "There's something you need to know. It could impact you."

Troy raised an eyebrow.

"A guy named Enrico Morales turned up dead in the New Mexico high desert about a week ago. It's not something you'll see in the newspapers. They're keeping it under wraps. We just found out about it. Do you remember Enrico?"

Troy nodded. This was not a path he really felt like going down. But there was no way around it. If Alex was asking the question, that meant he already knew the answer.

"Yeah. I remember him."

"He shot himself in the head," Alex said.

"Of course he did."

"He'd been out there for several days when they found him. He was partially eaten."

"Thanks," Troy said. "I'm about to eat lunch myself."

"He was under investigation for human rights violations in El Salvador. It stems from his time as part of a secret unit in the employ of the CIA and the Joint Special Operations Command. It was, or maybe is, called the Metal Shop or just the Shop. You might have heard of it. The Senate Intelligence Committee has apparently gotten a bee in their bonnet about this unit."

"A bug up their ass?"

247

Alex gave a half-hearted smile. "Yeah. Who's in it? Who controls it? Where does it go? What does it do? How much does it cost? Who pays for it? All those kinds of questions. They don't like to discover that they don't know what's going on."

Troy nodded. "Okay."

"Your name is in the documents."

Troy looked at the colorful bag of food on the table in front of him with the yellow flowers lying next to it. It would have been nice if some real delivery guy had shown up here and just dropped the food off. No flowers. No classified information. No Enrico Morales. No past at all. No memories.

"Let the dead bury the dead," he said. "That's my philosophy."

"Sometimes the dead get up and walk around," Alex said. "All that lived cries out to live again."

Troy sighed. He felt the air going out of him. Somehow, his injuries hurt more than they had just a minute ago. "I understand."

"It's coming," Alex said. "Bad ju ju."

"It always is," Troy said.

"We'll keep you updated about what's going on. Missing Persons doesn't want you blindsided by this."

"Thanks," Troy said.

"He likes what you're doing. He likes you where you are. You did an exceptional job on this one. He told me to tell you that. It comes straight from him."

"Really?" Troy said. "The place blew up and burned to the ground. A bunch of people died. A super collider and millions of euros worth of other machinery are a total loss. It doesn't look that good on paper."

Alex shook his head. "No. It's a big win. A couple of buildings and an old collider that was going obsolete anyway were blown up, but with negligible release of radiation. You saved a little girl from human traffickers. You killed some terrorists and busted a few others. The terror network was rolled up and destroyed. Their patron, Silvio Strukul, if that's what he was, washed up on a beach in Albania a few days ago, half eaten. The torso had three bullets in it."

Troy nearly laughed. "Did I mention I'm about to have lunch?"

"You should," Alex said. "The food's gonna get cold in a minute."

"You keep talking about dead people being eaten."

Alex shrugged that away. "Overall, it was a pretty good showing. That's the point. And everybody—CERN, Interpol, governments, research facilities of all kinds—learned a valuable lesson. No one is safe anymore."

He reached down, put a white envelope on the table and slid it across. It was a thick envelope. Troy picked it up and looked inside. There was a stack of euros inside. He thumbed through them. At a guess, he thought it was about ten thousand.

"What's this?"

"I told you. Persons thinks you did a good job. He was worried about these guys, that if they kept going, they were going to cause a disaster one day, like a Chernobyl repeat performance. Persons doesn't like to worry. I don't think you know that about him. Now there's one less thing to worry about."

"This is for the medical charity work?" Troy said.

Alex nodded. "Sure."

"I've been getting that money direct wire to my account."

"Well, call this a Christmas bonus," Alex said.

"It's not Christmas yet."

Alex nodded and smiled. "I know." He reached down again and placed a Rock Star Zero on the table next to the food bag. Troy didn't even see where it had come from.

"Look," Alex said. "I'll see you around, all right?"

Troy stared at Alex for a long moment and watched him fade. Slowly, he morphed into Aliz Willems.

Now it was night. Aliz had flown down here to Madrid to see him. Why not? It was one of her favorite cities. She stood before him, in nearly the same spot where Alex had stood. She was framed by the same window, only it was dark outside.

They had gone to dinner. Troy had rallied himself, taken a shower, and cleaned up. It was good. He needed to get out. He'd been spending too much time just hanging around this apartment alone. And besides, he could treat her this time. He was flush with cash from his Christmas bonus.

There was a half empty bottle of wine on the table. They had opened it when they came in. They were having a good, funny night. Troy had popped an extra painkiller so he could be especially witty.

"I've been waiting for this," Aliz said.

She was wearing a shimmering blue dress that hugged her curves. She reached behind her neck with both hands and manipulated something back there. Her eyes were on Troy the whole time.

She moved slowly toward him.

"Be gentle with me," he said.

She shook her head. "I don't know if I can."

* * *

Down on the quiet street, a man turned and walked away.

Up until a moment ago, he had been staring into a pair of binoculars, watching the tall windows of the Interpol agent Troy Stark's flat. The girl was very silly. Her whereabouts and activities were easy to track. She was perfectly visible in the middle window. Anyone who cared to look could see her.

A sniper could have shot her.

The man lit a cigarette as he walked. He pulled his jacket close around him. It was a chilly night.

He took out his phone and dialed a number. It beeped and booped for a moment, as the signal bounced across countries.

A male voice answered. "Tell me."

It was him. Luc Mebarak, the man who could not, or at least should not, be named. This was his direct line. Mebarak didn't like to hear things second or third hand. Apparently, this extended to news about his sister's affairs.

It occurred to the man, and not for the first time this evening, that he was in a very delicate position himself. He was now privy to personal information about one of Luc Mebarak's family members. Suppose Mebarak decided he didn't like that.

"I'm on the street outside the man's flat."

"And?"

"She's in there."

There was a long pause over the connection. For a moment, the man wondered if it had gone dead.

"Very good job," Mebarak said at last. He sounded pleased. The man supposed that could mean anything. Maybe Mebarak wanted his sister to date a policeman. Or maybe the information just solved a mystery that had troubled him.

"Expect to hear from me again," Mebarak said and hung up.

The man walked the city streets for a long time afterward, smoking one cigarette after another.

He couldn't decide if hearing from Mebarak again would be good or bad.

NOW AVAILABLE!

ROGUE TARGET
(A Troy Stark Thriller—Book #3)

"Thriller writing at its best. Thriller enthusiasts who relish the precise execution of an international thriller, but who seek the psychological depth and believability of a protagonist who simultaneously fields professional and personal life challenges, will find this a gripping story that's hard to put down."
--Midwest Book Review, Diane Donovan (regarding Any Means Necessary)

"One of the best thrillers I have read this year. The plot is intelligent and will keep you hooked from the beginning. The author did a superb job creating a set of characters who are fully developed and very much enjoyable. I can hardly wait for the sequel."
--Books and Movie Reviews, Roberto Mattos (re Any Means Necessary)

From #1 bestselling and USA Today bestselling author Jack Mars, author of the critically-acclaimed *Luke Stone* and *Agent Zero* series (with over 5,000 five-star reviews), comes an explosive new, action-packed thriller series that takes readers on a wild-ride across Europe, America, and the world.

Although elite Navy Seal Troy Stark was forced into retirement for his dubious respect for authority, his work in stopping a major terrorist threat to New York did not go unnoticed. Now part of a new, secret international organization, Troy must hunt down all threats to the U.S. and pre-empt them overseas—bending the rules if he has to.

In ROGUE TARGET (book #3), a new marvel of engineering is set to open with fanfare, heralding a new era of technology and attracting heads of state for the grand opening. But terrorists have their eyes on it, too—along with the high-value targets attending— and in this high-octane action thriller, Troy Stark may be the only person left standing between the terrorists and an event of mass destruction.

An unputdownable action thriller with heart-pounding suspense and unforeseen twists, ROGUE TARGET is the debut novel in an exhilarating new series by a #1 bestselling author that will have you fall in love with a brand new action hero—and turn pages late into the night.

Future books in the series will soon be available.

Jack Mars

Jack Mars is the USA Today bestselling author of the LUKE STONE thriller series, which includes seven books. He is also the author of the new FORGING OF LUKE STONE prequel series, comprising six books; of the AGENT ZERO spy thriller series, comprising twelve books; of the TROY STARK thriller series, comprising three books; and of the SPY GAME thriller series, comprising five books.

Jack loves to hear from you, so please feel free to visit www.Jackmarsauthor.com to join the email list, receive a free book, receive free giveaways, connect on Facebook and Twitter, and stay in touch!

BOOKS BY JACK MARS

THE SPY GAME
TARGET ONE (Book #1)
TARGET TWO (Book #2)
TARGET THREE (Book #3)
TARGET FOUR (Book #4)
TARGET FIVE (Book #5)

TROY STARK THRILLER SERIES
ROGUE FORCE (Book #1)
ROGUE COMMAND (Book #2)
ROGUE TARGET (Book #3)

LUKE STONE THRILLER SERIES
ANY MEANS NECESSARY (Book #1)
OATH OF OFFICE (Book #2)
SITUATION ROOM (Book #3)
OPPOSE ANY FOE (Book #4)
PRESIDENT ELECT (Book #5)
OUR SACRED HONOR (Book #6)
HOUSE DIVIDED (Book #7)

FORGING OF LUKE STONE PREQUEL SERIES
PRIMARY TARGET (Book #1)
PRIMARY COMMAND (Book #2)
PRIMARY THREAT (Book #3)
PRIMARY GLORY (Book #4)
PRIMARY VALOR (Book #5)
PRIMARY DUTY (Book #6)

AN AGENT ZERO SPY THRILLER SERIES
AGENT ZERO (Book #1)
TARGET ZERO (Book #2)
HUNTING ZERO (Book #3)
TRAPPING ZERO (Book #4)
FILE ZERO (Book #5)
RECALL ZERO (Book #6)
ASSASSIN ZERO (Book #7)